CW00820600

The Last Hunt

THE LAST HUNT

ALSO BY AUDREY J. COLE

THE FINAL HUNT SERIES

The First Hunt (JUNE 2025)

The Final Hunt

STANDALONES

The Pilot's Daughter

Only One Lie

The One

Missing In Flight (JANUARY 2025)

EMERALD CITY THRILLERS

The Recipient

Inspired by Murder

The Summer Nanny: A Novella

Viable Hostage

Fatal Deception

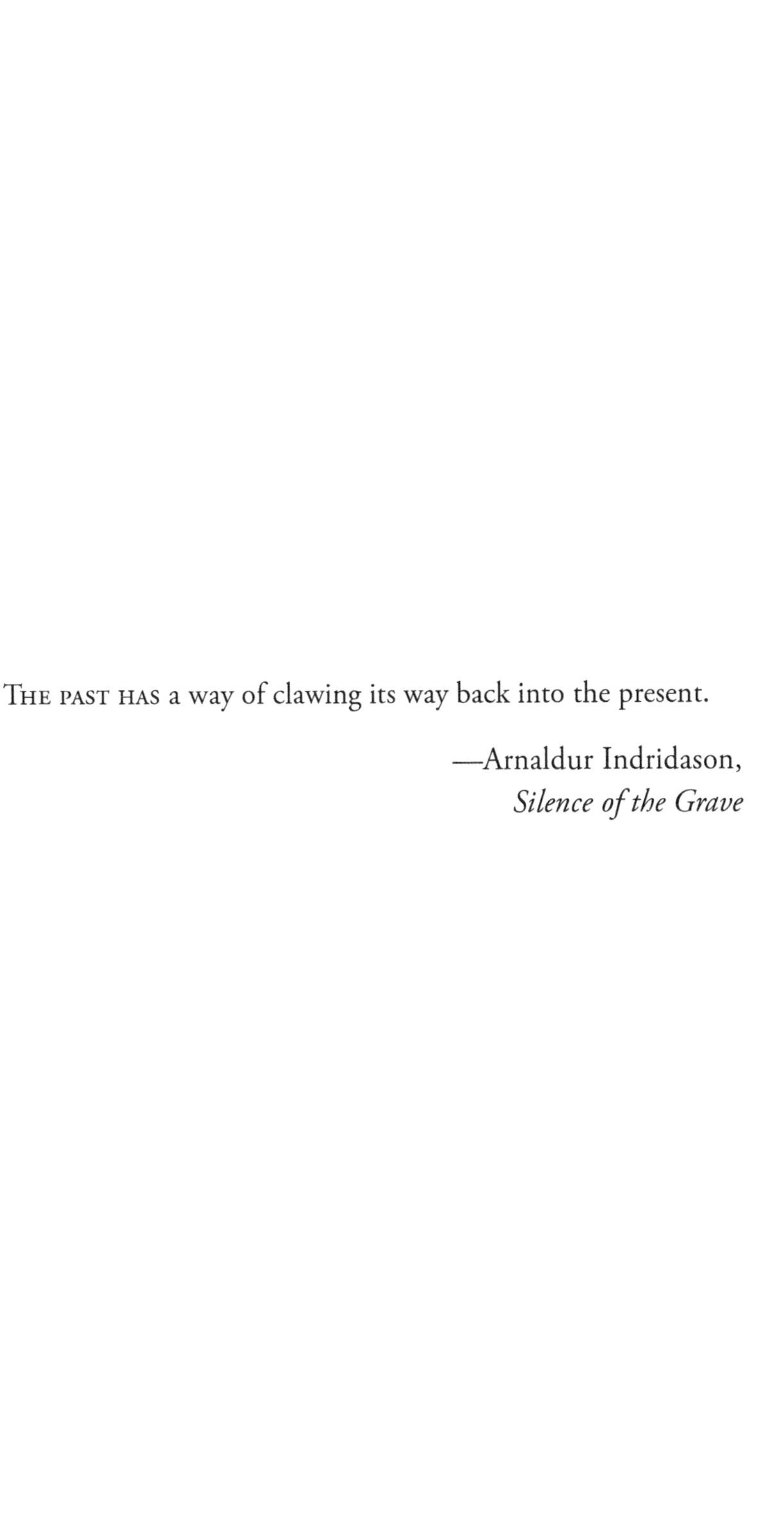

THE PAST HAS a way of clawing its way back into the present.

—Arnaldur Indridason,
Silence of the Grave

THE LAST HUNT

AUDREY J. COLE
USA TODAY BESTSELLING AUTHOR

PROLOGUE

Madison clamped a hand over her mouth to muffle the cry that escaped when her ankle rolled off the side of her heeled sandal. A *crack* split the air, and pain shot up the side of her foot. The sound hadn't come from a branch crunching beneath her feet but from bone. She stifled a whimper and forced herself to keep moving, gritting her teeth as her ankle gave out.

She sank to the uneven ground. With a trembling hand, she ripped off her sandals, straining to hear the man's heavy footsteps running after her. The handcuff still dangled from her wrist, fastened so tight she was losing feeling in her hand. She struggled to her feet, resisting the urge to grunt from the agony in her ankle, and ran through the woods with her arms out in front to keep from smacking into a tree.

She could no longer hear the man behind her. Maybe the setting sun had been a blessing in disguise. The darkness would give her a chance.

She tripped on a log and went down with a thud. Her palm scraped against a pinecone as a bright beam swept the branches hanging beside her. Madison crouched lower as the beam swung to the left, willing her shaking body to be still.

The man's voice drifted through the trees. "This will go easier for you if you give up. Trust me, Madison."

Madison closed her eyes and inhaled a shallow breath. The venom in his voice was obvious now. How had she been so stupid to get inside his car?

But when she met him outside the Wolf Pack Bar, he seemed so harmless. So *nice.*

"You need a hand with that?" he'd asked after she slammed the hood of her first-generation Ford Focus. He motioned to the adjacent parking lot in front of the diner. "I've got jumper cables if you need some."

Turning around, she found a dark-haired man standing a few feet behind her. "Thanks, but it won't help." This had happened before. Her car was a year older than she was, and it needed a new transmission. But she was hoping it would run for at least another year, so she could save up from her first year of teaching to buy something more reliable. She sighed, knowing that was no longer an option. "I'll have to take it into the shop tomorrow."

"I can give you ride."

"Oh." He had a kind face, and an attractive one at that, but she wasn't about to accept a ride from a stranger in a town where she knew no one. "That's okay. I can walk." The house she was renting was only a couple of miles from the bar.

After a few steps, the balls of her feet already ached. She looked down and remembered she'd worn her most uncomfortable shoes, not anticipating she'd be walking any farther than the ten feet from her parking spot to the bar.

The man put up his hands, his plaid shirtsleeves rolled up to his elbows. "Sorry, I wasn't trying to pick you up." He smiled sheepishly.

Even in the waning daylight, Madison could see his face change color. *Was he blushing?*

"It's just that we get a lot of truckers passing through here." He pointed his thumb over his shoulder where drunken laughter erupted from the row of semis parked outside the diner. "It's not the safest town to be walking around alone at night."

Despite it being only dusk, it was nearly midnight. And it would be dark long before she made it home. She remembered the college girl who'd gone missing last fall after her shift from this very bar. *Bethany.* When her body was found, it had been all over the Fairbanks news, where Madison did her student teaching. Like herself, Bethany had been an ed major.

"I didn't mean to make you uncomfortable. Just be careful."

She watched the man continue toward the bar, knowing she was likely being paranoid not to accept a ride from him. He was just trying to help.

More laughter reverberated from the other side of the parking lot. Madison glanced in the direction of the parked semis. She would have to walk right past them to get home.

She took a few steps in her cheap-heeled sandals before turning around. The man reached for the door of the bar.

"Hey," she called out.

He turned.

"Actually, I'll take you up on that ride. Thank you."

It wasn't until after he missed the turn for her house that his demeanor changed. The disarming man she'd met in the parking lot was gone. After ignoring her pleas to turn around, the man's voice had morphed into a vicious snarl as he sped along the Alaska Highway and announced that she wasn't going home.

He could be the same monster who killed Bethany.

Madison had reached for the door handle. The man cinched a metal handcuff around her wrist and yanked her arm away from the door. Fueled by terror, Madison grasped the handle with her other hand and threw herself out of his speeding car.

Now, she held her breath as the bright beam swept across the forest in the opposite direction from where she lay. A twig dug into the raw flesh on her elbow from where she'd skid across the pavement.

She exhaled, lowering her face to her forearm as branches crunched beneath his shoes a few feet from where she lay. Her lungs stilled as the beam shone onto her back, illuminating the forest floor around her. She pushed against the ground with her palms.

She was only a few inches off the ground when the weight of the man's knee on her back shoved her down. His grip clamped around her handcuffed wrist, yanking it behind her back. With her other hand, she frantically swept the ground around her until her fingers brushed the edges of a cold rock the size of a softball.

She gripped it, then twisted her torso and swung the rock into the side of her assailant's skull. The man's head recoiled sideways from the blow. He grunted in pain and his grip loosened. She pulled her arm free as he rolled off her back, cradling his head in his hands.

She got to her feet, pain shooting up the side of her leg like an electric shock. She bit the inside of her lower lip and limped in the direction of the highway.

When she reached the edge of the forest, she sagged forward, resting her hands on her knees. Ahead, the light from the moon drew the edges of an empty stretch of highway. A branch snapped on the ground several feet behind her.

She whipped around, envisioning the man creeping toward her through the darkness. But all she could see was the outline of the dark woods. As fast as her ankle allowed, she raced down the dry ditch separating her from the road when a pair of headlights appeared in the darkness. *Thank God.* She waved her arms above her head before her ankle gave out again, then crawled up the side of the ditch on her hands and knees.

When she reached the blacktop, she stood, stepping over the white line into the lane of the oncoming car, frantically waving her hands. The headlights slowed. Her chest heaved with relief.

She stole a glance over her shoulder, making sure the man hadn't followed her onto the road. Her breath stuck in her throat as the vehicle's bright beams illuminated a pair of eyes in the tree line. They stood much too short to belong to the man.

Something emerged from the trees as the car braked to a stop, the heat from its engine warm against her legs. The headlights illuminated the forest and lit up the figure's tail, and Madison watched in horror as the coyote ran beside the ditch in the opposite direction before tucking into the forest.

The driver's door opened, and Madison pivoted slowly on her bare feet, knowing who it was even before he stepped in front of the car. The road swayed beneath her as his plaid shirt moved in front of the headlights.

"There you are." A sick smile played at the sides of his mouth. Blood dripped down the side of the face she'd found attractive less than an hour ago. "I told you this wasn't a safe town to be walking alone at night."

Madison spun and ran in the opposite direction along the vacant highway as fast as her injured ankle would allow. *Please let there be another car. Someone.* As she strained to see through the darkness, the image of her parents waving goodbye to her from their Fairbanks driveway last week flashed to the front of her mind. Her dad wrapped his arm around her mom's shoulders as Madison backed out of their sloped drive. It had never occurred to her that it could be the last time she'd ever see them. The two-lane road was dark as far as she could see. She choked back a sob.

Behind her, the driver's door slammed. The car's engine revved seconds before tires squealed atop the pavement. Its beams grew closer. Madison darted for the ditch.

Before she crossed the fog line, the metal bumper struck the backs of her thighs, throwing her to the ground as everything went black.

CHAPTER ONE

DETECTIVE TANNER MULHOLLAND crouched to inspect the crusted brown stains on the saw-like teeth of the bear trap. He had no doubt it was blood, and if he had to guess, it wasn't from an animal.

"You want this?" Reed, a Fairbanks crime scene investigator, pointed a gloved finger toward the frayed rope lying around the base of the pine tree.

Tanner's gaze skirted to the weathered rope, blotched with the same dark stains as the bear trap. "Yes, definitely. Let's bag the trap too."

A long distant howl reverberated through the quiet surrounding forest. Tanner looked in the direction of the animal call. "I thought wolves only came out at night."

Reed shook his head. "That's a myth. They're most active at dawn and dusk. They're opportunistic, so they'll hunt during the day too. Be careful walking around here by yourself. This area is densely populated with them. Bears too." He gestured toward the trap at Tanner's feet. "We're going to need a bigger evidence bag for that. I'll be right back."

Tanner stood as the investigator strode toward the helicopter belonging to the Alaska State Troopers, parked in front of the cabin, in a small clearing that had been just big enough for them to land. When they'd flown that morning from Fairbanks over nearly two hundred miles of mountainous terrain, Tanner was struck by how remote the cabin was. In summer, it would be a several days' hike from the nearest airstrip, and not an easy one at that. For John—or Cameron, John's widow—to make the trek here in the dead of winter seemed close to impossible.

When the investigator returned, Tanner helped him fit the bear trap, open at a forty-five-degree angle, into the evidence bag.

Reed lifted the bag to inspect the contraption. "These kinds of traps aren't legal anymore, but it looks fairly new."

He carried the trap to the helicopter as Tanner moved around the tree, examining the ground before lifting his eyes to the surrounding forest. The sun filtered in through the thick canopy, and he was grateful he didn't have to do this in winter. He wished he would've requested a cadaver dog to come along, although, it might not have done much good. If there *had* been a body here, the remains could have been carried away by scavengers. There likely wouldn't be much left. And the surrounding forestland was so vast, not to mention filled with dangerous wildlife, that it could be like trying to find a needle in a haystack.

It was hard to fathom Cameron making it here, finding John, and killing him. But then, the whole story surrounding John Prescott and his wife Cameron was hard to fathom. How ironic was it that the serial killer who had faked his death through a supposed bear attack was now dead in much the same way—in the jaws of not one, but a pack of dangerous animals.

John Prescott's original plan to fake his death almost worked. It wasn't until the only witness to the bear attack last fall proved unreliable that Tanner seriously considered the possibility that the Teacher Killer was still alive, and that Cameron was not his accomplice.

As he walked toward the log cabin, a branch crunched beneath his shoe. They'd left no element of surprise with their helicopter landing, and he and a Fairbanks detective did a quick sweep of the small structure after their arrival. When Tanner had kicked in the door with his weapon drawn, he'd half expected to find Prescott's decaying body. While they didn't find Prescott, the dates on some of the canned foods suggested someone had inhabited the cabin recently.

And the large drops of blood smeared on the cabin floor confirmed Tanner's suspicion that something had gone down here. Like the bear trap, he'll have to send samples to the Fairbanks crime lab to confirm that it's human—and whether it was John Prescott's.

When he stepped inside, the second crime scene investigator, Katrina, was dusting the fire poker for prints. Tanner peered through the open doorway to the bedroom, which was void of any personal effects. Its small closet had been emptied of clothes, but Tanner had them bag the pillowcase to test for DNA.

"Looks like someone got a shot off."

Tanner turned.

Katrina pointed to the ceiling in the middle of the room. "But I couldn't find a casing."

Tanner took a few steps and tipped his head back to examine the small hole in the knotty pine.

"No gun either," the Fairbanks investigator added.

Tanner surveyed the room as the investigator returned her attention to the fire poker. It reminded him of Prescott's hunting cabin in the Cascades, where Tanner discovered the buried remains of Alicia Lopez and Olivia Rossi, two Seattle teachers who had gone missing on the same night fourteen months earlier.

He crossed the small space toward the kitchen and slowed when he passed a bookcase filled with literary classics, a contrast to the one at Prescott's cabin in Washington state, which was filled with hunting and outdoor guides.

Tanner scanned the worn-in spines. *Hemingway. Salinger. Fitzgerald.* His eyes settled on a faded copy of Jack London's *The Call of the Wild*, which he'd read in the fourth grade. Tanner recalled the teacher who'd introduced him to the famous tale, how she would excitedly jump to her feet when reading excerpts aloud to Tanner's class. Now looking at the worn spine, he cringed thinking of the pleasure John Prescott took reading those same words.

When he searched Prescott's Seattle home last winter, Tanner had seen a weathered copy of *White Fang* and *A Farewell to Arms*. He'd assumed they belonged to Cameron until he watched a local news interview of Prescott's law firm partner saying what a huge fan Prescott was of classic literature, particularly Jack London and Ernest Hemingway.

Tanner moved to the kitchen while Katrina took a photo of the bullet hole in the ceiling. The open first aid kit and empty bottle of betadine they'd found on the counter was already encased in an evidence bag, along with swabs from the dried blood running down the front of the cabinets onto the floor.

Tanner opened a cupboard beside the sink to find a half empty bottle of scotch. He withdrew the bottle and set it on the counter. It would've been careless and out of character for Prescott to have left his blood and fingerprints behind. Unless he'd been too injured to clean up. Or he didn't think anyone would ever find this place.

"Can you dust this for prints?"

The investigator turned. "Sure thing."

Tanner read the label on the bottle. T & N Scotch was mass

produced, one of the cheapest brands you could find. Prescott was a scotch drinker, but he had expensive taste. Still, Prescott's options would have been limited if he purchased it on his way here.

Before flying out to the cabin, Tanner had checked with the motel in Eagle—population eighty-nine and the closest thing to a town within one hundred miles of the cabin. Not surprisingly, they had no record of a John Prescott staying, nor did their staff recognize his Washington driver's license photo. One of them did, however, recognize Cameron, only with different hair.

But could she have made it here from Eagle in February? And killed John? After Cameron returned from Alaska, she'd seemed so certain John was dead, when she'd been so adamant before she went that he was still alive.

Tanner assessed the kitchen's empty waste basket before squatting in front of the fireplace. He used the fire poker to sort through the burned contents, but all he upturned was ash. He set down the poker and started to stand when he spotted a small piece of singed paper half covered in ash. He reached into the powder to grab the paper and wiped off the gray residue with his gloved hand. The paper was smooth and still held a glossy finish. It was triangular, like the page had been ripped from the corner. As Tanner stared at the words, he realized what it was.

A photo of a man's head wearing a camo hat covered part of the large white letters *NTING.* Tanner recalled the several editions of *HUNTING* magazine he found not only at Prescott's Cle Elum cabin, but also his Seattle home. Tanner stared at the smaller lettering in the top corner. *December 2023.* The magazine was dated one month after the bear attack that was believed to have killed Prescott. He felt a prickling sensation as his hair stood on end at the nape of his neck.

John Prescott didn't die that day in the Frank Church

Wilderness like he'd made the world believe. Tanner was certain of that now.

"Mulholland!"

Tanner whirled toward the sound of the Fairbanks detective's voice coming from outside the cabin's open front door.

"I found something!"

Tanner extended the magazine remnant to Katrina. "Let's bag this."

The investigator nodded as Tanner hurried outside and rounded the side of the cabin. Tanner spotted Detective Morton's salt-and-pepper hair and found him standing beneath a small carport beside a stack of kindling. Upon seeing Tanner, he motioned to a red five-gallon gas can at his feet.

"Found this behind the wood stack. It's empty." Morton extended his arm toward the edge of the covering. "This is just the right amount of space to house a snowmobile."

Tanner scanned the stacked logs that comprised the cabin's exterior wall. He had no doubt Prescott had been here. He could feel it.

His gaze fell to the gas can lying on the flattened grass. *But if Cameron had killed her husband, then where was his body?*

CHAPTER TWO

As CAMERON TURNED down the long tree-lined drive, her phone rang inside her purse. She reached inside her bag as her A-frame came into view, the snow-capped Alaskan Range protruding above the treetops in the distance. Seeing Dane's name on the screen, she put the phone to her ear.

"Hey babe."

"Hey. Am I still invited to dinner?"

At the sound of his deep voice, the sides of her lips upturned to a smile. It was hard to believe they'd been together for six months.

"You are." She peered through a break in the trees to his gravel drive next door, but his SUV wasn't there. Wind whistled through the call, followed by the sound of a door slamming. "Are you leaving the station?"

"I'm actually heading back from Dry Creek. A tourist hit a moose while doing about seventy-five on the highway."

"Oh no." Cameron grimaced. She braked in front of her home before killing the engine.

"It caused a few car pileups, but no fatalities. The driver's being airlifted to Fairbanks, and we just reopened the highway. Anyway, I should be back in about an hour. That okay?"

She reached over to the passenger seat and lifted the overstuffed bag from Three Bears, the only grocery store in town. "It's perfect." She cradled the phone between her shoulder and ear and opened her door. "My last patient needed an emergency root canal, so I'm just getting home."

"I guess that's what you get for being the only dentist in town. Even a town as small as Tok."

Cameron made for her front porch steps when the crunch of gravel behind her made her whip around. She didn't recognize the blue Ford Focus that slowed to a stop behind her truck.

"You want me to pick up anything before I come over?"

A tall blond man wearing a gray suit stepped out of the sedan. As he slid off his aviators, Cameron's breath stuck in her lungs.

"Cam?" Dane's voice echoed in her ear as Detective Tanner Mulholland's blue eyes pierced through hers.

They held the same intensity as they did when he'd sat across from her in the interview room at the homicide unit. There was a sharpness—a focus—that she'd nearly forgotten.

"Um." She swallowed. She hadn't seen the detective since he let her walk out of Seattle homicide without arresting her for what she'd done to Miles, her first husband. Had he changed his mind? Come to charge her with murder? Or maybe he was here because of what she'd done to John; perhaps he'd found out she'd killed her second husband as well—although, technically, *she* hadn't killed him. The wolves had taken care of that for her.

"Cameron? You still there?"

Dane's voice pulled her out of her spiraling thoughts. "Sorry, what?"

Tanner took a step closer.

"I said do you want me to pick up anything for dinner?"

"I have everything," she said, keeping her eyes trained on the detective's.

"Okay, see you soon."

Dane ended the call, and Cameron lowered the phone. Tanner's expression gave away nothing, but she was certain whatever he'd traveled nearly two thousand miles to tell her wasn't good.

"Hi, Cameron."

"What are you doing here?" A shiver snaked up her spine, despite it being one of the warmest days Tok had seen so far this year.

He didn't answer right away, and she resisted the urge to ask if this was about Miles. Had Tanner let her go only because he didn't have enough evidence to charge her?

"It's about John."

Her jaw dropped before she could stop it. She clamped her mouth shut, but it was too late; the detective hadn't missed her reaction. She composed herself as Tanner's watchful eyes assessed her.

"Mind if I come inside?" He motioned toward her house behind her.

She'd wondered many times since she killed John whether Mulholland would discover Miles' inherited cabin. It wasn't easy to find inside the national preserve one hundred miles north of Tok, and as the months went on, she'd felt more assured he wouldn't.

Not that he couldn't find it if he looked hard enough. She had no doubt of his competence as a detective. Rather, Tanner didn't believe there was a *reason* to look. He'd never bought her theory that John hadn't died on his hunting trip with Simon.

Had learning the truth about Simon changed his mind?

"Sure. Come on in." She shifted the grocery bag to her other arm.

"You need a hand with that?"

"I'm good. Thanks." She turned and led him up her porch steps.

CHAPTER THREE

When Cameron stepped inside, warm, stuffy air closed in around her.

"Nice place," Tanner said.

She left the front door open behind him, closing only the storm door, hoping for a breeze. She already felt flushed. She gestured for him to take a seat on her white, slipcovered couch.

"Quite different from your old one," Tanner added.

It was what she liked best about her new home. No reminders of the past. As he glanced around the room, she perched across from him on the edge of an overstuffed chair that had come with the house.

"I don't recognize any of your furniture," he said.

"I sold the Laurelhurst house furnished."

His jaw flexed as he chewed his gum, seeming to understand.

A bead of sweat dripped from the nape of her neck—whether from the heat or her nerves, she wasn't sure. None of the homes up here had air conditioning. There was rarely a day it got above eighty degrees, today being one of them. Without a breeze through the screen door, the air thickened and made it hard for her to draw a full breath.

His eyes settled on hers. She stared back at him, dying for him to explain what he was doing here. At the same time, she was terrified to find out. *Had he found John's remains?*

She realized Tanner might be waiting for her to offer him something to drink. There was an etiquette to these sorts of things if she remembered correctly.

"Can I get you something? Water? A Coke?"

"No, thanks."

Cameron scooted back in her seat, wondering how much of John was left after the wolves got to him. A vivid image of John welled up in her mind, tied to that tree, bleeding onto the snow from the bullet in his leg. She remembered the feel of the wolf call between her lips, the hard plastic, and her frustration when it didn't work. She'd thrown it aside in the snow, then howled to draw them in, watching the gray wolf pack appear on the summit of the nearest slope. John screamed at her to cut him loose, his ankle clenched in the steel bear trap.

The wolf call. I left it only a few feet from John. If Tanner had found the cabin—and John's remains—the wolf call would've been right next to him. With her DNA on the mouthpiece.

She drew in a sharp breath, praying Tanner didn't notice.

"I found the cabin," he finally said.

She used all her willpower to keep any shred of recognition from appearing on her face. "What cabin?"

He smiled. She fought the urge to shift in her seat.

"The cabin your first husband, Miles, inherited. About a hundred miles north of here."

She rubbed her forearm, trying to soothe the revulsion that crawled beneath her skin from hearing her abusive first husband's name. She should've known that if she had been able to find Miles's family cabin, hidden deep in the Alaskan National Preserve, that Tanner could find it too.

Cameron blinked, keeping her eyes trained on Tanner's. Before John became known as the infamous Teacher Killer, whose killings had plagued Seattle for over two decades, he was Seattle's most prominent criminal defense attorney. Cameron had learned enough from her time as John's wife to know the less she said, the better.

She tilted her head, feigning ignorance. Just because Tanner had found the cabin didn't mean he'd been there. This time of year, the only way in would be a several days' hike, and not an easy one at that. Not to mention the big game that was prevalent in that area, particularly wolves and bears. Surely, he hadn't taken that journey with a forensic team. Had he?

"Your fingerprints were on the door handle, if that helps jog your memory."

Cameron swallowed the lump of panic that rose to her throat. He *had* been there. The memory of biting off her glove to open the door while gripping the rifle in her other hand played in her mind like a movie. She resisted asking how he got there, knowing it would be an admittance of guilt. *He knows I killed him.*

Tanner's deep blue eyes bored into hers as he studied her reaction. "I don't know how you managed to get there in the dead of winter, but I'm guessing you had some help."

At least he's wrong about one thing.

He leaned forward, his elbows resting atop his knees as he interlaced his long fingers. "Outside the cabin, I found some bloodstained rope and a bear trap. I'm guessing it's not animal blood, but I'm having it tested to be sure."

Cameron sank against the soft back of her chair. *Was that all he found? No remains?* She also knew from her near decade-long marriage to Seattle's top criminal lawyer slash serial killer that without any of John's remains, it would be nearly impossible for Tanner to charge her with his murder, especially when John had already been declared dead.

Maybe the wolves carried John back to their den. Or a bear took what was left of him. Wouldn't that be ironic?

Tanner chewed his gum, watching her carefully from across the room. His eyes bore into hers, as if he could read her very thoughts. *If he was hoping for a confession, he's not going to get one.*

"And yours weren't the only fingerprints I found. John's were there too, on some canned goods in the pantry. From the dates on the label, he was likely there *after* he presumably died last November."

Likely. Not for sure. She could lie and tell him she and John stayed there before he died. But could Tanner prove her prints—or John's –had been put there more recently? Probably, she decided. Plus, she'd lied to him before, and knew it. So, she doesn't say a word.

Tanner sat up straight. "There was also a large amount of blood spill *inside* the cabin. I've submitted samples of it for DNA testing."

Cameron nearly choked on her own spit. Her memory of shooting John in the leg in the cabin's living room flashed in her mind. She'd forced him outside right afterward. When she'd gone back inside, there was hardly any blood on the floor.

As if on cue, a sudden breeze whipped through a window at the rear of her house, slamming the front door closed. Cameron jumped in her chair.

She shook her head. "I don't understand. John is dead."

"Then where's the body, Cameron?"

He waited for her response.

When he didn't get one, he added, "I found an opened first aid kit inside the cabin. It looked like someone had bandaged and disinfected some wounds. I'm guessing it was John, trying to patch himself up after you shot him. Unless that was you?"

Cameron didn't answer.

"Also," Tanner shifted forward on the couch. "There was an empty gas can on the side of the cabin beneath a covered area big enough to house a snowmobile. I'm guessing that's how John got to the cabin in the middle of winter."

Cameron remembered seeing John's snowmobile parked beside the cabin. Was Tanner saying it was gone? Unless Tanner was lying, trying to trick her into a confession.

"There was no snowmobile?"

She could see it in his eyes, him registering her surprise. She shouldn't have asked the question—an indirect admission that she'd been there. But she needed to know the answer.

He shook his head. "If you killed him, I can't protect you from being held accountable. But if you're truthful, it could lessen the severity of charges you face."

Despite the stuffy room, goosebumps traveled down her arms.

She held his gaze, thinking about the last time she saw John, tied to the tree outside. The wolves were so close. There's no way he could've survived. Or gotten back inside. But then how did all that blood get inside the cabin? The floor swayed beneath her chair. And where the hell was John's snowmobile?

"Where is he, Cameron?"

She stiffened. *There's no way John survived.* "The last time I saw my husband, he was alive." That, at least, was the truth.

Tanner placed his hands on his knees and inhaled deeply, nostrils flaring briefly.

"I've managed to keep these prints out of the news for now. But if the DNA from the blood comes back a match to John, I can't guarantee the word won't get out. I believe you tracked John to that cabin and left him for dead. But if whatever you did to him up there *didn't* kill him, you need to be very careful." Tanner maintained eye contact with her as he stood. "Because he's not the kind to let that go."

CHAPTER FOUR

Cameron flipped the steaks in her stovetop pan as Tanner's words replayed in her mind.

She'd never been much of a cook, but she'd been doing more of it since moving to Tok. After everything that had happened with John, it felt good to do something mundane. Normal. Nice.

But now, the sound of the steaks sizzling in the peppercorn olive oil did nothing to ease the constriction in her chest. She lifted her can of Alaskan White that she'd bought for Dane to her lips and stared out the window at a mule deer nibbling off a tree at the edge of her property. Even though it was past seven, the sun shone high in the sky. It wouldn't be dark until nearly midnight.

Tanner was wrong. He has to be. John is dead. She'd made sure John couldn't untie himself from the tree. And when she'd left, the wolves were so close.

I should never have gone back a second time. But what she'd done should have ensured John's death, not his survival.

She took another long drink. Tanner was flying back to Seattle tomorrow. Before the detective left, he urged her to call him immediately if she saw or heard from John. Although, there seemed no way that could be possible.

But then where was John's snowmobile? And what else could explain the blood and opened first aid kit inside the cabin? Maybe an injured hunter or hiker raided the cabin for medical supplies and used John's snowmobile to get back to civilization. But it still wouldn't explain how they could've gotten there without a snowmobile to begin with. And why there was nothing left of John's remains.

She remembered trekking through the snow so vividly, retracing her steps in the waning daylight as John screamed at her to untie him—she could almost hear him now. In response to her call, the wolves descended on the valley, where John lay tied to a tree outside his cabin, bleeding onto the snow. His cursing morphed into desperate pleas while she rushed through the white woods.

She tossed the salad in the wooden bowl on the counter before placing it on her kitchen table. Dane should be back any minute. She returned to the kitchen and flipped the steaks another time before turning up the heat on the burner.

After finishing what was left of her beer, she tossed it into the recycling next to the can she'd already finished. She wasn't much of a beer drinker, but it felt too warm for red wine, and after Mulholland's visit, she needed something to quell her nerves.

I should've stayed inside the cabin until the wolves had finished with John. Although, at the time, spending the night in that cabin among John's things after watching him get eaten alive was more than she could stomach. The wolves had been so close the last time she'd seen him. She hadn't imagined there would be any question that John wouldn't survive. But then, she'd thought the same thing when she'd heard the news of his disappearance in the Frank Church Wilderness on his hunting trip with Simon.

She closed her eyes, pressing her hands against the butcherblock countertop as she envisioned John withdrawing a pocketknife, cutting himself free as the pack of wolves tore through the snowy forest. Then came an image of John crawling through the snow, dragging the bear trap with his injured leg.

She forced the grisly scene from her thoughts. *He's dead. He has to be.* She remembered the life draining from John's eyes the last time she saw him. After she—

A large hand clamped onto her shoulder. Cameron screamed. She whipped around, half-expecting to see John standing behind her with a wicked grin on his face.

"Whoa!" Dane put his palms in the air. "It's me."

Cameron lifted a hand to her racing heart.

"Sorry, I didn't mean to scare you." The side of her boyfriend's mouth turned up into a half smile. He was still dressed in his state trooper uniform. His smile faded, and he stepped closer. "You okay?"

She nodded. "Yeah, fine." She glanced at the front of her house. "I didn't hear you come in."

"Your front door was open, so I came in through the screen door." He looked beyond her at the stove. "Is something burning?"

She turned to see smoke rising from the pan. She switched off the burner while flipping the smoking steaks with her other hand. "Oh, no."

Dane leaned over her shoulder and peered at the blackened meat. "Ooh."

"They're ruined." She transferred the steaks to a plate on the counter, knowing she wouldn't have been able to eat anyway.

"We might be able to salvage part of them if we cut off that burnt side."

Cameron faced Dane and tried to force Tanner's visit from her mind. "I'm sorry."

"Don't worry about it." He pointed to her beer. "You have any more of those?"

"Yeah."

"I'll get it."

Dane pressed his hand to the small of her back as she started toward the fridge. After retrieving a can of Alaskan White, he sat across from her at her small kitchen table. As Cameron cut away the charred meat with her steak knife, she pictured John withdrawing a pocketknife and shredding the rope she'd used to tie him to the tree.

"Do you want some help?"

Dane motioned to her half-cut steak, and she realized her hand had gone still.

"I got it. Thanks."

"You sure you're okay?"

"Yeah," she lied.

Cameron resumed her hopeless effort to salvage her steak as Dane lifted his knife to do the same. After giving up, she pushed her salad around with her fork before forcing herself to take a bite.

Just tell him. Dane knew what she'd done. Well, *mostly* what she'd done. Still, she hated to remind him. It was one thing for him to know what she'd done to John—and Miles—but it was another to bring it up when they promised to never speak of it again. But maybe Dane could reassure her that Tanner was wrong.

Tanner didn't know this area like Dane did. John was dead. There was no way he could've escaped. Dane knew how remote the cabin was. How treacherous it would've been for John to get out—even without a mangled ankle and a bullet in his leg. Not to mention the wound she'd inflicted on him after going back.

She lifted her gaze, seeing that Dane had hardly eaten

anything either. She met his eyes and noticed they were bloodshot. She must've been too startled when he came in to notice.

She set down her fork. "What's wrong?"

"Oh." He leaned his elbow onto the table. "The accident." His gaze traveled to the window beside them. "It was a dark SUV that hit that moose. When I first got there, it looked a lot like the scene when..."

Cameron reached across the table and rested her hand on the back of his. Six years ago, his wife's vehicle was struck by a semi when she turned out of the Tok State Trooper's Station one night after work. Dane had watched it happen from the parking lot.

"For a moment, it felt like I was reliving it."

She squeezed his hand. She'd been so distracted she hadn't even noticed the pain on her boyfriend's face. "I'm so sorry."

He returned the squeeze, pulling his gaze away from the window to meet her eyes, his face softening. "Are you going to tell me what made you so jumpy when I came in?"

She debated whether to tell him. "Actually—"

His phone rang from inside his vest pocket. He pulled it out and checked the caller ID.

"Sorry, I gotta take this," he said before lifting the phone to his ear. "Hey, Nelson." Dane straightened, his expression turning serious. "Where?" He pushed back his chair. "I'll be right there."

For the most part, the Tok troopers got called to car accidents, bar fights, and domestic violence incidents. Cameron wondered which of these this was.

Dane turned to Cameron as he tucked his phone into his pocket. "I've got to go."

"Another car accident?"

The two-lane Alaska Highway that ran through Tok and the surrounding areas was notorious for head on collisions and fatal T-bones.

Dane shook his head, his brown eyes grim.

"A body was just discovered in the tree line along the highway just outside of town." He planted a kiss on her head before heading for the door. "I'll call you when I can."

Cameron watched Dane hurry down her porch steps toward his SUV. She covered her mouth with her hand as Dane reversed out of her drive. *It can't be.* But in her gut, she already knew this couldn't be a coincidence.

The last body found in the woods on the outskirts of Tok was Bethany Long—her ex-husband's twelfth victim.

Cameron gripped the curved back of her kitchen chair as her bite of salad threatened to come back up. She took a deep breath, reminding herself that coincidences really do happen. Plus, Dane hadn't said whether the body was male or female. It could be a man.

If it *was* a woman, chances were that she was killed by an intimate partner, a boyfriend, not a serial killer back from the dead.

Her gaze fell to a reddish-brown object lying next to Dane's plate, thinking it was a bug. She started to swat it away then realized what it was. It must've fallen out of Dane's pocket when he answered his phone.

She lifted the trout fly Dane had caught his first trout with when he was a boy. The sharp end of the hook and barb had been snipped off and dulled. Cameron reached for her phone and dialed Dane. It rang three times before going to voicemail. She hung up, knowing he was likely on another call related to the crime scene he was headed to.

She twirled the fly between her fingers. Dane was superstitious about it, having carried it in his uniform pocket since his first shift as a trooper. He never went to work without it.

Cameron looked out the window, hoping he wouldn't need it tonight.

CHAPTER FIVE

Cameron sat up in bed. She hadn't imagined it. Something, or someone, scratched at her back door. She closed her grip around the 9mm on her bedside table and swung her legs onto the floor.

The sun had finally set, and her house was dark. But there was enough moonlight filtering in through her windows for her to see as she crept down her hall toward the noise. She wasn't about to tempt fate by putting a spotlight on herself. She paused when she reached the kitchen, her pulse pounding in her ears.

Last she checked, it was after one in the morning. Dane still hadn't returned home. Not surprising since he'd been called to a homicide. Still, as she'd lain in bed earlier, she'd been listening for the crunch of his tires on his neighboring drive, longing for the security of having him nearby.

Sweat dripped between her breasts as she stared at the door. It was still closed. She crept forward, squinting to see the lock. When she got closer, she saw the deadbolt was still turned to the right, just as she'd left it.

As soon as Dane had left, she'd closed all the windows despite the heat and locked her two doors. The scratch sounded again. Cameron tightened her grip on the gun and raised it at the door.

Meeeow.

She exhaled, lowering the gun. *A cat.* She pictured the black, long-haired cat that belonged to a house farther down the road, the only other home on the long, gravel street.

She filled a glass with water, downing it at the sink before returning to her bedroom. It was too warm to sleep without any windows open, but she had to keep them closed. This way, she could at least take some solace in knowing if John *was* alive, she'd hear him before he broke in.

She replaced her gun on the nightstand, a present Dane had bought her a few months ago, more for wild animals than anything else. She lay on top of her comforter, a thousand unanswered questions swirling in her mind. Was Tanner lying about the blood in the cabin and the opened first aid kit? Trying to trick her into a confession? Why hadn't he mentioned the wolf call? And where the hell were John's remains?

Maybe she should be grateful Tanner hadn't found them so she couldn't be charged with murder. But the possibility of John being alive wasn't much better.

She rolled onto her side and grabbed her phone lying beside the gun. After calling Dane, she pressed the phone to her ear. It rang three times before going to voicemail. She hung up without leaving a message. What would she say? She should've told Dane before he left.

She set the phone on her nightstand. The murder could have nothing to do with John. It was also possible it wasn't a homicide—although, dying of natural causes in a ditch along the Alaska Highway seemed unlikely.

If John *had* survived, would he really be so stupid as to kill a second time in a town of twelve hundred? If John wanted to taunt

Cameron, or come after her, he'd know better than to announce his presence to not only her, but to law enforcement.

There were countless other probable scenarios. In this town, the murder was most likely a result of a drunken brawl that ended in a gunfight. Or domestic violence. A dispute between neighbors. A robbery gone wrong. Road rage.

Dane might even already have a suspect in custody. She plucked her phone from the tabletop and googled *Tok Alaska homicide.*

When she read the breaking news headline that topped her search results, her blood ran cold despite the heat.

Tok, AK – Young woman's body found in ditch off Alaska Highway; Homicide investigation underway

CHAPTER SIX

TROOPER NELSON HELD the metal door to the station open for Cameron. "Hey Doc."

From the dark half-moons beneath his eyes, Cameron guessed that, like Dane, he'd been up all night. As they moved past the empty front office assistant's desk, the station was quiet, despite a murder victim being discovered the night before. Cameron remembered it was Saturday.

"Is Dane here?" The extra hot Americano she'd bought for him was practically burning her hand, despite the sleeve.

"Nice to see you too."

"Oh, sorry I—"

Trooper Nelson cracked a grin as Cameron walked beside him into the large open room in the middle of the station. Two tables had been pushed together in front of a large white board that hung on the wall. A fax machine beeped in the corner beside a makeshift coffee station.

"I'm just kidding. It's been a long night, and I'm sure Sergeant Waska will be glad to see you. He's in his office."

"Thanks."

Cameron moved toward the door marked *SGT. WASKA.* It was ajar, and Dane motioned for her to come in, his phone pressed to his ear. She closed the door behind her and set the piping hot coffee on his desk, along with a bag of blueberry scones.

After reading the short article last night, she'd lain awake, staying in bed and listening in vain for the sound of Dane's tires until the sun came up after four in the morning. The article hadn't given many details about the young woman's murder, which left Cameron's mind to run wild.

Cameron sat in the folding chair across from Dane's desk. A second article was published by a Fairbanks news channel over an hour ago, and he still hadn't returned her call. If she hadn't been too anxious to eat since Tanner's visit yesterday, she would've thrown up when she read of the young woman's profession. She was thankful it was the weekend, and her dental practice was closed. There was no way she could've stayed focused on her patients after reading that.

Dane pressed his fingertips against his temple as his gaze fell to the coffee. "All right." He sighed into his desk phone receiver, and she watched the color drain from his face. "Thanks for calling. I'd like to know when you've finished the autopsy."

"What's wrong?" she asked after he hung up.

"It's just this new case." He avoided her eye contact and reached into the bag with the scones.

He was being vague. What was he keeping from her? And why?

"I'm starving, thank you. Are these from Frontier Coffee?"

Cameron nodded. The mobile coffee stand was only open in the summer months when the town had more visitors. Their scones were wildly popular and sold out daily before noon. Dane was usually first in line.

He took a bite, and Cameron braced herself for what she'd come to tell him, although she now guessed he already knew.

"Detective Mulholland came to see me yesterday," she said. "About John."

Dane coughed, making a fist and pressing it against his lips. *"What?"*

Cameron glanced at Dane's closed officed door. Aside from her, Dane, and Detective Mulholland, the world believed John died from a bear attack last November. She lowered her voice.

"Mulholland found the cabin. He *went* there. I thought he'd come to accuse me of killing John. Instead, what he found makes me worry John might have survived. And escaped. Tanner warned me to be careful."

Dane's eyes narrowed and he took a drink from his coffee. "How could he be sure?" he asked, setting the paper cup on his desk. "Maybe he was trying to get a confession out of you."

Cameron shook her head. "His body wasn't there. According to Mulholland, there were no remains at all. But there was evidence of John trying to treat his wounds inside the cabin. And blood. And his snowmobile was gone."

At this, Dane raised his eyebrows. He hadn't been there, but he knew how remote the cabin was—too remote for someone to happen upon it and steal John's snowmobile.

"I think he killed Madison Youngblood," she added.

Dane's dark eyebrows knitted together. "Her death doesn't bear any resemblance to John's murders."

Cameron straightened. "But she's a teacher! I read she was hired as an elementary teacher by the Tok school district. She was going to start this fall."

"It's not John." Dane's voice was firm.

"But how can you know? She was twenty-four, a teacher, and

found less than two miles away from John's last victim. It's *him*. I know it is. He's taunting me."

"This isn't about you, Cameron!"

He shouted loud enough for Trooper Nelson to hear. Cameron recoiled in her seat. He'd never spoken to her like that before.

A phone rang outside Dane's office, and Cameron heard Trooper Nelson take the call.

"Of course, it's not about me. My point is that John killed her." She lowered her voice, aware of Nelson on the other side of the wall. "It's too much of a coincidence to not be him. I don't understand why you can't see that."

"Look, I'm sorry." Dane reached across his desk, extending his hand toward her. "I didn't mean to shout at you. This case, it's awful. And I don't want it to go unsolved any more than you do." His voice softened. "But it's not John."

How could he be so sure? "Don't you think it's strange that Detective Mulholland came to see me about John still being alive the same day this young woman's body was found?" She leaned forward.

Dane stared back at her, seeming to think it over. "I don't know, but I don't think we should jump to conclusions."

His cell phone rang, making her jump. He picked it up, keeping his eyes on hers.

"Sergeant Waska."

Dane held the phone to his ear, and Cameron strained to hear as he listened intently to the person at the other end of the call. The voice coming through his phone sounded female, but Cameron couldn't make out what she was saying.

"Okay," Dane said after a minute. "I'll meet you there." He slid the phone into his vest pocket of his uniform and stood.

"I have to go. Trooper Cox just identified the patron who

left the Wolf Pack Bar fifteen minutes after Madison. Madison's parents came down from Fairbanks this morning, and when they went to pick up her car, still parked in front of the bar, it wouldn't start. So, it's possible she was still in the parking lot when this guy came out of the bar." He grabbed his coffee and moved around his desk. "I'm going to go with Trooper Cox to interview him. He's the closest thing we've got so far for a witness—and a suspect."

Besides John, Cameron thought.

Dane patted the front of his uniform vest. "Have you seen my trout fly? I couldn't find it this morning."

"Oh. Yeah." Cameron reached into her purse and held it out. "I found it on my kitchen table after you left."

"Thanks." Dane's shoulders relaxed as he smoothed the Velcro closed after tucking it into his vest pocket. He closed the space between them and enveloped her in a hug. "I love you. Try not to worry about John."

Cameron nodded after Dane pulled away, knowing that was impossible.

He let her go and opened his office door to leave. She put her hand on his forearm before he could escape. "I love you, too."

She stayed in his office and watched him through the window as he walked to his SUV. After he pulled away, Cameron grabbed the bag containing an untouched scone, leaving Dane's half eaten one on his desk.

On her way out, she handed the bag to Trooper Nelson who'd just inserted a paper into the fax machine.

"Scone?" Buying one for herself had been wishful thinking. She still had no appetite.

Nelson peered inside the bag. The faint creases around his eyes and flecks of gray in his brown hair were the only giveaways to his age, but Cameron guessed he had to be at least fifty.

"Oh, these are the best. Thanks, Cam." He nodded, taking the bag.

"No problem. Thought you could use one."

She made for the door, and then stopped. Dane never told her what the medical examiner had said on the phone. *Why was he so adamant John hadn't killed this young teacher?*

She turned to see the trooper had only a bite of the scone left. "Dane didn't say much about this new murder victim. Do you know how she died?"

Nelson nodded as he swallowed. "She was run over. But it wasn't your typical hit and run. The sarge is a little worked up over it. We all are. That's probably why he didn't want to talk about it, but don't take it personal." He popped the last of the scone into his mouth before hitting a button on the fax machine.

A hit and run. So that's why he didn't think John killed her.

Nelson glanced around the empty room, his mouth forming a frown. He stepped toward her, lowering his voice. "The details of this killing are like a couple that happened in this town in the late nineties."

Trooper Nelson had worked in Tok as a state trooper even longer than Dane. Dane started as a trooper when he was twenty-three, which meant he hadn't been hired until the year 2000. But Nelson would've been here.

"She had markings from a handcuff on one of her wrists and bruising that looked to be from a knee in her back, same as the old cases." He shook his head. "Never solved. And they aren't something any of us want to remember."

"Why is that?"

He shot her a look as if debating whether to tell her. "Because the killer was someone who knew this area. Someone the victims trusted, both of which were in their twenties." Nelson looked up from the fax machine. "Sergeant Waska's dad and I were both working here, and it was a rough time for years afterward. Not just for us, but the whole town. It was believed—and still is—that the killer was law enforcement. And more than that, a state trooper."

CHAPTER SEVEN

Outside the station, Cameron dug inside her purse until she felt Tanner's business card. She typed in his number as she strode across the parking lot in front of the troopers' station, which was empty aside from her truck. Nelson must've parked his SUV in the back. Tanner's phone went straight to voicemail. He was probably on his flight back to Seattle.

She unlocked her truck. "Hey, Tanner. It's Cameron. Please call me when you get this. There's been a murder, and—"

"Cameron!"

Cameron stopped short of reaching for the door handle. She turned to see Valerie, one of the first people she'd met in Tok, standing on the other side of the Alaska Highway wearing jeans and a faded T-shirt with the Howling Wolf Motel logo on the front. She was the owner, and rarely missed an opportunity to advertise.

"—and I'm worried it might be John," Cameron finished before ending the call.

Valerie strode toward Cameron, shading her eyes with her hand after crossing the highway. "Beautiful day, ain't it?"

"Yeah," Cameron agreed, thinking it felt like anything but.

"You wanna join me for a walk?"

Cameron hesitated, exhaustion sinking in after her sleepless night. "Sure."

She locked her truck and dropped her phone in her purse before she crossed the rest of the parking lot to where Valerie stood. She doubted she could sleep yet even if she tried, and what else did she have to do besides go home and worry about John being alive…and this new murder?

Valerie resumed her pace when Cameron reached her side. "I'm on my way to get one of those scones. Even though those damn tourists probably cleaned them out already." She nudged Cameron when she didn't respond. "You know I don't really mind those *damn tourists.* They keep me in business." She motioned to her five-cabin motel over her shoulder. "Plus, you used to be one of them yourself."

"I know." Cameron's gaze traveled to the snowcapped Alaskan Range that jutted up like a Bob Ross painting behind the town.

Cameron doubted she'd ever be considered a 'local' in this town, but those she'd befriended during her time here under a fake name seemed surprisingly unfussed when she moved to Tok under her real identity: the widow of the infamous Teacher Killer, John Prescott.

She'd first assumed the Tok residents' warmth with her was because she was dating Dane. Or that being the only dentist in town meant that practically every resident became a patient at her practice. Then Valerie told her something one day that made her think otherwise. *You're not the first one to move to this remote Alaskan town to escape your old life. And you won't be the last.*

"You seem quiet." Valerie turned to her. "You okay?"

Cameron forced a smile. "Yeah, I'm fine." Aside from Dane, Valerie was her closest friend in town.

Valerie's eyes told Cameron she didn't believe her, but the motel manager returned her attention to the road as they walked along the shoulder.

"Actually," Cameron said after a few steps. "It's the murder last night. The young woman whose body was found just outside town. Did you hear about it?"

"I did. Tragic."

"Trooper Nelson was just telling me this case has some similarities to a couple of unsolved murders that happened here in the late nineties."

Valerie stopped in her tracks. "Is that so?" She resumed her stride, apparently recovering from her momentary shock. Cameron kicked herself. She probably shouldn't have said anything. They were likely not releasing that information yet to the public.

"And this is troubling you because of your late husband, yes? Something like this must bring up a well of emotions for you."

Cameron's throat tightened before she saw the look of concern spreading across her friend's face. *Valerie has no idea what I did to John,* she reminded herself. *She thinks John died of a bear attack.*

"I guess so." Cameron stared ahead. As they neared the coffee stand, she took a sidelong glance at Valerie, curious if her shock was personal. She had lived in this town her whole life. How old had she been when the murders occurred? Possibly the same age as the victims.

"Trooper Nelson said the suspect in the old murders was someone in law enforcement. A trooper."

"Yep." Valerie raised her hand at the driver of a truck that passed on the highway. Her jaw was clenched, despite her friendly gesture.

"It was terrifying," she added. "I was twenty-eight when the first murder happened. Back then, Tok didn't have many women my age. And to think we couldn't even trust our own police officers was...unsettling to say the least. I didn't sleep good for years." As they veered to the right into a mostly empty parking lot, her gaze drifted toward the mountain range. "When no one was caught, I wondered for a time if the troopers knew who'd done it—one of their own. But as the years went on after the second murder and no more killings happened, people believed the killer wasn't someone who still lived around here. Either that or the killer died. Otherwise, why would they stop?"

They reached the coffee stand in the middle of a small parking lot that fronted a seasonal gift shop. The trooper station was still in view about a half a mile behind them.

"But the main suspect in those murders wasn't just *any* trooper." Valerie squinted at Cameron beneath the midday sun. "It was Sergeant Waska."

The ground shifted beneath Cameron's feet.

"Dane's father," Valerie added, seeing the look on Cameron's face.

Valerie stepped up to the stand's open window while Cameron grappled with what she'd just heard. It had to be the reason Dane was so upset. Why he was so convinced John hadn't killed this young teacher.

Valerie rested her elbow on the open windowsill and peered inside the coffee stand. "Please tell me you're not out of scones."

Why didn't Dane tell me about his father?

The man inside the coffee hut shook his head. "I'm afraid we are. Sorry."

He looked at Cameron, but she was only vaguely aware of his gaze lingering on her. "Some tourist bought the last two."

"Figures. I knew I was probably too late." Valerie sighed. "Guess I'll take a muffin instead. And a large coffee. Two sugars. No cream."

The rest of their conversation faded into nothing as Cameron stood there in the bright August sunshine, waiting for him to pour Valerie's coffee, as if things like scones and coffee mattered anymore. It wasn't lost on Cameron that *she* was the 'tourist' who'd bought the last two scones. Normally, she would've been grateful for his discretion in front of Valerie, but right now, all she could think about was Dane.

Why hadn't he said something to her? After all this time? Did *Dane* suspect his father?

Valerie turned from the window after she paid, holding a large blueberry muffin wrapped in plastic wrap. "Damn tourists."

CHAPTER EIGHT

TANNER STEPPED OFF the jetway at SeaTac, then moved through the crowd with his phone to his ear. A family of four stood in line at the gate, the two young children wearing matching Disneyland t-shirts. Tanner smiled at the enormous grins on the kids' faces as Cameron's voicemail played.

"Hey, Tanner. It's Cameron." Behind her voice, he could hear the hiss of the wind. "Please call me when you get this. There's been a murder, and I'm—"

She paused. Tanner heard someone in the background.

"—worried it might be John."

Tanner stepped onto the escalator as the voicemail ended, replaying Cameron's words from his visit yesterday. *The last time I saw John, he was alive.* When she'd said it, he suspected she was lying.

When he told her what he'd found at the remote cabin, he'd detected fear in her eyes. At the time, he guessed it was fear of being caught and facing the legal consequences for what she'd done to her husband. But the tremor in her voice on his voicemail was unmistakable, making him wonder what exactly had gone down at that cabin in the woods.

He pulled a piece of gum from his pocket and popped it in his mouth, chewing as he searched the news for *Tok, Alaska homicide.* Three headlines topped his search. He clicked on the article posted eight minutes ago.

TOK HOMICIDE VICTIM IDENTIFIED AS TWENTY-FOUR-YEAR-OLD TEACHER

Tanner walked off the escalator, his eyes glued to his phone as he read the article. Madison Youngblood had recently moved to Tok after being hired as an elementary school teacher. She was last seen leaving the Wolf Pack Bar.

His stomach tightened. The same place where Bethany Long was picked up by John. By the time he'd reached baggage claim, Tanner had read through both articles. Despite Madison Youngblood being a young teacher, her killing didn't fit Prescott's MO. In fact, the article mentioned that the killing was similar to two unsolved murders in Tok from the 1990's. But he could see why Cameron was suspicious, especially if Cameron had reason to believe her husband was still alive.

Tanner waited until he was in the privacy of his car to call the Tok trooper station, and the desk clerk connected him to Dane's office. Tanner rolled his window down to pay for his parking while he waited through the hold music.

"Sergeant Waska."

"This is Detective Mulholland."

"Oh. Hi."

Tanner pulled out of the parking garage and rolled up his window. "I'm calling about the recent murder in Tok. I saw the victim was a teacher. I was hoping you could give me some details."

The last time Tanner checked, Bethany Long's case was still unsolved. At the time, Cameron had been convinced her husband killed the young woman despite the lack of evidence to support her claim. But back then, Tanner thought Prescott was dead.

"Because you think it has something to do with John Prescott."

Tanner waited, letting the silence drag out on the phone. Cameron must've told him about Tanner's visit.

"No," Sergeant Waska said, "I don't think this is connected to Bethany Long's death, but I'm not ruling out anything at this point. They *were* both last seen at the Wolf Pack Bar, but our new victim wasn't sexually assaulted, and she was run over, not strangled. We'll have to wait to find out if there was any foreign DNA under her fingernails."

If Prescott had killed her, Tanner doubted there would be. Prescott had been scratched by a victim once, when he was first learning how to hunt his victims. Prescott wouldn't have allowed his victim's body to be so easily discovered if it had happened again.

"But at this point, I don't see any evidence pointing to Prescott as the killer," the sergeant continued, "even if he is still alive somehow."

Tanner wondered if Waska was referring to Prescott's staged bear attack or if he knew what really happened at that remote cabin in the Alaskan wilderness. He turned onto the 518 from the Airport Expressway. The traffic was light, even for a Saturday. "Do you have any leads?"

Sergeant Waska breathed into the phone. "There are similarities to a couple of unsolved murders that happened here in the late nineties."

"Really." This confirmed what he'd read in the article. "I'd like to see those old cases. Can you send me the casefiles?"

A pause. "I can. But if you're looking for John Prescott, they won't help you. Those cases were nothing like The Teacher Killer murders."

"I'd like to have a look anyway."

"All right. I'll send them over."

"Thanks."

"And, Sergeant?" Tanner asked after giving the trooper his email address.

"Yeah?"

"You think there's a chance that John Prescott could be alive?"

The call went quiet. If Tanner's suspicions were correct, the trooper knew what had gone down between Cameron and her husband at the remote Alaskan cabin. Waska was likely debating what to say, not wanting to incriminate his girlfriend.

"I suppose there's always a chance without finding his body, right?" Waska finally said.

Tanner wondered if the trooper sergeant was referring to Prescott's alleged bear attack in Idaho or the grim scene Tanner had found at the isolated cabin. He presumed it was the latter. He thought it likely the trooper had even gone with Cameron to the middle of the national preserve. Tanner couldn't imagine Cameron getting there by herself.

"But my gut tells me he's dead," Waska added.

Tanner thanked him again and ended the call. After merging onto the 509, he sped past the exit that led to his neighborhood and continued north for downtown. Maybe Cameron didn't confide in her boyfriend as much as Tanner had thought.

As he neared the bridge over the Duwamish Waterway, there was something in Waska's tone that needled at Tanner. Not the typical resistance he usually met from small town cops who didn't like anyone in their territory. No, this was something else.

Tanner popped another stick of gum in his mouth, tapping his fingers on the middle console of his Ford Fusion. If Tanner was right, Waska knew something he wasn't telling.

CHAPTER NINE

CAMERON DREW THE yoke of her Cessna toward her chest as she climbed above the tree line beyond Tok Junction Airport. Ever since her walk with Valerie, she'd been trying to make sense of what the motel owner had told her about Dane's father. Cameron had driven aimlessly along the Alaska Highway before pulling into the airport, deciding to go for a flight. She hoped that separating herself from the ground would clear her head.

Cameron banked left as she continued to climb and flew over the two-lane highway, imagining the young teacher killed on this same stretch of road two nights ago. Next came the image of Bethany Long, the ed major John murdered last winter after the world believed he was dead, her body dumped in the woods that stretched beneath Cameron's windscreen.

Normally, when she lifted off the ground, she felt the tension dissipate from her shoulders, like the distance between her and the earth was also a removal of all her problems. But there were times like today—and when she learned that John was the notorious Teacher Killer—that the elevation did nothing to quell her spiraling anxiety.

Had John really survived? It seemed the only explanation for the blood inside the remote cabin. And the missing snowmobile outside.

She suppressed a shudder, recalling the day she'd discovered the truth about her husband. She'd gone flying, thinking obsessively about the ripple effect it had on her reputation and Seattle dental practice. She'd come so close to ending it all with one swift push on the yoke.

Her gaze moved out her side window to the trooper station in the middle of town as she headed north over the vast forested area. In her mind, she replayed what Valerie said about Dane's father being the prime suspect in the old Tok murders. Had John replicated those killings, knowing it would point to Dane's dad?

She found herself scouring the town's backroads below for a sign of John, half expecting to catch him strolling down one of them in broad daylight. It would be just like him, infecting her life again after she'd carefully rebuilt it.

When she soared over the Tanana River, she was low enough to spot a black bear and her cub moving slow along its rocky shore. It was ironic to think how heartbroken she'd been when she'd gotten the news that John had been attacked by a bear while hunting, believing he was dead, before she learned what kind of man he really was.

Cameron was lost in thought when Hunt Lake came into her view. She turned the plane toward the small body of water. When she got closer, she could make out Dane's and his father's cabins, the only two on the secluded lake. George's small fishing boat was tied to the end of his dock.

George practically lived up here, despite neither of the cabins having electricity. Dane's father even stayed at the lake for most of the winter months, which drove Dane crazy, since his father could have a heart attack, or an injury, and no one would know until it was too late. Cameron had always presumed that George lived up here to feel close to his late wife, Dane's mom. Although gruff on the outside, Cameron suspected he had a soft spot.

But maybe the reason for George's reclusive lifestyle was something else. A shudder grazed over her skin as she squinted from the glare of the sun reflecting off the water, recalling the weekends she'd spent at John's hunting cabin in the Cascade Mountains following John's supposed death. And the night she stumbled upon the evidence of his crimes.

Afterward, the Seattle media was so quick to accuse her of not only *knowing* about John's murders but being his accomplice. Cameron looked out her window, staring at the roof of George's cabin. Maybe Dane's anger surrounding this new murder stemmed from his father being misjudged, wrongly accused of something unthinkable.

She glanced at her fuel gauge and turned back for Tok, unable to keep herself from wondering what made everyone in that town suspect he was a killer all those years ago.

Her cabin was warm when she stepped inside. Almost immediately, her hair felt damp against the back of her neck. Dane's driveway next door was empty, and she collapsed on her slipcovered couch. She'd meant to only close her eyes for a minute when she woke to a sharp rap on her door.

Her pulse raced as she became aware that she'd dreamt of John. He chased her through the snow outside Miles's cabin, dripping blood onto the white ground. John came around a tree, leaving Cameron in shock, not that he'd caught up to her but what he was wearing. During the chase, his faded jeans and sweater had morphed into an Alaska State Trooper uniform.

It was still daylight, and she peered through her thin curtains at the figure standing on her porch. Her heart lurched in her chest. She opened the curtains a slit and sank against the couch. It was Dane. Not John.

She pushed herself off the couch and trudged to the door.

"Hey," Dane stepped inside after she swung the door open, holding a large pizza box from the town's diner in one hand and two Alaskan Whites in the other.

He'd changed out of his trooper uniform, now wearing jeans and a red flannel shirt with the sleeves rolled up to his elbows. She could see the exhaustion in his bloodshot eyes.

Cameron glanced at the sun, still high in the sky, before shutting the door behind him. "What time is it?"

"Just after eight. You hungry?"

Dane set the beers on her kitchen table, and Cameron followed him into her kitchen, trying to recall the last time she'd eaten. Yesterday?

"A little," she said.

"I'm starving." Dane pulled two plates from the cupboard and filled his with two slices of pepperoni with olives.

Cameron put one on the plate he left out for her and sat across from him at her kitchen table, the same seats they'd taken the night before. Dane reached his hand across the table to take hers. She met his tired, brown-eyed gaze.

"I'm really sorry that I shouted at you earlier," he said. "This new case struck a nerve with me."

After what Valerie said about Dane's father, she could understand why. "It's okay." Tanner's visit yesterday had struck a nerve with her too.

"But that's no excuse." Dane stroked her palm with his thumb. "I should never have spoken to you like that."

"It's all right, really. How's the investigation going?"

Dane took a large bite of his pizza and wiped his mouth with a napkin. "Not good. For now, we're pretty much at a dead end."

Cameron bit into her own slice, waiting for him to elaborate.

Dane took a swig from his beer. "Nelson and I spent the afternoon going through her social media, email, text messages, and phone logs. She just moved to Tok and had no boyfriend. All her close friends live in Fairbanks, and from what we can tell, they had good relationships. I don't think she knew her killer."

"What about the guy who left the bar right after Madison? What did he say when you talked to him?"

"He said when he left the Wolf Pack, Madison was already gone. And I believe him. He's got no criminal history and drives a Subaru Outback, which looked unscathed. It was negative for blood in the spots that we tested it, plus the tires are too small and have the wrong treads to be the ones that ran over Madison."

"What size tires are you looking for?"

Dane frowned. "Eighteen inch. Same size and same tread that's on most of the police-issued SUVs, like the one I drive." He stuffed another large bite into his mouth.

Cameron nearly choked on her beer. What if John did this? What if he planned every detail to get under Dane's skin? And hers? If John was watching her, he would know they were together. Plus, after what happened in her Seattle home last February, her and Dane's names were all over the news.

If Dane noticed her reaction, he didn't show it. He finished his first slice of pizza and reached for a second. Cameron set down her can of Alaskan White with a clunk, swallowing hard.

"What makes Madison's murder so similar to those old cases?"

Dane's eyes locked with hers. "Both the murders happened here in the summer of '97. The first victim was Amy Clarke. Twenty-six. Her husband's parents owned a gas station in town.

Amy and her husband both worked there. Amy called 911 one night when her husband was working and reported someone lurking around her property." A shadow came over his face. "My dad responded to the call. He searched around her place but couldn't find anyone, then left around one-thirty in the morning. When her husband came home from the nightshift at seven, he found her dead in the street in front of their property. She'd been run over."

Cameron's breath stuck in her throat as she stared across the table at her boyfriend. She could tell this was getting harder for him to talk about.

"Like Madison Youngblood, she hadn't been raped, and investigators suspected she ran out of the house before her killer got a chance. She had markings left by handcuffs on both her wrists and bruising on the small of her back from where she'd been pinned down. The same spot where police were trained to pin down suspects. There were no signs of forced entry. A neighbor half a mile down the road reported seeing a vehicle drive toward her house just after 2:00 a.m., which is right around the time of her death."

Dane's gaze traveled out the window. "My dad was a main suspect for lack of any other evidence or leads. It was hard. Even now, it's still not easy for me to think about—or say out loud. People in town started looking at him differently. At me and my mom too. I was home that summer from the University of Alaska. It was hard on their marriage, but mostly it was hard on my dad. It got worse after the second victim was found." His Adam's apple bobbed as he swallowed.

"That must have been tough." She watched him drain what was left of his beer, knowing all too well what it felt like to be falsely accused of helping John kill all those women.

"The second victim's name was Erica Lavine, and her car was

spotted with a flat on the side of the Alaska Highway a couple of miles out of town the day she went missing—not far from where Madison's body was found. Two witnesses remembered seeing a state trooper vehicle parked behind Audrey's car, but there was no record of any police response. That night, after she was reported missing, her car was found—with a flat and the jack still in place—abandoned in that same spot on the highway. There were no prints besides her own and a couple of members of her family."

Cameron shifted in her seat, realizing she'd been gripping the arms of the chair so hard her hands hurt. She studied Dane's expression. How hard it must have been for him to get yesterday's call and dredge all this up. She felt guilty for even thinking Dane was hiding something from her.

Dane swallowed hard, the color draining from his face. "She wasn't found for a while. She went missing in September, and in February an ice fisher drilled his auger into her body, encased in the frozen surface of Yarger Lake."

She pushed her plate away, her appetite gone. Last winter Dane had taken her ice fishing on a nearby lake. An image of him drilling the silver corkscrew through the ice flooded her mind.

Dane's gaze returned to hers. "The day after Erica Lavine went missing, my dad and Trooper Nelson responded to a call near Yarger Lake in separate vehicles. They were both interviewed by an investigator from the Fairbanks Major Crimes Unit, although it was obvious the investigator—and the town—suspected my dad the most."

"Did you ever think it was him?"

A pained look flashed in Dane's eyes, and Cameron regretted her question. But she had to know.

"No." Dane shook his head. "But I believed it was likely a state trooper. Or someone with a police scanner and access to a patrol vehicle. They knew the area, but I don't think they were local. The killings stopped, and eventually people seemed to believe the killer moved on. Or died. Maybe both. It faded in people's memory, but my dad never forgot how quick people were to think he was behind it."

Cameron took a long drink of beer. "From my experience, some people are ready to think the worst of you, given the chance."

When he leaned back, her wooden table chair creaked. Although, Cameron thought, Dane believing his dad to be innocent didn't mean that he was. She'd been married to John for nearly a decade and hadn't known he was The Teacher Killer.

"It's why he hides away all year at his cabin," Dane said. "Only comes to town when he has to. After it happened, he and my mom both lived up there as much as they could." Dane sighed. "There's still something I need to follow up on, but I should probably go see my dad about this new murder. It's not going to be fun, but he remembers those old cases better than anyone. He was obsessed with solving them for years afterward, especially when all leads pointed to him."

Dane's eyes met hers, and the pain in his eyes softened. "You okay?"

"Yep. Of course."

"I thought maybe…this brings up some difficult feelings for you too."

She rubbed the back of her neck, and her palm came away slick with sweat. The cabin felt like it was growing hotter. She got up to open a window.

Behind her was the clink of the beer bottle on the table. "You ever sorry you hooked up with a guy who deals with death all the time?"

She turned and shook her head. "Never." She offered him a small smile.

He pushed away from the table, his second slice untouched, and gave her a quick kiss before enveloping her in his strong arms.

Cameron leaned her head against his chest, unable to shake the feeling that Madison had died at the hands of John. For him, it made the perfect crime. It upended Cameron's new life by throwing suspicion onto Dane's father, while no one but Cameron suspected that it was John. It was exactly how John—

Her phone rang, interrupting her thoughts. Dane lowered his arms, stepping back as she moved toward her purse, which she'd left on the kitchen island when she'd gotten home. It was still ringing when she withdrew her phone from her bag.

She recognized the Seattle area code, and the number she called earlier.

Detective Mulholland.

CHAPTER TEN

SIENNA CHECKED THE time on her phone after closing out of the news article. She stood from her seat behind the desk at the Howling Wolf Motel, frowning at the lack of progress she'd made today on her novel. Despite being left with practically nothing to do at the motel after a late cancellation and no show, she'd hardly written anything during her entire shift. The second graders in the class where she worked as a teacher's assistant could probably get more done in the same amount of time. She snapped her notebook closed.

"Goodnight," she said to the large stuffed wolf mounted on the wall beside the motel's front office door, imagining her aunt Valerie shooting the enormous beast in the middle of some remote forest before dragging it onto the sled behind her snowmobile.

Normally, her evening exchange with the taxidermied apex predator made her crack a smile. But tonight she was too disturbed by the town's recent murder to find any humor in it. She'd spent most of her shift on her phone, reading about Madison Youngblood.

She flicked on the lights for the motel's *VACANCY* sign and flipped the sign on the door that gave the phone number of the caretaker's cabin where Sienna was living for the summer. She stayed fifteen minutes longer than usual tonight in case her no show arrived, and when Sienna stepped outside, the sun had already set beyond the mountain peaks on the horizon.

She gazed across the highway at the Wolf Pack Bar, where Madison was last seen alive—and likely picked up by her killer—right across the road. She and Madison were the same age, new to this town, and lived alone. Even though she didn't know her, Sienna felt a strange sense of grief for the life so similar to her own that had been lost. They even looked alike, both having long, blond hair. And they had almost the same job. During the school year, Sienna worked as a teacher's assistant in Anchorage.

The last time she refreshed the news search on her phone, Madison's killer was still at large.

A chill ran down her arms as she walked through the gravel path that led to the motel's six standalone cabins. *What if Madison's killer had a type?* She zipped up her hooded sweatshirt and pulled the hood over her hair. This was the first time all summer that she'd stayed on the motel's premises without a single guest on the property.

She quickened her steps, passing through the tree line behind the motel that shielded the guest cabins from the view of the caretaker's property and large maintenance shed. Most nights, she liked the seclusion of her temporary quarters, and how the spruce trees made her feel like she was staying in the wilderness, alone to work on her novel away from the distractions of the outside world.

Now, it felt *too* remote, making Sienna wish she was spending the night at Aunt Valerie's home a few miles away. She chided herself for her pounding heart when she reached the door to her cabin, wishing she would've locked it before leaving that afternoon.

After stepping inside, she twisted the deadbolt. She eyed the empty cabin and flicked on the lights, glad it was too small for some intruder to hide. Her gaze lifted to the tiny loft, where her bed remained unmade, exactly how she left it.

For a moment, she debated calling her aunt and asking to stay. There were no guests tonight anyway. But she decided against it. Aunt Valerie was one of the toughest women she's ever met. A *wolf* hunter. Despite her growing fears, Sienna didn't want to seem weak. Plus, she knew Valerie would want her to be onsite in case the no show arrived in the middle of the night.

She sat at the kitchen table and opened her laptop, hoping that diving into her manuscript would force her fears from her mind. You're *not* in a remote forest, she told herself. You're two blocks from the Alaska Highway. The diner and bar are right across the road.

You're perfectly safe here.

She stared at her laptop screen and her fifty-page work-in-progress, feeling a loss of inspiration for plotting murder after the reality of one happening in this very town. Sienna's phone chimed. When she withdrew her phone from her pocket, she saw that she'd been sitting there for over ten minutes and hadn't written a word.

It was a text from her mom. *You sure you can't come back early? I'm worried about you up there.*

Sienna's mother couldn't be any more different than Aunt Valerie. For Mom, living anywhere smaller than Anchorage was unthinkable. Before Sienna took the job at the motel this summer, she'd warned Sienna not to let Aunt Valerie 'put any crazy ideas in your head.'

Her mom had called as soon as she'd seen the news about Madison Youngblood's murder, asking Sienna to come back to Anchorage. Even before hearing about the murder, she hadn't been a fan of Sienna's summer plans. But Sienna had been coming to stay with her aunt every summer since she was a kid. And she loved the seclusion of Tok at the junction of the Alaska and Glenn highways, surrounded by forest land for hundreds of miles. With the Alaska Range as its backdrop, the town had a unique beauty that she'd hoped would inspire her writing when she took the summer job.

Sienna and Aunt Valerie had always been close, bonding over their shared love for the outdoors, crime fiction, and a need for independence—all things Sienna's mother could never relate to.

Sienna glanced at her novel's word count on the lower left of her screen. She bit her lip.

This was why she'd taken the summer job with her aunt, rather than her usual two-week visit. She had to supplement her income over the summer break, and this job afforded her the time and seclusion to finish her novel in peace. Or so she'd thought.

She only had two weeks left before she had to return to Anchorage, and her novel was only halfway done. She'd always wanted to be a writer, but finishing her first book was taking her much longer than she planned. At this rate, I'll never finish, she thought with a pulse of anxiety.

She closed her laptop before replying to her mom, because she just wasn't in the right headspace to write tonight. *Don't worry mom, I'm fine. And I'll be back in just two weeks.*

She pushed back her chair and moved to the cabin's couch, where she'd left the faded Seattle crime thriller she borrowed from her aunt. She lifted the novel off the seat and rested her feet on the coffee table, then opened to the bookmarked page.

Five minutes in, she found herself unable to concentrate on the words, her thoughts returning to the news articles she'd read about Madison's killing. *If Madison didn't know her killer, what if he was still here, in Tok, watching, waiting to strike again?*

One article said that Madison's murder resembled two

unsolved murders that happened here in the nineties. *If this was a copycat, would there be two murders this time too? Or, has the original killer come back?*

She set down the novel, deciding to go to bed before her thoughts ran wild anymore. She was halfway up the ladder to the loft when she heard the crunch of gravel outside her cabin. She stopped cold, turning in the direction of the noise, waiting to see if she'd hear it again.

She descended the ladder, her pulse pounding in her ears as she peered through the front window. All she could see in the waning daylight was the row of trees that separated her from the motel. After a steadying breath, she opened the door and scanned the gravel pathway that led to the trees.

"Hello?" she called.

No response. *There's no one here. You're just being paranoid from plotting a serial killer thriller all summer.* She stepped inside and locked the deadbolt behind her. *It was probably an animal.*

She climbed up the ladder again and crawled into the double bed, not bothering to get undressed. No sooner had she closed her eyes, they snapped open as she recalled the two phone calls she'd gotten at the motel office earlier that evening. *How could I have forgotten?*

The phone had rung twice, and when she'd answered, there was no one there. Just silence on the end of the call until she hung up. Cell phone reception outside of Tok was spotty, and at the time, she'd assumed it was someone calling to see if they had vacancies. Or the no show calling to say he'd be late.

But what if it was something else?

She turned onto her side, willing her mind to stop imagining crazy scenarios. She gazed at the knotty pine ceiling, grateful for the fading daylight that still filtered in through the windows. Things always seem scarier in the dark.

CHAPTER ELEVEN

TANNER DIALED CAMERON's number and leaned back in his desk chair at Seattle Homicide, pressing his phone to his ear. The unit was quiet this Saturday evening. There was only one other homicide detective working at the adjacent cubicle.

Cameron answered after the first ring. "Hi, Tanner."

Even though she'd only spoken two words, her greeting felt stiff. Perfunctory. He thought back to how she sounded in her voicemail. *This new murder really has her rattled.*

"Hi, Cameron. I got your message. And I spoke with Sergeant Waska earlier today about the recent murder in Tok."

"Oh." A pause. "He didn't tell me."

"He also sent me two casefiles from a couple of unsolved murders in the area from the late nineties that he believes share some similarities to this new homicide." Tanner stared at the scanned pages of Erica Lavine's autopsy report from 1997 on his laptop screen. "I reviewed this new case, and I can see your concern after my visit, especially her being a teacher." He moved his gum to the other side of his mouth. "But I'm not convinced John had anything to do with this new murder."

He was met with silence. Tanner checked his phone to make sure they were still connected. They were.

"Did Dane tell you that Madison was last seen leaving the Wolf Pack Bar?" Cameron asked. "The same place as Bethany Long?"

"He did. But there's no hard proof that John killed Bethany either."

Again, she was quiet.

Tanner wondered what she was holding back. "At least that *I* know of."

"How can you not see that this is John? I mean, you warned me about him only yesterday."

Tanner swiveled in his chair. "Well, Madison Youngblood wasn't strangled. She wasn't sexually assaulted either."

"Maybe it didn't go as planned. She tried to escape."

He can hear the doubt in her voice, despite her effort to sound convincing. They both knew that if John *had* killed Madison Youngblood, it likely went exactly as he'd planned.

He returned his gaze to the case file on his laptop. "I can see why Sergeant Waska believes this new murder is connected to the two unsolved cases from the nineties. Especially the first victim, Amy Clarke."

He's met with silence. "Unless you know something that I don't?"

"No," she said after a moment.

"Hmm. Okay. Regardless of whether John killed Madison Youngblood, I think you should be careful."

"I will."

"And Cameron?"

"Yeah?"

"I appreciate you calling. Don't hesitate to call again."

"I won't."

After Cameron ended the call, Tanner returned his attention to Erica Lavine's autopsy findings. Despite being dumped into a cold lake, and her body frozen into the lake's surface probably less than a week after her death, she was too decomposed for the ME to determine whether she shared any of the same markings on her wrists or lower back as Amy Clarke or injuries consistent with being run over—or whether she was sexually assaulted. Erica Lavine's hyoid bone was fractured, however, and the ME ruled her cause of death homicide by strangulation.

There was evidence suggesting the two women were killed by someone in law enforcement. Or at least who had access to a state trooper vehicle and police scanner.

Tanner scrolled to the witness report on the last page of the casefile that he'd reread now several times. The witness was Karl Sadler, and he came forward after Erica Lavine's body was discovered in Yarger Lake, stating that he'd been fishing on the lake the day after Erica Lavine was last seen alive. Leaving the lake at dusk, Karl passed a white Ford Explorer headed toward the lake before he reached the Alaska Highway. Recognizing who the vehicle belonged to, he waved at the driver, who didn't wave back.

Despite a note in the report questioning the reliability of the witness after he admitted to having several beers before leaving the lake, the Ford Explorer Karl claimed to have seen was searched by Alaskan authorities. But no evidence was found linking Erica Lavine to the vehicle.

Nevertheless, the owner of the Ford Explorer remained one of three names listed as the top suspects in Erica Lavine's murder. Tanner studied the three names listed at the bottom of the casefile while chewing his gum. There were two he recognized, but it was the one at the top of the list that concerned him most.

CHAPTER TWELVE

WHEN CAMERON HUNG up with Tanner, Dane had already left the kitchen table. She'd had her back to Dane while they spoke, staring out her window. She'd nearly told the detective that John had confessed to killing Bethany Long, the ed major who was murdered in Tok last November. That was right before she left him for dead. Or at least *thought* she had.

She closed her eyes and recalled John's panicked screams that morphed into cries of agony, echoing through the remote wilderness, along with the howls and yips of the pack of gray wolves that descended into the valley where she'd left John wounded, bleeding, and tied to a tree. As she trekked through the white woods, she'd been certain she heard him die.

She replayed her conversation with Tanner in her mind. He was right. Madison Youngblood's murder didn't completely fit with John's other killings. And there were similarities to the town's unsolved case from the nineties. But Madison *was* a young teacher.

If John had survived—and had come after her—he would be stupid to kill exactly in the way he was famous for. John was a lot of things, but stupid wasn't one of them.

She moved toward the rhythmic sound coming from her living room and found Dane asleep on her couch, feet hanging over the armrest. She padded closer, admiring his thick dark hairline and high cheekbones, and the way his plaid shirt was pulled tight around his biceps. He was ruggedly handsome, even as he snored with jaw slightly open.

She sank into the chair across from him, the same one she'd sat in when Tanner came to tell her he thought John was still alive. *Why was Tanner so doubtful that John killed Madison? And why hadn't Dane mentioned that he'd called?*

Her gaze settled on Dane's palm resting on his chest, rising and falling with each breath. What must it have been like for Dane, living in a town where everyone suspected his father of being a killer? Even more unsettling was that the killer was never caught.

She recalled the photo of Madison Youngblood from that morning's news article. She looked different than John's victims, all of whom had dark hair. In her photo, Madison had long blond hair, much like Cameron's during her marriage to John. The twenty-six-year-old beamed with a broad smile, full of life and a bright future. The article stated Madison's parents lived in Fairbanks.

Cameron had been twenty-six when her parents died in a car accident on their way to her graduation from dental school. She'd taken it hard, and her boyfriend, Miles, proposed not long after. A shudder coursed through her, thinking of their marriage—and its catastrophic end.

Cameron lifted her gaze to the window. Daylight streamed through the glass despite it being after ten. How hard it was for Madison's parents not to have answers right now. Cameron couldn't imagine what it was like for the surviving family members of the two victims killed in Tok in the nineties.

What if Dane's father *had* been the killer? How easy would it be to get away with murder if you were the one investigating it? Tanner didn't believe John killed Madison. Could Dane's father have killed those women all those years ago? And now had the urge to scratch an old itch? She watched her boyfriend sleep, then pushed aside the thoughts about his father, feeling guilty for even thinking it. Maybe her years being unknowingly married to a vicious murderer had left her jaded.

She yawned. Even after her own nap on that couch, she still felt exhausted, like the day had hollowed her out. She pushed herself up from the chair and locked the front door. After double checking the back door was still locked, she headed to her room to try and get some rest.

She eyed Dane again, sound asleep on her couch, as she moved through the living room, which was still lit from the lingering daylight filtering in. She was glad he'd stayed, even if only on her couch.

Maybe with him here, she'd be able to sleep through the night.

CHAPTER THIRTEEN

Sweat trickled down the back of Sienna's neck when she sat up in bed. Outside, it was dark. Her heart raced from her dream of being chased by bright headlight beams as she ran down the Alaska Highway.

She reached for the cup of water she kept on her nightstand, wishing she hadn't read every article on Madison Youngblood's murder during her shift at the motel. When she lifted it to her lips, the glass was empty. She replaced it on the nightstand and felt her way down the loft's ladder in the darkness.

When she reached the bottom, she had one bare foot on the floor with her other still on a rung when a large, gloved hand clamped around her forearm, yanking her limb behind her back as cold metal cinched around her wrist with a sharp *click*. She screamed in terror as she released her free hand from the ladder.

Her second foot hit the floor and she stumbled backward. Her attacker gripped her other arm, holding her upright as a shriek of horror escaped Sienna's throat. An image of Madison in her final moments sprung to her mind as she registered the feel of the handcuff on her second wrist.

She screamed again, writhing to free her arms from the restraints. A leather-gloved hand clamped over her mouth.

"Shh."

She tried to shake free of the man's hold as she felt his warm breath on her cheek.

"This will go easier for you if you don't fight it."

She drew her knee to her chest and drove her heel back with a force heightened by the adrenaline coursing through her.

"Ahh!"

When her heel connected with his kneecap, the hand fell away from her mouth. She shook out of his hold and ran for the cabin door. She'd only gotten a few feet when her head whipped backward, her attacker's hand gripping her hair. She tried to lift her hands to the burn in her scalp, stopping as pain seared through her shoulder blade.

She stood still, head tilted back as the man pressed himself against her back, his gloved fingers digging into the flesh of upper arm. She stifled a whimper as her assailant stroked her hair, causing goosebumps to prickle her forearms.

"That's better," he whispered.

The calmness—and control—in his voice made Sienna's blood run cold. She had no doubt this was the same man who'd killed Madison.

Breathing hard, Sienna eyed her pathway to the door in the darkness. She could still run despite her arms being restrained. If she could make it outside, she could scream for help. She wouldn't have far to go to reach the highway.

"Just relax." He stroked the back of her head, tucking her hair behind her shoulder.

She resisted the urge to shiver beneath his touch, reminded of her Aunt Valerie's advice about wolf encounters. *Never let them sense your fear. They can sniff it out, and they'll take it as an opportunity to turn you into their prey.*

She willed herself to remain still as she waited for Madison's killer to lean his head toward hers. When she felt his breath on her face, she cocked her head to the side and bit the base of his neck, her teeth sinking into the collar of his shirt and the flesh beneath. He cried out when she clamped her jaw shut.

His gloved hands closed around her face, shoving her away with enough force that she fell against the back of the couch.

"You *bitch!*"

His hand flew to his neck as Sienna pushed herself to her feet. Even in the darkness, she could see his rage. Sienna raced for the door, knocking over a table lamp as she rounded a corner. The man's heavy footsteps tromped after her, but she didn't dare slow down to look.

When she got to the door, relief flooded her. She was met with resistance when she reached for the doorknob and remembered the handcuffs around her wrists. She twisted, frantically feeling for the knob behind her back as the tall figure moved toward her through the darkness.

Her hand closed around the knob. She twisted and pulled. The man's pace slowed, the outline of his form moving with a slight limp, probably from Sienna's blow to his kneecap. She pivoted through the open doorway and ran down the wood porch steps as a beam of speeding headlights shone through the tree line.

In bare feet, she sprinted across the grass. Hearing the drone of the semi's engine on the highway, hope flickered in her chest. *It's not that far. You can make it.*

"Heellp!"

She was silenced by the gloved palm that clamped over her mouth. With his other arm, the man encircled the front of her chest. She kicked and flailed beneath his hold as he dragged her back toward the cabin, digging her bare heels into the grass.

When they reached the cabin's front steps, he lifted her into the air and pulled her inside, slamming the door behind them. She screamed as he threw her onto the wood floor, thinking of the phone calls to the motel earlier that day—and the eerie silence on the other end of the line.

She bent her knee and pressed it into the floor to crawl away from him. But with her hands cuffed behind her, the effort was useless. His knee came down hard on her back. She let out a grunt from his weight crushing her spine. She writhed beneath him as his palm shoved her chest against the floor.

He released his knee from her back and turned her over to face him. It was too dark for her to clearly make out his face, but her eyes had adjusted enough to see his mouth upturn to a smile.

"That was fun."

He knelt over her, pressing his palm over her mouth, muffling the sound when she screamed again. *I should've stayed with Aunt Valerie.* She'd known in her gut that she was in danger. Now it was too late.

She pressed her feet into the floor in a futile attempt to slide away, sickened by the realization that this was all a game to him.

The pressure on her mouth released seconds before his hand closed around her neck. She shook her head wildly from side to side, trying to escape his grip tightening around her throat. She opened her mouth to scream again as the man wrapped his other hand around her neck, but her vocal cords were squeezed shut.

Sienna frantically tried to free her wrists as the man's fingers dug into her flesh, squeezing her airway shut. As the pain dulled, and her vision blurred, an image of Madison in her final moments filled Sienna's mind. She felt a strange connection to the young woman she'd never met, knowing they would both die at the hands of the same man. The bright headlight beams from her dream overtook her thoughts as she was enveloped by darkness.

CHAPTER FOURTEEN

Cameron opened her eyes. There was just as much daylight streaming through her bedroom curtains as when she'd fallen asleep. She rolled over and checked the time on her phone. It was almost 7:00 a.m.

She climbed out of bed and padded toward her living room, remembering Dane asleep on her couch. But her couch was empty.

"Dane?"

She checked the kitchen, but there was no sign of him.

"Dane?"

She returned to the living room and peered through her front window and at his driveway next door. His SUV was gone. *He must've gone back to work already,* she thought as she wandered back to the kitchen to brew a pot of coffee.

She filled the coffee pot with water at her kitchen sink, remembering Dane saying last night that he still needed to follow up on something. Or maybe he'd decided to go to the cabin on Hunt Lake to talk to his dad.

Out of the corner of her eye, she caught a dark flicker of

movement through the trees behind her house. She turned and peered through the window beside her back door, crossing her arms as she scanned the patch of spruce trees. A crow emerged from the forest and disappeared above her house. An uneasiness crept over her as she stared outside. Whatever had caught her eye seemed much bigger than a bird. The figure had seemed human, skirting between the evergreens. She watched her yard for another minute. Maybe it had just been the crow after all.

She turned, freezing in place when she saw her unlocked deadbolt above the back door handle. She was certain she'd locked it last night before going to bed. Had Dane unlocked it? Maybe he'd gone out back for some reason. She frowned and flipped the deadbolt when a knock sounded against her front door.

She jerked her head toward the sound. Her gun was still on her nightstand. She stepped slowly through her kitchen, keeping her eyes trained on her front door as she debated whether to get the pistol. The figure on her porch moved to the side, and she recognized Trooper Nelson in full uniform through the window.

Cameron released the breath she'd been holding before she opened the door.

"Hey, Cameron. Sorry to disturb you so early," he said.

"That's okay." Cameron stepped on the porch, squinting from the bright morning sun, suddenly aware of not wearing a bra beneath her t-shirt. At least she was wearing pants.

She rubbed at the goosebumps that prickled her forearm. Despite it being August, with high temperatures in the sixties during the day, it was getting close to freezing at night. The temperature dropped each day as they got closer to September. Dew glistened the patch of grass beneath one of the larger spruce trees in her front yard.

"I'm looking for Dane. Is he here?"

An involuntary shiver ran down her arms. She'd found it

hard to believe when Dane told her earlier that month that Tok occasionally sees snow in the month of August. But there were still a few days left in the month and the temperature was dipping into the thirties at night.

"No." She glanced at his empty drive next door. "He fell asleep on my couch last night, but when I woke up, he was gone."

"Huh." Nelson put his hands on his hips. "He's not answering my calls. Did he say where he was going?"

Cameron shook her head. "Sorry. I don't know. Maybe to see his dad?"

"It's possible, but I don't think so. We were planning to go talk to him together a little later today."

Cameron thought back to their conversation last night before Tanner called. "There was something Dane said he needed to follow up on. Can't remember what it was. Actually, I don't think he said."

"Well, I'm sure he'll turn up." Nelson started down her porch steps. "He must be somewhere out of cell range."

Cameron nodded. She'd discovered since moving up here that you didn't have to go far from town to lose your cell signal.

"Will you let me know if you hear from him?" Nelson asked when he reached the bottom step.

"Yeah, of course."

"Thanks." Nelson nodded and strode toward his SUV.

After going inside, Cameron retrieved her phone from her room, then called Dane on her way to the kitchen to finish making her coffee. It went to voicemail like Nelson said.

"Hey, it's me. Trooper Nelson was just here looking for you. I hope you're okay." She stared at the deadbolt on her back door after pouring coffee grounds into the filter. "Call me when you get this."

Cameron pulled into the Wolf Pack Bar's nearly vacant parking lot, braking to a stop beside Karl Sadler's truck. It would be an understatement to say Karl, a longtime Tok resident, was a regular of the bar. If the bar was open, Karl was here. His truck hardly ever left the parking lot.

It was almost noon, and Cameron still hadn't heard from Dane. Unable to sit around her empty house any longer, she'd decided to come into town. Aside from the library, which was closed on Sundays, there were only two options: the diner or the bar.

When she stepped inside, Karl sat hunched over the bar nursing a beer with his eyes glued to the pre-season football game on the bar's TV. Seeing Cameron, Joan slung a towel over her shoulder and came to the end of the bar, singing along to the Loretta Lynn song playing from the jukebox.

"Haven't seen you in a while," Joan said. "What can I get for you?"

Cameron slid onto the barstool. "I'll have a Coke. Thanks."

Joan slapped her palm on the counter. "You got it."

"You haven't seen Dane today, have you?" Cameron asked when Joan returned.

"Not today." Joan tucked a strand of graying hair behind her ear. "He was here yesterday though. About that new murder." She shook her head. "I can't believe another young woman's been killed. After what happened to Bethany last year and all."

Joan had been working the night Bethany Long went missing after her shift at the bar last November.

"How long have you lived here?" Cameron asked.

"Too long." Joan leaned an elbow onto the counter. "Why?"

"Were you here in the late nineties?"

A knowing look came over the bartender's dark eyes. "You mean when those *other* two women were killed? Yep. I was here."

Cameron took a sip from her Coke, swallowing her hesitation to ask what she needed to know. "Did you suspect Dane's father?"

Joan lowered her eyes to meet Cameron's. "Once word got out that the killer was likely law enforcement, I suspected all the troopers in this town, including Dane's father. It was a scary time to be a young woman in this place."

Cameron paused before asking her next question, a sharp sense of betrayal rising up. But she asked anyway. "And what about now?"

Joan shot a glance at Karl, still engrossed in the game on TV, before she answered. "I think whoever committed those crimes in this town moved on. Probably killed again somewhere else. I don't know. I like to think they're dead."

"Wahoo!" Karl raised his arms in the air. "Touchdown!"

Joan turned away to refill Karl's beer, leaving Cameron alone with her thoughts. On the TV behind the bar, the kicker set up for the extra point. Cameron reached inside her purse for her phone to see if she had any messages from Dane. Not feeling it, she looked in her bag, moving her wallet and lip balm to peer underneath.

She swore under her breath. *Did I leave it at home?*

She slung her purse over her shoulder and slid off her barstool. "I'll be right back," she called to Joan before leaving the bar.

She dug around inside her bag while she walked to her truck, but still didn't feel her phone. Hopefully, it fell out of her purse in the truck. Across the parking lot, a man stepped out of the diner. He looked in Cameron's direction before donning sunglasses.

Cameron's jaw fell slack. He had the same build and same beard as John when she last saw him.

Cameron stood still, assessing the way he walked as he strode beside the diner. *It's him.*

"Cameron!"

A hand landed on her shoulder. She spun around. Karl stood behind her, holding his nearly full beer glass in his other hand.

Cameron exhaled. "Karl, you scared me." She looked back at the diner, but the man was gone.

She chided herself for being so paranoid. Even if John *was* alive and *was* here, he wouldn't be so brazen to be walking around the town in broad daylight.

"I heard you ask Joan about those old murders," Karl said, scratching the white stubble on his jaw with a wiry hand. "I was a trooper here at the time."

Cameron turned to him with wide eyes. "You were?"

He nodded. "I got fired shortly after. Some asshole accused me of drinkin' on the job." He took a long drink from his beer. "But I heard you ask her about Dane's dad."

"Yeah?" The image of John striding beside the diner burned in her mind. She glanced another time over her shoulder.

"It wasn't Dane's father that *I* was worried about." Karl gripped her by the upper arm with surprising strength.

When she met his troubled gaze, there was a sudden sobriety in his bloodshot eyes.

"I saw him that day, driving away from the lake where they ended up finding the dead girl."

"Saw who?"

Cameron smelled the IPA on Karl's breath when he stepped toward her.

"Dane Waska."

CHAPTER FIFTEEN

Cameron tightened her grip around her truck keys. The jagged metal dug into her palm.

"Have you seen Sienna?"

Startled, Cameron turned to the sound of Valerie's voice, still reeling from Karl's accusation against Dane. The motel owner was striding across the parking lot, and despite it being ten degrees colder today than yesterday, Valerie wore a similar t-shirt to the day before, advertising the Howling Wolf Motel.

"No, sorry," Cameron called, distracted. There *had* to be an explanation for why Dane was at the lake that day. *If* Karl's memory was even accurate.

"Hey, Val." Karl swayed slightly as he gave Valerie a lopsided wave, his sudden sobriety disappearing as fast as it had come on.

Cameron squinted in the midday sun. It wasn't until Valerie stopped within a few feet of them that Cameron saw the worry written on her friend's face.

"Sienna was supposed to relieve me at the motel an hour ago. I had asked her to come in early today, and I can't find her anywhere. She's not at her caretaker cabin, but her car's there. I checked all the motel rooms."

Valerie sounded out of breath. One look at her face told her it was from panic, not due to her speed-walk from the motel across the highway.

"Her cabin was unlocked," she added. "And her phone was still there. I know it's only been an hour but…" She heaved a sigh, worry lines spreading across Valerie's forehead.

Cameron pressed her lips together, picturing the young blond woman she'd met at the start of the summer. With a sinking realization, it hit her that Sienna was in her early twenties—and looked a lot like Madison Youngblood.

Cameron shielded her eyes from the sun with her hand, glancing toward the diner, where she thought she'd seen John moments before. The parking lot was empty. *She has to be fine. This was Valerie's niece they were talking about.*

It had only been two days since Madison Youngblood had been killed. *If John wanted to scare me and send a message that he was still alive, he'd accomplished it. He wouldn't kill again so soon.*

Would he?

Valerie followed her gaze as Cameron scanned the row of spruce trees behind the motel across the highway. It was a beautiful day, and she remembered Valerie saying that Sienna had come up here to write a novel. One of her patients at her Seattle dental practice was a famous author and had once told Cameron that long walks were the best way to work through a storyline in your head.

"Could she have gone for a walk?" Cameron worked to keep her tone light, hoping to quell her growing trepidation as well as Valerie's.

Valerie shook her head. "I've already driven around on the roads behind the motel."

The motel owner turned around and peered at the Alaska Highway in both directions. From where they stood, you could practically see the whole town.

"You check Three Bears?" Karl gestured to the grocery store in the adjacent lot over his shoulder.

Cameron was again struck by the slur of his words that had been absent when he spoke about Dane.

"No, but I will. Thanks." Valerie started in the direction of the store. "Hopefully, she just forgot she was supposed to start early."

Valerie's effort to convince herself did nothing to slow Cameron's increasing dread. If John was watching her, he could've seen her with Valerie. And might've targeted her niece.

"Let me know if she's not there," Cameron calls after her. "I'll help you drive around to look for her."

"Me too!" Karl raised a hand in the air as he turned back for the bar, unsteady on his feet.

"Thanks, Karl," Valerie said. "But you better stay here in case she turns up."

Cameron's gaze followed Valerie as she continued toward Three Bears. Hopefully, like Valerie said, Sienna forgot she was supposed to start early and ran to the store. Or took a long walk without her phone.

Because if not, and John took Sienna, she would already be dead.

CHAPTER SIXTEEN

Cameron sat next to Valerie in a back room at the trooper station. She draped her arm around the back of the older woman's folding chair.

Across the table from them, Trooper Nelson's eyes fell to his notepad. "So, the last time you saw your niece was yesterday at 4:00 p.m.?"

Valerie nervously tapped her fingers against her thigh. "That's right."

Valerie wasn't a woman who was easily rattled, but her anxiety over her niece's whereabouts was palpable.

Nelson lifted his gaze. "Were there any guests at the motel last night who might've seen her afterword? Or this morning?"

"No." Valerie leaned an elbow on the table, cradling her forehead with her palm. "The motel was vacant. The only reservation we had was a no-show."

"Do you have a name for the no show?"

"Yes, back at the hotel."

Nelson nodded, making a note in his notepad. "Does Sienna have any friends she might've gone somewhere with?"

Valerie shook her head. "Not in Tok. She came here for the quiet, hoping to finish writing her novel before the summer was up. She jokes about being a loner." A hint of a smile reached her lips. "Said she takes after me."

Cameron glanced at the two-handed clock on the wall above Nelson's head. It was nearly three hours since Valerie came looking for her niece at the bar. After not finding her at Three Bears, she and Cameron had scoured the town in their separate cars.

Tok only had so many roads, and she and Valerie had driven down every one of them more than once. If Sienna had gone somewhere by foot, they would have found her by now. Afterward, Valerie had insisted on waiting at the motel until the time Sienna normally started her shift while Cameron had checked the library, the diner, the gas station, and the medical center.

Not finding her, Cameron had met Valerie back at the Howling Wolf Motel. When Sienna failed to show up after three, Cameron had gone with Valerie to file a missing person's report.

Nelson set down his pen and pushed back his chair. "I'd like to take a look at Sienna's cabin. Make sure there's no sign of forced entry or anything unusual."

"I'll take you."

Valerie stood, and Cameron put a hand on her friend's back as they followed Trooper Nelson out of the room. The station was quiet, which was typical for a Sunday, although it seemed odd, considering that there'd been a murder less than forty-eight hours ago.

When they entered the open area in the middle of the station, Cameron watched Valerie's gaze travel to the white board on the wall. Madison Youngblood's photo hung from the board's top corner. Details of her case were handwritten below. A line was drawn through a short list of potential witnesses. Beside it a map marked the location where Madison Youngblood's body had been found.

She heard Valerie draw in a sharp breath. Nelson turned at the sound. Cameron had seen the board when they came in, but Valerie must've been too worried about her niece to notice until now.

Valerie stood still, staring at the girl's photo. "My sister's already on her way from Anchorage." Her lower lip trembled. "What am I going to tell her?"

It was one thing reading it in the news, Cameron supposed. Being here and seeing the beautiful young woman's photo with the ongoing details of her investigation made the reality of the girl's senseless killing sink in. She recalled the night she found John's crime scene photos by mistake and discovered who he really was. Even then, she didn't fully believe it until Detective Mulholland confirmed it the next morning.

"My sister called Sienna yesterday. Begged her to come home after reading about the murder." A whimper escaped Valerie's throat. "Said Sienna looked just like her."

Cameron squeezed her friend's hand.

Valerie cleared her throat. "I told Sienna that she was much safer here than in Anchorage, where murders happen all the time. But this isn't Anchorage…" Valerie covered her mouth with her hand, keeping her eyes glued on the white board. "I should've offered to let her stay with me last night. We didn't even have a guest at the motel. I was responsible for her. I…" A sob broke her voice.

"This isn't your fault," Cameron said.

"And we don't even know what's happened yet," Nelson added.

Valerie gave a silent nod and continued to follow Nelson out of the station.

Cameron peered inside Dane's empty office, remembering Nelson looking for him on her doorstep that morning. "Trooper Nelson, did you ever hear back from Dane?"

She knew he was working, and she'd been too preoccupied by Sienna's absence to worry about where Dane was, especially since he'd been so busy at work. But she'd called Dane twice while driving around town to see if he could help them look for Sienna. Both her calls went to voicemail.

"Yeah, he called right before you two came in." Nelson held the front door of the station open as she and Valerie stepped outside. "He was just getting back into cell range. Went up to see his dad after all. I thought we were going to talk to him together, but he decided to go alone." Nelson shrugged. "Although, after the way this town treated Dane's father about those old murders, I can't say I blame him. I'm sure it was a pretty tough subject to bring up."

The sun was still high in the cloudless sky when Cameron stepped out of the building. She reached into her purse for her sunglasses. Valerie started toward her motel, then paused and stared at the row of semis parked at the truck stop beside the diner.

Valerie seemed to be doing the same thing Cameron was, looking for Sienna's abductor everywhere. But Valerie didn't know about John—at least not about Cameron finding him alive last February and leaving him for dead, even though it was her friend's intrinsic knowledge of wolves that sparked Cameron's plan. Valerie looked away, continuing toward her motel alongside Trooper Nelson when an SUV pulled into the parking lot, coming to a stop in front of the station. Cameron recognized Dane behind the wheel before he hopped out.

He looked from Nelson to Valerie. "Something wrong?"

"Her niece is missing."

Dane pulled off his sunglasses. "For how long?"

Valerie clasped her hands together. "Cameron and I have been looking for her for a few hours. But I haven't seen her since late yesterday afternoon."

Dane looked from Valerie's face to Cameron's, his face stricken. He put his hands on his hips and glanced at Cameron.

"We're on our way to search her cabin. You want to join us?" Nelson asked.

Dane looked in the direction of the motel before responding. "Yeah. Of course."

"Do you want me to come with you, Val?" Cameron asked as the three of them started across the parking lot. "Or should I keep looking?"

"Keep looking," Valerie called over her shoulder. "Thanks, Cam."

Cameron watched them walk toward the motel. The worry Valerie carried was visible in her shoulders. Cameron prayed Valerie's niece was okay. She couldn't bear the thought of someone else in this town losing someone they loved.

CHAPTER SEVENTEEN

Tanner quickened his pace as he jogged along the paved waterfront path at Lincoln Park, replaying last night's phone call with Cameron, and her suspicions that John was responsible for the recent murder in Tok. He gazed out at the Sound, reminded of all the runs he'd taken on this same path during the years he'd investigated the Teacher Killer murders. There was enough early morning light for him to make out the piles of driftwood along the beach, and the water lapping against the shore.

Prescott's killings had consumed him for the ten years they'd plagued the city. Each year a Seattle teacher had been murdered, leaving Tanner tormented with the weight of responsibility in their deaths. He'd become obsessed with the Teacher Killer cases, going without sleep a few nights a week, running along this path at all hours, until he finally uncovered the killer's identity.

Tanner would never forget the moment in his cubicle that he got the call from the Washington State Patrol Crime Lab linking DNA evidence from the Teacher Killer's first victim to John Prescott.

Knowing now that Prescott was likely alive last November

when Bethany Long was killed, he thought it very possible that Prescott killed her. But Tanner was doubtful Prescott was responsible for the recent hit and run since it was so similar to a Tok murder in the nineties. It wasn't Prescott's style. Plus, if Prescott survived whatever Cameron did to him, he'd be coming after *her*.

Tanner ran past a playground, empty at this time in the morning. He hadn't planned to get up so early on a Sunday, but he'd woken up at four, unable to go back to sleep. He couldn't stop thinking about the witness statement in the Erica Lavine cold case, accusing Dane Waska of being at the lake where her body was dumped the day after her disappearance over twenty years ago.

Several things about Karl's report didn't sit right with him.

It wasn't until after Erica Lavine's body was discovered that Karl Sadler claimed to have seen Dane Waska leaving Yarger Lake the day after her disappearance. The level of detail Sadler provided was exceptional for anyone to remember three months later, especially someone who'd admitted to having a few beers at the time. Karl said he remembered the date because it was his birthday. That made it more plausible. But he'd also supposedly recalled Dane's Explorer having a headlight out, Dane wearing a black knit hat, the time of day, and damage to the vehicle's front bumper.

Tanner neared the parking lot for Lincoln Park, the Fauntleroy Ferry coming into view as it left for Vashon Island. He slowed to a walk when he reached the nearly empty parking area and crossed the street to his neighborhood. He'd read in the case notes that Sadler had been a state trooper, fired for drinking on the job not long after the two murders. Tanner found it interesting that despite Sadler being a trooper at the time of the killings, he wasn't one of the three names listed on the suspect list.

He contemplated the case note questioning the reliability of

Sadler's account. Tanner wondered if the unreliability was due to him fabricating the incident on purpose. Dane's father, Sergeant George Waska, was likely the one who'd fired Sadler. Had Sadler sought revenge by accusing the sergeant's son?

Tanner strode up the hill to his house as the glow of an orange sunrise peeked above Mount Rainier. Or could Sadler have had a darker motive for wanting to cast blame on someone else for the murders? Tanner broke into a jog at the end of his street, struck by something he should've done last night. When he reached his house, he moved through the sparsely furnished space where he'd lived for ten years and went straight for his work laptop on the kitchen counter.

He typed *Karl Sadler* into his Accurint database. He refined his search to Alaska and hesitated before narrowing it to Tok, knowing the likelihood the man still lived there was slim. Instead, he selected *Fairbanks (and vicinity)*. It was also likely that Karl Sadler was deceased, given it was over twenty-five years now since he'd made that witness report.

His search yielded one result. Tanner's pulse quickened when he clicked on the name. He stood tall after his eyes moved to the address. Not only was Karl Sadler still alive, he still lived in Tok.

CHAPTER EIGHTEEN

Cameron pressed down on the foot pedal to sit her elderly patient up in the dental chair, then stifled a yawn from her lack of sleep before pulling off her mask. She'd stayed up most of the night, assisting with the search for Valerie's niece.

"Thanks, Doc." The woman smiled, exposing her newly filled front tooth.

"You're welcome," Cameron said, helping the frail woman to her feet. "Next time use a nutcracker, not your teeth."

The woman raised a finger in the air toward Cameron as she shuffled toward the door. "You got it."

Gwen, her dental office's only hygienist, appeared in the room's doorway. She backed against the doorframe to allow the woman through.

"I've got the patient prepped for the root canal next door," Gwen said.

"Thanks, Gwen." Cameron slid off her latex gloves and tossed them in the trash. "I'll be there in a minute."

Gwen nodded before retreating from the doorway.

"Dr. Jenkins will be here in just a few minutes," Cameron

heard Gwen say from the adjacent room. It still felt strange to be called by her maiden name, having only reverted to it after everything came out about John's crimes. "You feeling numb?" A pause. "Okay, good," Gwen said.

Cameron moved to the sink beside the wall. As the warm water flowed over her hands, her thoughts drifted to Valerie, and her niece who was still missing. After leaving the trooper station, Cameron had driven around the area for the rest of yesterday afternoon, turning down every side and back road she could find. As she drove, her mind kept returning to the photos that she'd accidentally stumbled upon last winter in the cabin she and John shared, when she was still grieving the loss of someone she'd truly believed was a good man. Her thoughts ran wild, envisioning finding Sienna dead on the side of the road, looking like the deceased woman in the photo she'd found on John's SD card last winter. Cameron shivered, recalling the woman's lifeless eyes staring into the lens of John's Nikon, and John's shirtless reflection captured in the photo by the mirror above the bed's headboard. It was an image she could never unsee.

Afterward, she'd helped comb the woods behind the Howling Wolf Motel, along with Dane, Trooper Nelson, and others who volunteered to join the search.

Dane sent everyone home after it got dark, and she hadn't seen him since. While he and Nelson went back to Sienna's cabin to search for a clue to her whereabouts, Cameron drove around for a few hours more. She found herself driving slow on the two-lane highway away from town, eyes scouring the ditch on the side of the road for Valerie's niece—the place where Madison Youngblood's body had been found.

Cameron had felt nauseated when she realized she was looking for a dead woman, already expecting to find Sienna's body.

On the other side of the wall, she heard Gwen making

small talk with Bill. If it weren't for the recent events, Cameron would've smiled. Gwen had a gift—if you could call it that—of carrying on long, one-sided conversations with her patients. She could converse with a rock if it came in for a teeth cleaning.

When she'd gotten home last night, Dane's SUV was already in his drive, but when she'd left for work the next morning, it was gone. She'd texted him after getting to work, asking if they'd found Sienna, but he replied that she was still missing.

As she lathered her hands with soap, her mind filled with an image of John the last time she saw him. And the evil in his eyes that she'd been too blind to see before.

Cameron turned off the faucet, catching a glimpse of her freshly dyed, short red hair in the mirror as she dried her hands. Sometimes she was still surprised by her reflection, expecting to see the long blond waves she had until coming to Tok under a fake name when she was looking for John last winter.

"Did you hear about the woman who went missing?"

Cameron stood still, hearing Gwen's question on the other side of the wall.

"When?" her patient asked.

"Yesterday. Another patient just told me this morning. She's young—college-age—and was working at the Howling Wolf Motel this summer. I guess she's the owner's niece."

Cameron held her breath, steeling herself to interrupt the conversation as she made for the hallway.

"They think she might've been taken by the same person who killed Madison Youngblood," Gwen continued. "They're asking for volunteers to help look for her."

A gasp. "That's awful. And frightening."

"I know."

Cameron stood frozen in the doorway of room three, stricken

by guilt for what she's brought back to this town. For not finishing the job. *I should've stayed to make sure he was dead.*

Madison Youngblood's murder and Sienna's disappearance reeked of John. It had to be him. Madison was a teacher, and Sienna was going to school to become one—just like Bethany Long. Madison wasn't strangled, but that didn't mean it wasn't John. Why couldn't Tanner see that?

Cameron stepped into the patient room, consumed by her thoughts.

Both Madison and Sienna were the age of John's victims, and both had long hair. But they were blond like Cameron was while she was married to John—not brunette like the rest of John's victims. Still, she knew John was too smart to recreate his killings to a T. Plus, in a town the size of Tok, John would have to broaden his type.

"There she is." Gwen beamed at Cameron with a wide smile of pearly white teeth.

Cameron took a seat on the wheeled stool on the opposite side of the patient. "Hi, Roger."

Gwen's smile faded.

"It's Bill," the man said.

"Oh." Cameron looked down at his disgruntled expression. "Sorry." She cleared her throat. "That's right. Hi, Bill. You ready to get this over and done with?"

"Yes, ma'am." As Cameron donned a new pair of gloves, he was still frowning from being called the wrong name.

The front door chime drifted into the examination rooms, followed by a low voice speaking with their front office manager. She glanced at the clock. She didn't think they had another patient for an hour.

"Open wide," Gwen said. "I'm going to place this bite guard in for you to rest your jaw on while we work."

Bill-not-Roger opened his mouth as Cameron assessed the instrument tray Gwen had laid out for the procedure. She reached for the rubber dam.

"Dr. Jenkins?"

She spun toward the front office manager, Jennifer, standing in the doorway behind them.

"Yes?"

"Trooper Nelson is here."

Cameron straightened. *Had they found her?*

CHAPTER NINETEEN

"He's asking about some dental records." She cast a cursory glance at Bill. "For a missing person's case."

Cameron exhaled, hope evaporating and replaced by tension in her shoulders. She recalled Nelson saying yesterday at the station that they would need the records if Sienna wasn't found. Sienna had come in for a cleaning and x-rays at the start of the summer, right after she arrived. And when Cameron had spoken with Nelson earlier, she'd offered to provide them if needed.

"Should I ask him to come back later?" Jennifer asked.

Bill's eyes followed the movement of Cameron's hand as she replaced the rubber dam on the tray.

"Can you give me a few minutes, Bill?"

He nodded, waving his hand toward the door. "Go ahead," he managed to say through his bite guard.

"Here." Gwen reached a gloved finger inside his mouth and withdrew the piece of plastic. "I'll take this out while we wait."

Cameron turned to her front office assistant. "Can you take Nelson into my office?"

"Sure."

"I can wait a little longer to be tortured," Bill said once his mouth was clear.

"Thanks. I'll be right back." She forced a slight smile at her patient despite the dread surfacing from Nelson's request—a reminder that the odds of Sienna being found alive were becoming progressively slimmer.

She found Nelson waiting for her by the door to her office. She nodded to him as she stepped inside, gesturing for him to take a seat. He followed her in and ignored the chair, standing in the middle of her office. The dark circles beneath his eyes matched his navy duty vest.

"Thought I'd come in person to get Sienna's dental records," he said, the usual hint of humor absent from his voice. "Plus, Valerie asked me to pass these around."

Cameron recognized the smiling photo of Valerie's niece on the printed paper he extended toward her. *MISSING* topped the page in bold letters.

"I figured you might want to put one up here," he added.

"I do." Cameron set the paper on her desk before moving around behind it. "So, there's still no trace of her?" She glanced at Nelson before logging onto her computer.

He came a few steps closer to her desk. "Nothing. Valerie and her sister are very distraught, as you can imagine."

She could, knowing how close Valerie was to her niece, and how responsible she felt for the girl's disappearance yesterday. She pulled up Sienna's x-rays while making a mental note to check on her friend when she got off work.

Nelson folded his arms. "We sent Sienna's phone to a data extraction expert at Fairbanks PD, but it could be a few days before he'll be able to unlock her device."

He heaved a sigh as Cameron sent Sienna's records to the front desk printer. "It's maddening we don't have more to go on. And with the recent murder, everyone's fearing the worst, especially now that we know the two women shared a similar profession." His tired eyes met Cameron's. "Myself included," he added. "Although, both women being in the education field could very well be coincidence. And we don't know yet what's happened to Sienna."

Cameron looked up from her computer screen, her heart dropping into her stomach. "I thought Sienna was getting her MFA while writing a novel." She was sure Valerie had told her this. Nelson had to be mistaken.

He nodded. "That's right, but she also works as a teacher's assistant at an elementary school in Anchorage."

Cameron imagined John stalking Sienna before abducting her without a trace. *This has to be John. Had Dane known this? Why didn't he tell me?*

"I'm sorry." Nelson's thick brows knitted together in concern. "I'm sure this brings up a lot of things with your late husband. But their professions could very well be a coincidence."

Cameron was tempted to tell him everything, from finding John to leaving him to the wolves, even though she'd be facing criminal charges. If John *was* alive and on a new killing spree, how could she not? But Dane knew it all, and even he hadn't believed that John killed Madison. Maybe he'd feel differently after learning that Sienna worked as a teacher's assistant.

"You okay, Doc?"

Cameron exhaled the breath she'd been holding in and tore her blank stare from her computer screen. "Yeah. You're right, this does bring up painful stuff with my late husband. But I'm worried about Sienna. And poor Valerie."

"I know. But we shouldn't give up hope yet. There was no sign of forced entry or a struggle at Sienna's cabin. With luck, her phone will give us a lead as to where she is." He shifted his gaze out the window, adding, "And who she's with."

Cameron could only hope Nelson was right. Although it seemed slim, there was still a chance that Sienna had left of her own accord and would turn up alive and well. But in her gut, she knew that was only wishful thinking.

Karl's words from yesterday in his seemingly sudden moment of sobriety popped into her head. *I saw him that day*, driving away from the lake where they ended up finding the dead girl. She forced the nagging thought from her mind, surprised to find herself even thinking about it. She'd never seen Karl sober. Surely, you couldn't trust a word he said.

She returned her attention to the computer. "I printed Sienna's records at the front desk."

"Thanks." Nelson started for the door.

As she followed him, the image of Karl standing outside the bar, and the eerie certainty in his eyes, invaded her thoughts for a second time.

"Hey, Nelson?"

He turned.

"I spoke to Karl yesterday." A sense of betrayal weighed down her steps for bringing it up. But Nelson was around during that time, and he could easily dispel Karl's accusation. "He said something about seeing Dane at the lake where one of victim's bodies was found in the nineties. Like he suspected Dane. I know it's ridiculous, and you were probably also a suspect, like every other trooper in town." *But that sobriety on Karl's face. His voice.* "But Dane wasn't even a trooper yet. Right?"

"Oh, yeah." Nelson waved his hand in front of his chest as if swatting a fly. "He accused Dane all right, but we all knew it was bogus. Karl made a statement that he'd seen Dane leaving the lake where Erica Lavine's body was found the same day she went missing. Karl was drinking heavily, even back then. I don't think he could remember what he had for breakfast, let alone an event a few months back. Karl also made the accusations soon after he was fired by Dane's dad for drinking on the job." He shook his head. "I still don't know how Karl managed to get hired as a trooper in the first place. Anyway, we knew he'd likely done it out of spite. But we had to follow up on it just the same, especially since Dane's dad was the sergeant at the time. We couldn't let it look like he was getting special treatment. Dane was brought in for questioning and his vehicle was processed, but of course nothing was found." His gaze fell to the floor. "It was a hard time to be a trooper in this town."

"I shouldn't have even asked."

Nelson looked up. "It's okay." He put his hand on her shoulder. "Don't let Karl get under your skin. The whole town is on edge again. People are quick to want someone to blame. Hell, some even blamed Dane when his wife died, accusing him of having something to do with it." His hand fell from her shoulder as his mouth formed a frown.

The room went cold. She'd never known this. "I thought she died in a car accident."

"She did. It was nonsense—just like Karl's accusations—and nothing came of it. It was after word got out that she was about to leave him for someone else. And the argument they got in right before she died."

"What?" The floor rocked beneath her feet. Why hadn't Dane told her? He'd spoken about his late wife on more than one occasion but always made it sound like they were incredibly happy. "Was it true?"

Nelson's head and shoulders recoiled as if she'd hit him. "That he killed her? Of course, not."

"No! That she was having an affair."

The shock on his face dissipated. "I thought you knew." His eyes searched hers. "It crushed him when he found out."

"No. I…he never said anything."

"Oh." Nelson shifted uncomfortably. "Sorry. I didn't mean to…I should—"

The office door swung open as he reached for the handle.

"Oops!" In the doorway, Gwen flashed Nelson a white smile as he reflexively stepped back to avoid getting hit by the door. "Didn't realize you were there." She turned to Cameron. "Did you want me to give more numbing to the patient in room three?"

"No, that's okay." Despite her shock, Cameron stepped through the door. "I'm coming."

"Thanks for the records," Nelson said.

"Of course." Cameron started for room three, trying to clear her mind of what she had just learned. But she knew she wouldn't be able to until she talked to Dane. "Jennifer can give you Sienna's records up front. That should be everything we have from her visit in June," she said over her shoulder. "But let me know if you need anything else."

"Will do." Nelson cast her an apologetic look before she continued down the hall.

As she neared room three, she heard Gwen launch into a story about her dog that Cameron had heard her tell another patient that morning. As Gwen's laugh filled the hall, Cameron's mind reeled with questions.

Why would Dane lie about his late wife? The next question that entered her mind nearly caused her knees to buckle. *Are there other things he's lied about too?*

She forced herself to keep walking toward the sound of Gwen's voice. When Bill looked up from his reclined chair, she plastered a smile on her face.

Gwen was in the middle of telling Bill how her husband mistook a coyote for their German Shephard and tried to call it inside their house in the middle of the night before realizing their dog was already inside. She saw Cameron and trailed off with a smile.

Gwen patted Bill's arm. "I'll tell you the rest in a second. You won't believe it. It's so funny." She lifted her gaze to Cameron and redonned her surgical mask. "Let's get this party started!"

CHAPTER TWENTY

After seeing the last patient of the day, Cameron climbed into her truck. She put her phone to her ear as she started the engine and called Dane. As it rang, she replayed what Nelson had said in her office. *Why had Dane never told her about his late wife's affair?* She wouldn't ask him now, on the phone. But soon.

Dane knew her secrets. Things she'd never told anyone else. Was there a reason Dane couldn't trust her with his? Had he done something he knew she would find unforgiveable?

Her call went to voicemail. "Hey, it's me. I was just calling to see if there were any updates on Sienna. I'm heading down to join the search of the woods behind the Caribou RV Park."

She tossed her phone on the bench seat as she pulled onto the highway. Valerie had texted her a few hours ago asking if Cameron would come help with the search, adding that Dane had managed to get a cadaver dog and its handler to come down from Fairbanks to help comb the wooded areas around town. Cameron agreed to help as soon as she finished with work. The large, wooded area behind the RV park was less than six blocks from the Howling Wolf Motel.

She glanced at the time on her dash. *4:30.* The sun was high in the sky. It was fortunate it wasn't winter, Cameron thought, and there was still nearly seven hours of daylight left to search for Sienna.

She passed the trooper station on the right and surveyed the empty parking lot as she drove through the very spot where Dane's wife was killed. An involuntary shudder coursed through her upper body. Dane had made it sound like he and his wife were happy. In love. He never once alluded to any serious problems between them. Why had he lied? *Was it too painful to talk about, or something else?*

She stared out the windshield at the empty stretch of highway, wondering if she even knew Dane at all. She'd trusted the wrong man before. *But I've learned from that, haven't I? How could this possibly happen to me again?* It was like lightning striking multiple times. First, Miles beating her whenever he flew into a drunken rage, then the horror of finding out her second husband was a serial killer, and now Dane?

She drummed her fingers against her steering wheel. She'd heard once from a therapist that women who are abused often end up in an abusive relationship again. *Why was that?* She rubbed her forehead, trying to recall the rationale behind it. It was like predators had a sixth sense in selecting their victims that hunters like John keyed in on. As if they could smell them. *Is that what this is?* Was she going to be attracting every predator in every town she settled in, for the rest of her life?

Or is there something in me *that seeks out men that are monsters?* Her mind flashed to her childhood. She grew up with two loving parents. No trauma. No abuse. Her father could be distant at times, but she'd always known that he loved her.

She nearly missed the turn into the RV park and slammed on the brakes, tires skidding to a halt atop the gravel beside Valerie's

Subaru. Her heart sank at the sight of the motel owner's car, knowing its presence meant they had yet to find Sienna.

Cameron got out and slammed her truck door harder than she meant to. As she strode past the parked motorhomes and trailers, decked out with American flags and hanging outdoor lights, she fixed her attention on the densely wooded area beyond them where they were searching for Sienna. She quickened her pace and pushed aside her suspicion of Dane. There had to be a good explanation for why he hadn't told her about his late wife's affair. Her muscles tensed with guilt for allowing herself to think he was anything like John or Miles.

She neared the path leading to the woods, which looked identical to the forest on the other side of town where Bethany Long's body had been discovered last winter. *John killed Madison.* And she was letting him get to her. Mess with her head.

She prayed John hadn't taken Sienna too. If he had—

"Cameron!"

Joan waved when Cameron reached the end of the short trail into the woods. A branch snapped under her shoe as she continued over the ungroomed ground toward the bartender.

"Thanks for coming." Joan patted her back as Cameron fell in step beside her.

"Of course."

"We're trying to search the entire woods before nightfall." Joan tucked a loose strand of her short dark hair behind her ear and pointed straight ahead. "Going north until this hits that dirt road, then covering new ground on our way back toward the RV park. Valerie and her sister, Pam, are right over there."

Cameron followed Joan's gaze to their left, spotting Valerie's gray hair from behind, walking beside a blond woman a few inches shorter than her. Valerie looked to be wearing the same blue motel t-shirt as yesterday even though it was barely over fifty degrees. Cameron supposed that when you were used to negative temperatures throughout the winter, fifty degrees didn't feel so bad. Or, more likely, Valerie was too distraught over her niece to care about being cold. The two women appeared too intent on sweeping the surrounding forest to notice Cameron's arrival.

Cameron fell in step beside Joan in silence, keeping her face tilted toward the ground as she scanned for a sign of Sienna. It wasn't until they reached the dirt road—one that Cameron had driven yesterday—that Cameron spotted Karl. Reminded of her earlier conversation with Nelson, she paused, surveying his unsteady gait as he weaved around trees, holding an open beer can in one hand.

Was Karl capable of making a false report, accusing Dane of murder, out of spite for being fired by Dane's father? Or could Karl have had another motive for pointing the finger at Dane? Karl tripped on a stump, stumbling forward before catching himself, somehow managing to keep hold of his beer. The sudden clarity in Karl's eyes when he'd accused Dane outside the bar made the skin on her forearms prickle.

"You okay, honey?"

Joan watched her with concern when Cameron tore her gaze from Karl. They moved up the tree line along the road before turning back toward the direction they'd come.

"This must be triggering for you after your late husband well…you know," Joan added.

Cameron stepped over a stump, envisioning John with his hands around Sienna's neck, squeezing the life from her as the petite young girl writhed beneath—

A dog barked in the distance. Several trees over, Cameron spotted Valerie, her head snapping in the direction of the sound. Valerie ran through the trees as the barking continued, her sister following close behind. Cameron and Joan ran too, careful not to trip over the roots and stumps protruding from the uneven ground.

Cameron's heart sank as she raced through the woods. No one made a sound as they ran, knowing the cadaver dog's bark could mean only one thing.

CHAPTER TWENTY-ONE

As THE HIGH-PITCHED yapping grew louder, it was evident it wasn't the cadaver dog. Valerie slowed as an elderly-sounding woman scolded the Beagle on the other side of the trees. Cameron stopped, realizing the dog belonged to someone at the RV village.

When Valerie turned, the color had drained from Valerie's face. She threw an arm around her sister and let out a sob. Cameron's throat tightened as she watched the sisters refocus their attention on the forest floor without a word.

Cameron felt Joan's hand on her arm as Valerie and her sister disappeared behind a thick patch of trees.

"Cam? Are you okay to be out here? I worry what this might bring up for you."

Having a husband turn out to be a serial killer isn't something you can really forget. Seeing the motherly worry on Joan's face, Cameron knew she meant well.

"I'm fine."

Joan flashed her a look that said she didn't believe her. "Sweetheart, I've been a bartender in this town for nearly as long as you've been alive. I've seen and heard it all."

It struck Cameron that Joan had been the first to tell her about the accident that killed Dane's wife. It was at the bar when she'd first come to Tok looking for John.

Joan brought her face toward Cameron's. "And I can tell when someone's lying."

In the next row of trees, Cameron heard a stream of water pouring onto the ground. She cocked her head to find Karl's back to them. Cameron's jaw dropped. *He's taking a piss.*

In disgust, she looked away, turning to Joan. "Can I ask you something?" She felt terrible for asking, but it wouldn't stop gnawing at her. "About Dane?"

Joan's eyebrows knitted together. "What?"

Cameron lowered her voice. "Was Dane's wife having an affair?"

Joan held Cameron's gaze before inspecting the forest floor around them. "Yes."

Cameron glanced in Karl's direction, who had resumed walking. "Did people in this town really believe that Dane had something to do with her accident?"

Joan pursed her lips.

"Because of the affair? And her planning to leave him?" Cameron added, swallowing the guilt that rose to the back of her throat.

Joan studied the others moving between the trees in the distance. "People like who? Karl?" She shook her head. "You know you can't believe everything he says." She whirled toward Cameron, her eyes serious. "Of course, Dane didn't. How could he? It was a car accident, and she was alone." She stepped over a fallen log toward Cameron. "Don't let this new murder and Sienna's going missing mess with your head. This town nearly did itself in back in the nineties—suspecting every trooper in town."

Karl whistled in the distance when Cameron and Joan neared

the edge of the woods that backed up against the RV village. Cameron felt the slightest bit of tension ease from her shoulders. Joan was right. Dane might not have told her the whole truth about his marriage, but that didn't make him a killer. It was *John* who was messing with her and terrorizing this town.

Beyond the trees, a car rolled to a stop atop the gravel. She and Joan moved to the left to cover new ground.

"I saw the accident happen that day," Joan said when they neared the path that led to the RV park. "From the bar."

Cameron slowed.

"I'd stepped outside to have a smoke when Krista, Dane's wife, tore out of the trooper station parking lot."

On the other side of the trees, two car doors slammed before heavy footsteps crunched atop the gravel pathway leading to the woods.

"If you ask me," Joan continued, "it almost looked like she pulled out in front of that semi on purpose." Joan lifted a hand for emphasis, her palm facing the sky. "But of course, those pills were in her system."

"Pills?" Cameron spun toward the bartender, but before she could get an answer, Dane emerged from the trees a few feet in front of them.

"Where's Valerie?" Dane's face was somber.

When Dane's eyes locked with hers, she recognized the look. She'd seen it once before. Dread rose in her chest, knowing what it meant. She pointed in the direction of where she'd last seen Valerie and Pam, who'd now disappeared amongst the trees.

"Is Valerie's sister still with her?" he asked.

Nelson appeared behind him.

Cameron nodded. Dane drew in a heavy breath before striding toward the two sisters. Cameron stood frozen, her eyes glued to Dane until he disappeared from view.

Joan seemed to search Nelson's eyes for what Cameron had already seen in Dane's. The three of them stood in silence, unmoving, when a wail erupted from the woods.

Joan's hand flew over her mouth. *"Dear God."*

"Noooo!!"

Cameron recognized Valerie's throaty scream, and her knees felt like they might buckle.

Joan stepped closer to Nelson. "You found Sienna?"

He nodded, looking grim. "We believe so, yes. A couple camping near Yarger Lake found a woman's body floating near the shore."

Cameron closed her eyes. *Sonofabitch.*

Joan gasped. Cameron opened her eyes and started toward the lake. She broke into a jog, dodging spruce trees and stumps as she raced through the woods toward the sound of Valerie's cries.

CHAPTER TWENTY-TWO

Amidst the comings and goings around his cubicle at Seattle homicide, Tanner kept his attention focused on the casefile on his laptop. He scrolled to the last page of Bethany Long's autopsy report from last November, vaguely aware of the shift change happening around him. The rest of Tanner's squad that had arrived alongside him early this morning were on their way out of the building. As usual, Tanner kept working.

Beneath his noise-cancelling headphones, Tanner could tell the decibel level of conversation in the unit had increased. Tanner didn't listen to anything while he worked, just kept them on to prevent his coworkers from stopping by his desk to tell him about their weekend.

Tanner heard the muffled sound of a phone ringing moments before two detectives stood from their desks in his periphery. A skull bobblehead appeared in between him and his laptop, making Tanner recoil in his seat. He cocked his head to see Detective Richards standing over him.

Tanner slipped off his headphones, knowing what being passed the bobblehead meant.

"You're next up." Richards gestured to her partner as Tanner reluctantly accepted the creepy figurine. "We just got called to a double shooting in Rainier Valley."

Tanner perched the bobblehead on the edge of his desk as Richards hurried with her partner out of the unit. Tanner looked away from the jiggling skull, intently returning his attention back to his screen, now that he'd likely be forced soon to drop everything for a new case.

There was a time in his career at Seattle homicide when he could make it through a week on call without getting called out. Now, he'd be lucky to go a few days without getting assigned a new homicide.

Tanner finished reading the end of Bethany Long's autopsy report, recalling when Cameron phoned him in the middle of the night, convinced her husband had killed the woman. Tanner argued it wasn't possible—John was dead. His lungs stiffened, knowing now he was wrong. Unfortunately, without any DNA evidence, there was no way to prove Bethany Long's killer was Prescott.

Tanner lifted his coffee mug. Seeing it was empty, he set it back down. He'd been too immersed in Bethany Long's autopsy report to notice he'd finished his fourth cup of the day.

He'd go refill it in a minute. First, he opened Madison Youngblood's casefile that Sergeant Waska had sent him after they spoke. That morning, Tanner hadn't been able to find much on Karl Sadler aside from two DUIs a decade apart and the fact that he'd lived at the same Tok address for over thirty years. There wasn't much more he could do from another state. Investigating John was one thing, but Madison Youngblood's murder was out of his jurisdiction.

He folded a stick of gum into his mouth as he studied Madison's case file. Unlike Cameron, he was not convinced John had killed her.

Tanner glanced at the time on the lower corner of his laptop screen. Yesterday, he'd tracked down a potential witness to a fatal stabbing that happened last month on Capitol Hill. He had to leave in less than an hour to interview her and needed to review his notes on the stabbing before he left.

He closed out of Madison's case file and opened his notebook with handwritten notes he'd been keeping on the Capitol Hill case. He flipped to the page where he'd written a list of questions he wanted to ask this witness while wondering if Karl Sadler was ever a suspect in the Tok murders from the nineties. *Or had Sadler's stigma of being the town drunk, and constantly incapacitated, caused him to be overlooked?*

Tanner reread the same question on his notepad a few times before pushing it aside and running an Internet search for news updates in Tok, Alaska. His stomach dropped, seeing the headline that topped the results.

YOUNG ANCHORAGE WOMAN MISSING IN TOK DAYS AFTER HIT AND RUN MURDER

After reading through the article, Tanner leaned back in his chair. The twenty-three-year-old was last seen at the Howling Wolf Motel the day before yesterday and had disappeared without a trace. A familiar unease grew in the pit of Tanner's stomach, a feeling he'd grown accustomed to over the years of being a detective.

Tanner found Sergeant Waska's number in his recent logs on his cell phone and put the phone to his ear. As it rang, he swiveled in his chair. The homicide unit had grown quiet.

Tanner readied himself to ask Waska about Karl Sadler, wondering how Waska would respond to Tanner questioning Sadler's statement placing Waska at the site where Erica Lavine's body had been dumped. The trooper's phone rang four times before going to voicemail. Tanner hung up without leaving a message.

Tanner agreed with the assessment in Erica Lavine's case file that Sadler's statement was unreliable. But *why* was it unreliable? Tanner wasn't sure. He tapped his forefinger on his desk. *Did Sergeant Waska suspect Sadler now?*

Tanner glanced at his notepad before pulling up Madison Youngblood's file again. If Karl Sadler was Madison's killer and also responsible for the Tok murders in the nineties, it would mean he took a nearly thirty-year break from his killing sprees. Unless he killed elsewhere and was never caught. While it was possible, Tanner found it unlikely. He'd been wrong before about John killing Bethany, and he couldn't shake the trepidation that he was missing something again.

He knew from the look on Cameron's face when he visited her that she expected John to be dead—and not from his alleged bear attack. What he'd told her had visibly rattled Cameron.

But was she afraid of him knowing what she'd done to her husband or had Prescott's missing body come as a surprise?

It had to have, he surmised, because now, Cameron was certain her husband was alive.

Cameron had showed no reaction when he said John was up at that cabin. She became fearful only when Tanner said no body had been recovered, and she'd become even more alarmed when he told her the snowmobile was missing.

Tanner reread Madison's autopsy report, struggling to find any similarities to Prescott's previous victims. There'd been no sexual assault, no letter markings anywhere on her body, and she'd been run over—not strangled. She was, however, a teacher and last seen at the Wolf Pack Bar like Bethany Long.

Tanner reopened his web browser and found the article he'd read at the airport that displayed a photo of Madison, beaming beneath a cap and gown at her college graduation. Laughter broke out in the adjacent cubicle. Tanner donned his headphones again as he leaned closer to the screen.

Madison was the right age for John's victims, but her appearance didn't fit the profile. All of Prescott's victims had long, dark hair—including Bethany Long. Madison's blond waves reminded Tanner of Cameron's hair when he'd met her. He zoomed in on the photo. Fifteen years ago, Cameron probably looked a lot like Madison. *Was this John's way of sending Cameron a message?*

Prescott had broken his MO before when he killed two Seattle teachers at his hunting cabin rather than inside their homes. And if he'd killed Bethany Long, he'd also refrained from making his trademark letter grade markings on her back, likely because the world believed he was dead.

His phone rang, tearing him from his thoughts. It was the Washington State Crime Lab. He sat forward. Getting a call from them usually meant they had a result on a pending DNA test or a hit on a new DNA sample that had entered their system. Being the department's cold case specialist, Tanner had scores of open cases that could be solved by a DNA match.

A wave of excitement ran through him as he lifted his phone. The crime lab was backlogged and their testing could take up to six months, so he never knew when he might get a call with a result.

"Detective Mulholland."

"Hey, Mulholland. It's Fresia from the state crime lab. We got a hit in CODIS on the DNA profile collected from Sally Hickman in 1984."

Tanner sat forward. CODIS, the acronym for Combined DNA Index System, was a software program that worked to match DNA profiles from a database of convicted offenders, unsolved crime scene evidence, and missing persons.

"The DNA recovered from her autopsy is a direct familial match, likely the father, to another profile you submitted earlier this year."

He knew Sally Hickman's case well. Weeks after she was raped and brutally murdered, her naked body was found in the woods in South Seattle by a man walking his dog. She'd been a prostitute and was last seen getting into a sedan off Aurora Avenue. The thing that had struck Tanner about the case was that a witness recalled seeing a child—a young boy—in the backseat of the sedan that picked up Sally when she was last seen.

"You're not going to believe who it is," Fresia said. "Are you able to check your email if I send it now? It's going to blow you away. Blew me away."

"Yeah, I'm at my desk."

"Okay, it just sent. Let me know if you have any questions after you read it."

As Tanner ended the call and waited for the email to appear in his inbox on his laptop, his mind ran through a dozen possibilities. His foot jiggled with anticipation beneath his desk. Hickman's murder reeked of serial killer. For nearly two decades, detectives suspected she was a victim of the Green River Killer until advancements in DNA technology disproved the theory following Ridgway's arrest in 2001.

Tanner opened the email from Fresia seconds after it appeared in his inbox. He held his breath as he scrolled to the name of the DNA profile of the child of Hickman's killer. Up until now, the DNA recovered from her body hadn't been a match to anyone in their system.

His leg went still as he read the name. *John Prescott.* Tanner leaned back in his chair, staring at the screen.

Prescott's father killed Sally Hickman. Like father, like son. John's father was a sadistic killer just like John. Or rather, John became a sadistic killer just like his father.

CHAPTER TWENTY-THREE

Cameron spotted Dane's blue state trooper uniform and rushed toward Valerie, who'd sunk to her knees on the dirt near Dane's feet. Valerie enveloped her sister in her arms, who was seated on the ground, crying with her face against Valerie's chest.

Cameron sank to the ground behind Valerie and placed her hand on her back that heaved from her gut-wrenching sobs. A lump formed in Cameron's throat. The two women's grief was so raw, it was tangible.

She lifted her eyes to Dane. He averted his gaze, but the pain on his face was obvious. With his mouth downturned, he looked to be blinking back tears. He'd likely known Valerie his whole life.

Valerie's sister looked up at Dane, clearing her throat. "Are you sure it's her?"

Nodding, Dane crouched beside them. "We compared her dental records." His voice was soft. "They're a match."

An agonizing sound escaped Valerie's throat.

"Can I—" Pam heaved a sigh, wiping a tear from her red cheek with the back of her hand. "Can I see her?"

"Yes. We'll be sending her body to Fairbanks for an autopsy, but I can arrange for you to see her before she goes." Dane stood. "Would you be willing to come with me now? I have some questions I'd like to ask."

Pam sniffed. "Okay."

Cameron helped pull the two women to their feet.

"I'm so sorry," Cameron said when Valerie's red eyes met hers.

Valerie squeezed Cameron's arm before taking her sister's hand and following Dane out of the woods.

After embracing Valerie in a hug, Joan waited for Cameron by the path to the RV park as the two troopers led the sisters to the lot where Valerie was parked. The SUV's engine roared to life as she and Joan walked along the tree-lined pathway out of the woods. They emerged from the woods into the RV park as Valerie and Pam pulled away.

A Beagle yapped at them from inside a screened window of a motorhome, same dog they'd heard earlier.

Joan's gaze trailed after the police vehicle. "What senseless brutality. It's maddening. Inconceivable that someone could do that to another human being."

Cameron had no words as her mind filled with an image of John, a sick smirk of enjoyment on his face, while he choked the life from Valerie's niece.

"Evil won't seem to leave this town alone." Joan surveyed the highway when they reached Cameron's truck. "Why don't you let me drive you home?"

Cameron shook her head. "I'm okay."

Joan shot her a knowing look. "You don't look it."

"It's less than a five-minute drive to my place," Cameron insisted. "I'll be fine."

"Look, I shouldn't have said anything about those pills. It's none of my business."

"It's okay. I'm the one that asked about it." Cameron was too flooded with emotion over Sienna's death to dwell on Dane and his late wife now.

John is here. And he killed Valerie's niece.

"It has to be a sensitive subject for Dane. I'm sure he'll tell you everything when he's ready."

Cameron forced a nod. Joan was probably right. She half-opened the door to her truck and paused, turning to Joan.

"Did Nelson tell you if they know how Sienna died?"

Joan's expression darkened. "He said they won't know for certain until the autopsy, but they think she was strangled."

Cameron's stomach somersaulted. She pressed her palm against her truck, thinking she might throw up.

"I don't know if I can take any more killing in this town."

Cameron registered the pain in the bartender's voice as Joan's gaze traveled to the Alaska Range.

"I'm sorry."

Cameron knew the wound Sienna's murder was reopening for Joan. Joan had been one of the last people to see Bethany Long alive, the bartender who was strangled last fall after leaving her shift at The Wolf Pack Bar. Like Valerie, Joan had felt responsible for her employee, whose killing remained unsolved.

Rage burned inside her chest as Cameron mentally replayed John's sickening confession to killing Bethany. She pictured the triumphant look in his eyes after she bested him, tying him to the tree. Right before she—

"I mean it. You drive careful." Joan studied Cameron, her voice firm. "I know it's not far—but accidents happen."

"I will. You want a ride to the bar?"

Joan shook her head as she started along the shoulder of the highway. "It's just a few blocks, and I need the fresh air."

Cameron climbed into her truck. She watched Joan wave to an oncoming car as Cameron sat behind the wheel without starting the engine. There was nothing she could do now to help Valerie's niece.

These new murders had nothing to do with the ones from the nineties. John had killed both Madison and Sienna, and he had to be stopped before he killed again.

When she tracked John down before, he hadn't known she was coming for him. Now, John was on the offense, seeking revenge. If she was going to stop him, she needed help from the person most likely to believe her that John killed Sienna.

She dug her phone out of her purse and dialed Tanner.

CHAPTER TWENTY-FOUR

TANNER BROUGHT A hand to his chin, letting the information sink in. While it made sense that John Prescott was raised by a killer, it still surprised him. Tanner pictured an eight-year-old John Prescott in the backseat of the sedan when his father picked up a prostitute, a little kid being told to wait in the car while his father raped and murdered Sally in the woods.

Hickman couldn't have been John's father's only victim. This wasn't the sort of crime someone committed only once in their life. And Hickman couldn't have been the first. One doesn't commit a brutal rape and murder for the first time while your kid waits in the car.

After Prescott's alleged bear attack, Tanner tried to find Prescott's parents and discovered they were both deceased. His mother had died in 1979 when Prescott was only three. His father, Hickman's killer, hadn't passed away until 2000—sixteen years after Hickman's murder.

Tanner opened his Accurint database to check the Prescott's address in 1984. He reached into his pocket and pulled out a stick of gum, keeping his eyes on his search results. Louie Prescott,

John's father, lived at the same Tacoma address from 1978 until his death.

Sally Hickman might've been the only woman Louie Prescott killed in *Seattle*, which would explain why Tanner hadn't gotten a hit with Prescott's profile on any of his other old cases. But that didn't mean there weren't others.

He drummed his fingers atop his desk. He needed to put out a bulletin to law enforcement in other jurisdictions to check their old cases for a possible connection to Prescott's father.

"Hey, I thought you said you had to go to Capitol Hill?" Tanner turned to the sound of his sergeant's voice. McKinnon stood at the edge of Tanner's cubicle, checking his watch. "It's after two."

Hearing the time, Tanner swore and pushed back his chair. "I'm late."

He was supposed to be meeting with his Capitol Hill witness right now. He'd have to review his questions for her in the car.

His phone rang in his hand. Recognizing the Alaska area code, Tanner pressed his phone to his ear.

"Hey, Morton."

Tanner tucked his notebook under his arm as he strode past his sergeant, still reeling from the news of John Prescott's father having murdered Sally Hickman. He cradled his phone with his shoulder while he speed walked out of the homicide unit and tried to focus on whatever Morton had called to tell him. He hadn't talked to the Fairbanks detective since he'd helicoptered with him to the remote Alaskan cabin, and he wasn't expecting to hear from him so soon.

Tanner's phone beeped with a second incoming call. Checking his screen, he saw it was Cameron. He pressed *decline* and replaced the phone to his ear. He would have to call her back after he heard what Morton called to tell him.

"Hey, Tanner. I just got some news I thought you should know."

Tanner slowed after stepping out of the unit, glancing out the seventh-floor window to his left at the glimmering Seattle waterfront.

"First, I called our state crime lab and was able to expedite the DNA sample I submitted from the blood on the bear trap we bagged back at the cabin, given the risk to the public if the Teacher Killer is still alive."

"Great." Tanner started past the elevators, heading for the door that led to the adjacent rooftop parking garage. He knew it was too soon for Morton to be calling with the results, even with the rush on the DNA sample.

"But the reason I'm calling is because unidentified human remains were discovered earlier today."

Tanner stopped. Two detectives emerged from one of the elevators, each holding a bag from Taco Bell.

"The remains were found about one hundred miles upriver from Eagle, less than fifty miles east of that cabin. A couple of kayakers found the body caught against a fallen tree near the river's edge. It looked to be male but badly decomposed. The snow gear suggests whoever it was likely died last winter or late spring. Do you have John Prescott's dental records on file?"

"Yeah." Tanner's mind raced.

"Oh, good. Could you send them to me? The body still has to be transferred here to Fairbanks for the autopsy. We had a triple homicide this morning. You're probably used to that sort of thing in Seattle, but it's pulling a lot of our resources, and our ME will be performing those autopsies first. But if the remains *are* Prescott, we should have the dental records confirmed in the next few days."

"Great," Tanner heard himself say.

"Yes. I hope it is him. One less serial killer sucking up air on this planet. I hate the idea of Prescott out there somewhere, alive, hunting another young woman. I'm sure I speak for you too, that I'll sleep better knowing without a doubt that he's dead."

"Yeah." Tanner's thoughts raced as he stared at the parking garage door at the end of the corridor, having nearly forgotten what he was doing.

"Anyway, send me those dental records, and I'll call you as soon as we have an ID."

Tanner lowered his phone, feeling his notebook under his arm, and stepped into the garage. His legs had gone numb, and not from relief at the possibility that Prescott was dead.

He marched toward his Fusion, thinking of Cameron up in that town, and her track record for picking the wrong men. An involuntary shiver ran down his torso despite the sun on his face.

If Prescott didn't kill Madison Youngblood—and possibly the missing young woman—who did?

CHAPTER TWENTY-FIVE

Cameron peered out her front window at the sound of gravel crunching, spotting headlights coming down her neighboring drive. In the twilight, she recognized Dane's tall frame and his familiar gait as he got out of his SUV and strode toward his house.

She'd wanted to check on Valerie that afternoon, her heart breaking for what her friend must be going through. But her sister was with her, and Cameron knew from her own experience with grief that there was nothing she could do to ease Valerie's pain. Knowing Valerie, she likely wished to be left alone.

Cameron recalled the vulnerable state she was in during the months following her parents' fatal car accident. It was during that time that her first husband, Miles, proposed. She wondered if she would've said yes if she hadn't felt so lost after losing her parents so suddenly.

A shudder ripped through her, thinking of the dark years of the marriage and what she'd had to do to end it. Soon after, she'd met John. After Miles, he seemed like a saint. So charming, attentive, sweet. In all the years they were married, he'd never once raised his voice at her. It was ironic to think that part of the reason she fell for John was that he made her feel safe.

Cameron let go of her curtain, letting it fall over the window. She started for her door, then stopped, deciding to give Dane a minute to get inside before she marched over. She gathered her own thoughts while she waited, even though she'd been alone with them for hours already.

She was dying to ask Dane about his late wife, and why he hadn't told her about the troubles in their marriage. Part of her was also afraid to hear the truth. When Dane first told her about his late wife's car accident, Cameron felt a connection, having lost her parents in the same way. But what if she'd misjudged him entirely? Blinded by their shared tragedy, she saw only what she wanted to see. *Could that be possible?*

She closed her eyes, forcing the thought from her mind. First, she needed to know about Sienna and if Dane had any evidence that pointed to John. Tanner hadn't returned her call. She'd thought about calling him again after she'd gotten home, but decided to wait until she learned Sienna's official cause of death.

If Sienna's cause of death *did* turn out to be strangulation, would that be enough to convince Tanner—or Dane—that John was responsible? She recalled with detail the look on John's face when she last saw him. And then there was the part she'd left out when she recounted to Dane what happened.

Cameron returned to her living room window as lights came on inside her boyfriend's house. She wasn't sure why she'd kept the last part from Dane. After everything John did, it's not like she should feel guilty about it. But for some reason she hadn't been able to tell him.

She watched Dane's silhouette move past a side window toward the back of his house. Maybe he had a similar reason for withholding the truth about his marriage. She turned for her front door, her thoughts drifting to Valerie and the awful grief she and her sister must be experiencing right now. It made Cameron's heart ache.

She had been certain she'd left John for dead that day in the remote wilderness. She'd even gone back to make sure he wouldn't survive. But she'd told Dane only the first part: that she'd left John tied to the tree, injured, and lying in wait for the pack of wolves she called in. She'd trekked through the woods, ignoring John screaming her name as she'd snowshoed back the way she'd come.

But as she went, listening to John's cries, she hadn't been able to shake the way he'd smirked when he'd confessed—no, bragged—to killing Bethany. The gloating gleam of enjoyment in his hazel eyes when he recounted taking the young woman's life.

John was too much of a monster to be left only to the wolves. In that moment, she needed to make sure John suffered. And to see it with her own eyes.

Cameron stopped in her tracks, unsure whether her heavy breathing was due to her physical exertion from snowshoeing through the forest with the pack on her back, or from the fresh spurt of rage pulsating through her body. She blinked through the falling snow, envisioning the cocky grin that spread across John's face when he admitted to killing Bethany Long.

In Tok, Cameron had seen firsthand the devastation on the faces of Bethany's parents, and the physical toll Bethany's death had on her younger sister, Grace. Remembering the teenage girl, and what had happened to her days earlier, made Cameron's limbs tremble with anger.

A wolf howled in the distance, sounding closer than it had only a few minutes before. She turned back toward John, who still screamed her name through the isolated woods.

She was sure the wolves would take care of John if she didn't go back. But she felt overcome with the need to see John suffer. To make sure he didn't stand a chance against the wolves. She broke into a jog, awkward with the snowshoes strapped to her boots, retracing her snowshoe tracks as quickly as her movements allowed.

By the time John's writhing form came into view, sweat trickled down her chest. As soon as he saw her, his face sagged with relief.

"I knew you couldn't leave me."

At his words, Cam felt a wave of disgust. His gaze darted toward the creatures as they reached the bottom of the steep hillside across the valley below.

"Hurry! We need to get inside before they come!"

Cameron marched straight for the cabin.

"Cameron! Did you hear me? What the hell are you doing?"

Cameron pushed open the front door and stepped inside. Her snowshoes rapped against the wood floor as she rushed to the kitchen. She yanked a knife from a weathered butcher's block while John's screams resounded from outside. As she moved past a window, she caught a glimpse of him, wriggling like a worm beneath the rope.

Outside, she trudged down the porch steps over the blood-stained snow. A howl echoed through the forest from the valley beyond. Cameron glanced toward the sound. They didn't have long.

Cameron stopped a few feet from her husband. "You should quiet down, John. You're making them hungry."

"There's no time for jokes! We don't have time to waste." Panic flickered in his eyes, the gold flecks of his hazel irises catching the waning light before his gaze fell to the knife in her hand. "It would be easier if you untied me than trying to cut through the rope with that."

She stood still, awestruck at his placating tone, and the realization that he thought she'd come back to cut him free.

"Hurry!" he shouted, unable to keep the ferocity from leaking into his voice.

Cameron stepped back, assessing the man she thought she'd loved for nearly a decade.

"Cam. Sweetie. Come on. We'll talk inside. Untie me now!*"*

Cameron didn't move, hearing a branch crack beneath the heavy gait of the wolf pack tearing through the valley below. "Even now, John, you have the audacity to think you have the upper hand. Order me around. It's remarkable."

John's face turned to pleading. Fear sparked in his eyes. "Please."

"This is for Bethany."

John's eyes doubled in size. His jaw fell open without a sound as Cameron raised the knife in the air and lunged forward.

"Ahh!"

She plunged the knife into John's torso, feeling resistance as the blade sliced through the flesh of his abdominal muscles. It came to a stop with the handle butted up against his shirt.

Their eyes locked, only inches apart. John's lips parted, and he grunted through gritted teeth. Cameron started to withdraw the blade when she felt John's strong grip enclose her wrist. She looked down, seeing he'd managed to move his limb beneath the rope. She tried to pull away, but his hand clenched harder over hers. She withdrew the knife in one swift motion, and startled, Cameron released it, watching as it flew through the air and landed several feet away, speckling the surrounding snow with John's blood. Another wolf howled at the base of the hill below the cabin.

Cameron struggled to free her hand from John's grip. He kept hold of her wrist despite her attempt to twist free, squeezing tighter as panic ripped through her. Cameron thrust the gloved thumb of her free hand into his eye socket. He screamed and released her wrist. He attempted to grab her other arm but was caught short by the rope that bound him to the tree. Cameron stumbled backward out of John's reach, falling onto the snow.

John let out another grunt, peering at the blood seeping onto his shirt. "You stupid bitch! I'm going to kill you!"

Cameron scrambled to her feet. She ran toward the knife, tripping over the bear trap clamped around John's ankle. John cried out in pain as she landed in the snow on all fours and crawled toward the blade. Hearing a wolf howl from the base of the hill below, she froze. She got to her knees and peered down the hill as John screamed her name.

The alpha wolf had broken away from the pack, gaining speed as he ascended the hill toward her and John. Her heart thumped against her chest as the wolf's amber eyes bore into hers. He was close enough for her to clearly make out the black stripe of fur between his eyes, leading down his snout to his nose. Foam dripped from the side of its mouth. The wolf lowered his head and lengthened his strides as Valerie's warning about rabid wolves in this area echoed in her mind: The disease threw them into a violent rage. And what's more… they lost their fear of people.

If she wanted to live, she needed to move. Now.

She pushed herself off the snow, glancing at the weapon in the snow before turning to John, still bound to the tree. His chest heaved as blood streamed from his abdomen. His ankle remained mangled, clamped in the bear trap. There was no way he could reach the weapon.

As fast as her snowshoes allowed, Cameron lifted her legs, numb from the cold, one in front of the other.

"Cam—eron!" John cried through ragged breaths as she passed the tree. "Get your ass—ugh, shit—back here and help me inside!"

Cameron kept moving, spotting the alpha already halfway up the snow-covered hillside. His amber gaze had shifted from her, its eyes firmly trained now on John.

Something leapt inside her as she propelled herself to trek faster through the snow. She'd done it. She'd won.

"Don't worry, I'm sure the wolves can gnaw through that rope for you."

She kept moving without looking back, commanding her legs to move faster with each step. Ignoring the burn in her lungs from the frigid air, she pushed herself to maintain an uncoordinated jog as the decibel of John's screams intensified with his growing panic as the alpha—and his pack—closed in.

CHAPTER TWENTY-SIX

"HEY." DANE SWUNG his front door wide.

He'd taken off his blue uniform shirt. His fitted white undershirt was untucked from his trousers, a stark contrast to his tanned skin and dark brown hair.

Cameron stepped inside. "Hey."

He lifted the opened beer can in his hand. "You want one?"

"I'm good."

When he closed the door behind her, the outline of his pectoral muscles shifted beneath his shirt. Despite everything, it was impossible not to notice how good he looked.

"You want to sit down?"

She followed him into his living room and sat beside him on his leather couch. His house was newer than hers by a few decades. Dane had bought the house with his wife a few years after they were married. Cameron adjusted a throw pillow behind her back as her eyes were drawn to the ornate owl woodcarving displayed on the knotty pine bookshelf. She'd been surprised to learn earlier this summer that Trooper Nelson, who hand carved various animals for a hobby, had made it. Aside from the owl, she wondered how much of the home's décor had been picked out by Dane's late wife.

She swallowed over the lump that formed in her throat, turning to the man she'd gotten close to over the last six months. Why hadn't he told her the truth about his marriage?

She would ask him, but first, she needed to know about Sienna. "How is Valerie?"

Dane took a deep breath and reclined against the back of the couch. "She and her sister took it pretty rough after seeing Sienna's body."

A heaviness formed in her chest at the image of Valerie and Sienna's mother viewing Sienna's corpse. That feeling quickly morphed into a renewed hatred for John.

"Do you know how Sienna died?"

Dane took a long drink from his beer before warily meeting her gaze. There were dark half-moons beneath his eyes, and she realized for the first time how exhausted he looked.

"We won't have the official autopsy results until tomorrow." He looked away, his gaze settling on the wood burning stove in the corner. As he continued, it felt as though his mind had drifted somewhere else. "But I spoke to the medical examiner in Fairbanks after she did an initial exam. Sienna's hyoid bone was broken, and from the markings around her neck—"

John. "She was strangled."

It was the knife. I should've never gone back a second time that day. It must've been how he escaped.

She pictured the kitchen knife, lying in the snow several feet away from John where she'd left him for the last time, bleeding out and bound to the tree. She was certain he couldn't have gotten untied. As she'd retreated through the darkening woods, she'd heard his screams transform into cries of agony when the wolves reached him. It was nearly unfathomable to think he survived, even if he had managed to reach the knife.

"Cameron?" Dane studied her with concern. "You okay?"

"It was John. I know it. I can *feel* it, Dane. He's here."

Dane slowly shook his head.

Cameron felt a rush of heat rise to her face. "How can you be sure? I told you what Tanner said. He's alive."

Dane frowned.

How could he not see the obvious? "I wasn't completely honest with you about what happened with—"

Dane's phone vibrated atop his coffee table, startling her. She'd startled easily ever since being married to Miles. Even though that was long in the past—she'd never been able to stop the reflex.

Dane lifted his phone, keeping his eyes on Cameron. "Have you seen the news today?"

She sat up straight. "What news? About Sienna?"

"Not Sienna."

Cameron drew in a sharp breath. *Has John killed again?*

Dane checked the caller ID. "Sorry, I have to take this." He stood from the couch and moved toward the kitchen as he put the phone to his ear. "Sergeant Waska."

Cameron heard a male voice on the other end of the call before Dane left the room. She leaned forward and retrieved her phone from the back pocket of her jeans. A search for news updates in Tok yielded nothing newer than the article about Sienna's body being found, something she'd already read. There was no other news from today.

She'd broadened her search to news updates in Alaska when her phone rang in her hand. It was Tanner. Her pulse quickened. She hoped Tanner, of all people, would believe that John killed

Sienna after he learned that Sienna was strangled. *How could he not?*

"Hey. Thanks for calling me back."

"Hi, Cameron."

"They found Sienna's body today. In a lake. She was murdered."

"I saw that." His voice was calm, as always.

"But there's more. She was strangled. They don't have the official autopsy report yet, but Dane spoke with the Fairbanks medical examiner. This has to be John." Cameron stood from the couch. "He's here!"

"Cameron, I don't—"

She paced back and forth. "It's what you came to tell me, right? That he's alive!"

"Cameron!"

She stopped. "What?"

"Have you seen the news today?"

Her heart froze. "No. Why?"

He breathed into the phone.

"Tell me Tanner, what is it?" *What had John done now?*

"Unidentified male remains were discovered this morning north of Eagle. Roughly fifty miles east of your late husband's cabin."

Cameron stood still, her breath stuck in her throat. "Is it John?" she asked once she managed to speak.

"I don't know yet. The body's being transferred to Fairbanks. I sent them John's dental records, but they likely won't have an ID for another couple of days. The person looks to have been deceased for several months. They were wearing snow gear and likely died in winter or early spring."

Cameron closed her eyes. She'd left John tied to the tree in February.

"The remains were found on the shores of the Yukon River. An abandoned snowmobile was found less than one hundred feet away."

"Do you think it's John?" she heard herself ask.

"I think it's very likely at this point, yes."

Cameron sunk to the couch as Dane returned to the living room with his phone at his side.

"But then who…"

"I don't know," Tanner said. "But I thought you should know. And I'll call you when they have an ID."

Dane eyed her inquisitively when she met his gaze.

"And Cameron? Did John ever speak to you about his father?"

"His father? No, not much. Both parents were alcoholics, and they didn't have much of a relationship. At least that's what he told me. I never met them. The only memory John ever shared about his dad was that he took him to Fairbanks a few times as a kid."

A pause. "Did John say what they did?"

Cameron strained to recall the details. "Not that I remember. Just that his dad loved it up there. Why?"

"It's not relevant right now. I'll tell you another time. And we still don't have all the facts. So, promise me you'll be careful, all right?"

"Okay."

As she ended the call, Dane gave her a curious look. "Who was that?" he asked.

"Tanner. Did you know about the male remains that were found north of Eagle?"

"Yeah." He crossed the room and sat beside her. "That's what I was about to tell you before I got that call."

Her mind whirled. *If John didn't kill Sienna and Madison…*

She shifted to face Dane. He looked pensive. Wary.

"Do you suspect someone in Madison and Sienna's deaths?"

The look in his eyes told her he did.

"Who?"

He set down his phone and lifted his beer can. "I can't tell you."

Cameron stiffened. "Why the hell not?"

"I just can't, Cam." He averted her gaze and took a drink. "Not yet."

Cameron stared at him in disbelief. "I've told you everything." The memory of her driving the blade into John's torso flashed in her mind. *Well, almost everything.*

His eyes locked with hers. "I know. I will tell you as soon as I can. I promise." He put his hand on her knee. "For now, I need you to trust me."

She remained still, resisting the urge to recoil from his touch.

"What were you going to tell me a few minutes ago?" he asked.

Cameron tore her eyes from his. She stared at the wood-carved owl on the bookshelf as an image of John, dead, floating face down in the freezing Yukon River seared in her mind. If John was dead…

She turned to Dane, studying his face as she debated whether to tell him about what she'd done to John, knowing now that it likely no longer mattered.

"Why didn't you tell me your wife was having an affair?"

CHAPTER TWENTY-SEVEN

Dane sank against the couch cushions, looking deflated. "Who told you that?"

"Does it matter? You told me you were happy. Made me think you had the perfect marriage. Why didn't you tell me she was about to leave you?"

Dane ran his hand through his thick, black hair. "I thought we *were* happy. But she'd been having an affair for over eight months when I found out. Right under my nose, and I'd had no idea." He shook his head. "I investigate crimes for a living, but I had no clue my own wife was being unfaithful."

"You lied to me."

Cameron watched Dane finish what was left of his beer, waiting for him to respond. He averted his gaze when he set down the can. Cameron wondered if it was a sign of guilt for not telling her the truth.

"The morning of her accident, I drove by the medical center on my way to work and spotted her leaning against her car, kissing a doctor she worked with. A man I'd known for years. At first, I thought it couldn't be her. But I turned around and drove by a second time. I watched my wife pull away from him before she laughed and threw her arms around his neck. I kept driving and told Nelson when I got to the station." Dane's gaze fell to the floor. "I was so angry, I was shaking." He cleared his throat. "Nelson admitted to seeing them together before. He'd even confronted Lucille about it a week before, and she convinced Nelson not to say anything, promising she would tell me herself." Dane picked at the paper label on his beer, seemingly lost in his thoughts. "I called her from my office in a rage, and she admitted everything. I hung up on her, and she left her shift and came to the station. Told me they'd been seeing each other for eight months." He scoffed. "*Eight months,* and I never suspected a thing."

Cameron recalled the shock that ripped through her when she stumbled upon the disturbing photos that proved John was The Teacher Killer. She reached for Dane's hand.

"I screamed at her," Dane stared blankly at his beer on the coffee table. "Made her cry. Asked her how she could do such a thing." He pulled his hand out from beneath hers. "I…called her a selfish bitch and hurled our framed wedding photo against the wall. I was furious that people in town knew while I didn't. Even Nelson. I felt like such an idiot." He lifted his gaze to meet hers. "I was so angry, Cameron. Nelson was at the station in the middle of booking Karl for a DUI. I'm sure they both heard everything. I was still seething with rage."

His voice broke. He heaved a sigh before continuing.

"If I hadn't made her so upset…"

Dane leaned forward, and Cameron rested her hand on his back. "It's not your fault."

"I had no idea she was taking painkillers. She stayed at the station for a half hour after my outburst, crying. I ignored her, hiding in my office like a coward. They did a tox screen postmortem, and from the amount of oxycodone in her system, the medical examiner estimated she took a handful of pills within an hour of her death. Maybe if I had come out of my office and comforted her, she'd still be alive."

"I wish you would've told me the truth."

"I'm sorry." When he turned toward her, there were tears in Dane's eyes. "It's not easy for me to talk about. But you're right, I should've told you."

Cameron studied him. *Does he not trust me?* Her body tensed as her thoughts returned to the male remains that had been discovered near Eagle.

"Why can't you tell me who you suspect killed Madison and Sienna?"

"I just can't, Cameron."

She sensed a touch of agitation in his voice.

He rubbed her knee before pulling his hand away. "I should get some sleep. You want to stay here?"

"I think I'll go back home."

Dane's eyes searched hers. "I wish I could tell you. But first, I need to be sure."

Cameron stood, unable to hide the annoyance on her face. She had clearly trusted Dane more than he trusted her.

He reached for her arm. "I'm sorry."

"I think we both should get some sleep."

He followed her to the door, where she allowed him to envelope her in a hug. "I should've told you the truth about my marriage…I just—"

"It's okay," she said, pulling away. "I get that you didn't want to talk about it." Although she couldn't shake her disappointment after believing they told each other everything.

Almost everything.

She stepped outside onto his porch.

"Goodnight, Cameron."

"Goodnight."

Dane stayed on his porch as Cameron crossed his yard to her own. She gave him a wave before going inside, locking the deadbolt behind her, then leaning against her door as she looked around her empty house.

If John was dead, she had no reason to be afraid. But why didn't she feel relieved?

CHAPTER TWENTY-EIGHT

Tanner took a drink from his coffee after reading through Amy Clarke's casefile for the second time that morning. After what Cameron told him about Prescott's father taking him to Fairbanks as a kid, Tanner wondered if Louie Prescott might've returned to Alaska in the nineties and gone on a killing spree in Tok. Unfortunately, nothing in the '97 cold case was spurring new connections for him to the 1984 Seattle murder of Sally Hickman, despite pouring over the new murders in Tok that seemed so similar.

It struck Tanner that the one person John Prescott might've confided in about his father's killings was his law firm partner. The one who, as it turned out, knew Prescott better than anyone else. Tanner sat back in his chair. Too bad the attorney was no longer around for Tanner to ask, although Simon likely wouldn't have opened up to Tanner about Prescott even if he *was* still alive for him to interview.

When Tanner's alarm went off at four-thirty, he'd been surprised he hadn't gotten called out in the middle of the night to a homicide. After a short run along the shores of Lincoln Park, he'd been the first in his unit to arrive that morning. He glanced at the skull bobblehead on the edge of his cubicle. With six more nights being on call, he doubted he would make it through many more without getting called to a new case.

A laugh erupted from the cubicle adjacent to his. Tanner pulled on his headphones, reflecting on his brief conversation with Cameron last night when she told him about Sienna Lovell, the girl they'd found murdered yesterday. Her body was dumped in the same lake as Erica Lavine, the woman murdered in Tok less than three months after Amy Clarke.

According to Amy Clarke's casefile, George Waska had been the trooper to respond to her home the night she was killed. Her husband had found her body less than four hours after Waska had been called to her house. According to Tanner's Accurint database, the only other trooper working that night was now deceased.

Before opening Clarke's casefile that morning, Tanner had reread Karl Sadler's witness statement claiming to have seen Dane Waska leaving the lake where the second victim's body was discovered. Tanner minimized the casefile and ran an internet search for Sergeant George Waska, Tok, AK. He clicked on an image from a news article in 2002. A photo of George Waska and three other uniformed troopers standing in front of the trooper station topped the article headlined *NEW TROOPER STATION OPENS IN TOK.*

Tanner recognized Dane Waska standing beside his father. The two men looked strikingly similar: same build, same height, same thick dark hair and pronounced cheekbones. If Karl Sadler *had* seen someone leaving the lake that day, Tanner wondered how Karl could be certain at a glance that it had been Dane—and not his father.

He closed out of the article and pulled up Amy Clarke's

casefile again, scrolling to the three names listed as prime suspects. He stared at the list while finishing what was left of his coffee, debating whether to make the call. This wasn't his case. Not even his jurisdiction.

He reached for his phone and dialed anyway.

"Trooper Nelson," a male voice answered after the second ring.

"This is Detective Mulholland from Seattle Homicide."

"Oh. If you're calling to speak with Sergeant Waska, he's not here."

"I actually wanted to speak to you. I had some questions regarding the unsolved homicides of Amy Clarke and Erica Lavine from the 1990s."

A pause. "I don't know if you've read the news, but we're very busy up here today. Just had our second homicide of the week. Plus, I'm not sure what your interest is in these cases. They're pretty far out of your jurisdiction, no?"

Tanner leaned back in his chair, not surprised to get pushback from a trooper in another state. "I'm investigating a link between last year's murder of Bethany Long and some of my homicide cases. With these new murders happening, I want to make sure I'm being thorough."

Tanner heard a phone ring in the background of the call.

"I can give you a few minutes," Nelson said. "But that's all. What do you want to know?"

"What can you tell me about Karl Sadler?"

Nelson scoffed. "Karl? These days, he's a drunk. Couldn't hurt a fly even if he wanted to. Back in the nineties, he was more of a functioning alcoholic."

"What do you think of his witness statement placing Dane Waska at the lake where Erica Lavine's body was found? You believe it was accurate?"

Nelson exhaled into the line. "I'm still not sure. Although, it doesn't surprise me that Karl waited until after he was fired to point a finger at the boss's son. He wouldn't have dared to do it before. It would've cost him his job as a trooper."

"Why is that? According to the casefiles, I thought Dane and George were both already suspects at that time."

"They were. I was too, given I was a trooper. That's why the investigation was taken over by the Major Crimes Unit out of Fairbanks. But George Waska had a lot of authority here in the nineties. People in town suspected him, but they were also afraid of him. If there *were* any other witnesses, I doubt they would've come forward."

Tanner rocked forward in his desk chair, floored by what Nelson was saying. He hadn't expected him to say much, especially not to make an accusation. "You sound like you think George Waska was guilty."

"I'm not saying that. Just that the investigation was…complicated. For all of us."

"I read in Amy Clarke's file that it was George Waska who was dispatched to her house the night she was killed."

"That's right."

Tanner waited, hoping Nelson might elaborate. When he didn't, Tanner asked, "Do you have a phone number where I could reach George Waska? I'd like to ask him about it. See if he's willing to talk to me."

"I do, although I can't guarantee that you'll be able to reach him. There's no cell service up at his lake cabin, but he does have a satellite phone. You ready for the number?"

As Tanner jotted down George Waska's phone number on a post-it, he wondered about Nelson's implication that George Waska's 'authority' in the small town likely jeopardized the murder investigations. It was never good to find out one of your own had violated the public trust.

He finished the call and hung up, hoping that for once, he was wrong.

CHAPTER TWENTY-NINE

"I've got George ready for you in room two." Gwen caught Cameron's eye as soon as she stepped out of room three, where she'd been performing an emergency root canal for the past hour. "I just finished his cleaning."

"George Milton?"

Normally, Cameron checked her patient schedule at the start of her day, but she'd been too distracted that morning. She'd managed to get a few hours of sleep but was still reeling from learning John was possibly dead after believing he was still alive, wondering who Dane suspected and why he wouldn't tell her, and worrying about how Valerie was coping with her niece's murder.

"No. George Waska."

Cameron paused in the doorway of room two, recognizing Dane's father reclining in the dental chair. She was surprised he'd come back into town for his scheduled cleaning appointment, especially with the new murders. She'd had a tough time convincing him to go to the dentist last winter after suspecting he had a tooth abscess, and she imagined the previous dentist in town had implored him to come back more often without much effect.

"Hi, George." She smiled as she sat on the stool beside him.

He tilted his head toward her. "Hey, Cameron."

Despite his tough exterior, the older man had warmed to Cameron in the last several months she'd been dating his son.

"How's life at the cabin?" she asked.

"Oh, same."

Cameron grabbed her stomatoscope off the tray Gwen had laid out and lifted the mirror above George's mouth. "All right, open wide."

After completing his exam, she set down the scope and pulled off her gloves. "Well, George, everything looks great. Keep up the good work."

"So, you're saying I don't need to come back so soon next time?" He winked.

Cameron grinned. "Nice try. But we'd still like to see you every six months."

He let out an exaggerated sigh. "I guess I can't complain about getting to chat with this beautiful young lady for an hour." He motioned to Gwen sitting on the other side of him. "And seeing you, of course. How's my son by the way? I tried calling him the last few days, but he didn't answer."

Cameron felt her brows furrow. "I thought he came to see you the day before yesterday?"

Now George was the one who looked confused. He shook his head. "No."

Cameron studied him, searching for a sign he was joking. He was getting close to eighty. Could he be losing his short-term memory? But Dane hadn't mentioned him having any cognitive trouble. Plus, George had remembered his cleaning appointment today.

"Oh, I thought Dane came to see you to ask you about those new murders." The second part left her mouth before she could stop it.

George's expression turned serious. "He did. Two nights after that young woman was found in the ditch." George pushed himself upright in the reclined chair. "Are you saying there was another one?"

Gwen's eyebrows lifted. "You haven't heard?"

Cameron's stomach dropped. George turned toward the hygienist as Gwen launched into a wide-eyed, detailed account of everything the news had released about Madison's and Sienna's deaths.

Cameron touched George's arm as he listened in earnest, too shaken by Dane's lie to keep hearing Gwen's animated retelling of the discovery of Sienna's body. "Good to see you, George."

He patted her hand. "You too," he mumbled. The color had drained from his face. He turned back to Gwen while she continued animatedly sharing details of the murders.

When she stood and left the room, Cameron felt lightheaded. She stopped at the front desk on her way back to her office.

"Do we have any more patients today?" she asked Jennifer, the office manager.

Jennifer looked up from her computer. "Nope. George was the last one."

The floor swayed as Cameron retrieved her purse from her office and told Jennifer she'd see her tomorrow. She called Dane as soon as she reached her truck. Her hand trembled as she put the phone to ear.

Dane didn't answer, and she hung up without leaving a message, turning onto the Alaksa Highway. A half mile up the road, she spotted a trooper SUV parked in front of the trooper station and pulled into the parking lot. When she stopped alongside of it, she recognized the bear-shaped air freshener hanging from Nelson's rearview mirror. She got out of her truck anyway, hoping Nelson could tell her where Dane was.

Her fist was already clenched when she knocked on the locked metal door. A few moments later, Nelson opened it. His face looked strained.

"Cameron, hey."

"Hey, Nelson. I'm looking for Dane. Do you know where I might find him?"

He frowned. "No. I was hoping to ask you the same thing. I've been trying to get ahold of him for the last hour, but I can't reach him."

"Oh. Why?" She searched Nelson's eyes, praying there hadn't been another murder. "Has something happened?"

Nelson pursed his thin lips together as if debating whether to tell her. "I just need to talk to him," he finally said.

Cameron looked beyond Nelson to the station's office manager sitting behind the front desk. Her eyes met Cameron's briefly before she returned her gaze to her computer screen.

"I'm actually headed out," Nelson said.

Cameron stepped aside for him to come outside, watching him speed walk toward his SUV.

"Call me if you hear from him," he said over his shoulder.

Cameron stood still as Nelson sped out of the parking lot and pulled onto the highway. *Where* was *Dane? And why did he keep disappearing?*

As she slowly returned to her truck, she wondered if she should've told Nelson that Dane hadn't visited his father like he'd told Nelson he had. Her stomach flip-flopped.

The morning of Sienna's disappearance, when Nelson came to her house looking for him, Dane had already left. Then he didn't return until after Valerie made the missing person's report. Plenty of time to kill Sienna and dump her body in the lake.

She cringed at the thought as she started her truck engine, berating herself for even thinking it. Surely, Dane had a good explanation for lying to Nelson about going to see his dad. *But what?*

Cameron braked before turning left on the highway. She'd been planning to stop and see Valerie but was too shaken.

After pulling into her driveway, she checked her phone in case she'd missed Dane's call. But he hadn't called her back. Neither had Mulholland about the identity of the human remains found near Eagle, but he said it could take a couple of days. She glanced in the direction of Dane's empty drive, a sickening sensation spreading in the pit of her stomach.

She sat in her truck wondering why Nelson was looking for Dane. The worrisome look on Nelson's face at the station replayed in her mind. Even more concerning was Dane's lie to Nelson about going to see his dad. And where was he?

She typed *body found near Eagle, Alaska,* into the internet search bar on her phone. The only article her search yielded was the one posted yesterday reporting that the unidentified remains had been found.

She surveyed the front of Dane's house another time before throwing her truck in reverse and backing out of her drive.

CHAPTER THIRTY

Tanner pulled his Ford Fusion to a stop along the curb across from the white two-story home. Two cars were parked in the drive side by side: a white Tesla and a black Audi. The end of the driveway had already been secured with crime scene tape. Tanner spotted his sergeant's SUV parked in front of the house, along with a patrol car.

He had just finished going through every detail from Sally Hickman's casefile and was about to review his other unsolved cases around the time of her death when his phone rang, dispatching him to a double homicide in the waterfront neighborhood.

Tanner crossed the street, avoiding the gaping stares from an elderly couple standing on the sidewalk. He regarded the manicured lawns illuminated by streetlamps that lined the street. It wasn't often he got called to this part of the city. The last time he'd visited a home in Laurelhurst, the next neighborhood over, he was heading to Cameron Prescott's home in the wake of the Teacher Killer revelations.

Thinking of Cameron—and John Prescott—along with the new murders happening in Tok, filled him with a current of frustration. He was still waiting to learn the ID of the unidentified male remains, and when he'd called George Waska that afternoon, his call had gone straight to voicemail.

The officer assigned to the front of the house nodded at Tanner as he stepped over the crime scene tape and flashed the officer his badge.

"Bodies are upstairs. Master bedroom. It's the worst domestic bloodbath I've ever seen."

Tanner paused at the front door to pull booties over his shoes as a CSI van pulled up. He folded a stick of gum into his mouth while he climbed the polished wood staircase, hearing one of the CSI members step inside after he reached the top. When he got to the master bedroom, he took a large step over the blond woman's body splayed out on the carpet in the open doorway to the room, careful not to step too close to the casing lying beside her open palm.

From what he could tell, she'd been shot three times: twice in the forehead and once in the chest.

"Hey, Mulholland." His sergeant stood at the edge of the room with her arms folded, taking in the scene beside a patrol officer Tanner recognized. After Tanner graduated from the academy, he and Neil had worked for four years out of the same precinct. It felt like a lifetime ago.

"Hey, Sarge."

Tanner withdrew a pair of latex gloves from his suit jacket pocket as he surveyed the large splatter of blood and brain matter on the once white wall above the body. A CSI member appeared in the doorway. After stepping over the deceased, the crime scene investigator followed Tanner's gaze.

She swore before raising her phone to take a photo of the wall. "That's a lot of blood."

Tanner stepped aside for the crime scene investigator to place a numbered placard on the carpet beside the pistol lying a couple of feet away from the woman's body. Tanner took another photo.

The patrol officer came toward Tanner when he turned toward the second victim lying on the bed.

"Hi, Neil," Tanner said, examining the bloodied mess of sheets.

Tanner heard another CSI member swear when they entered the room behind them.

"My partner and I were the first on-scene," Neil said as they moved beside the large picture window offering an expansive view of Lake Washington below. Across the water, lights twinkled from the city of Kirkland.

Tanner chewed his gum while he assessed the second victim. His lungs stiffened at the grim scene. Despite having been called to countless homicides over the years, Tanner found it no less disturbing seeing a murder victim than he had at the beginning of his career. The woman in the bed had been shot multiple times. She wore only a lacy black bra and matching panties. Her torso and head were so covered in blood it was difficult for Tanner to determine how many bullet wounds she'd sustained.

Neil pointed to the blond woman lying in the doorway. "We believe she was the initial shooter. She's been identified as Megan Wallis. Her husband returned fire with a 9mm his girlfriend"—Neil gestured to the blood-covered body on the bed—"kept in the bedside drawer. He called 911 and was rushed to Bayside with two bullets in the chest. He's pretty badly injured, but he managed to tell us that the girlfriend, Natalie Thomas, met him earlier tonight after work at his real estate office. They stopped for a drink at Bottom's Up, that new bar in Belltown, before driving here to the girlfriend's house together. The husband said his wife must've followed without them noticing." Neil shook his head. "They even left the front door unlocked."

Tanner stepped closer to the dark-haired woman lying on her back on the bed. Her lifeless blue eyes stared blankly at the ceiling fan.

Neil stood next to Tanner, following his gaze. "She was shot from behind and was lying prone when we arrived. My partner and I turned her over to see if we could resuscitate her. But it was obvious she was beyond saving. It looks like she was shot four times."

Tanner bent forward to get a closer look at the bullet wounds as Neil continued.

"Three times in the torso and once in the head. According to the husband, his wife shot his girlfriend first then turned her gun on him when he pulled the pistol out of the drawer and returned fire."

Tanner assessed the woman's long, dark hair, which fanned out over the pillow above her head, reminding him of Prescott's victims. Unlike The Teacher Killer victims, hers was matted with blood. Tanner felt his gaze fall to the lower part of her torso, looking for the Teacher Killer marking that he knew wouldn't be there.

He turned to Neil. "The husband was conscious when the medics took him to Bayside?"

"He was in and out."

"I want to interview the neighbors," Tanner thought aloud. "See if anyone witnessed the wife arriving after her husband and girlfriend."

"You need me to do anything for you, Mulholland?" his sergeant asked.

Tanner tore his gaze from the victim on the bed. Unlike the rest of the detectives in his squad, Tanner had no partner. While he preferred working alone, it could prove difficult when working a new homicide, especially in a case where time was of the essence. But this case appeared to have solved itself.

"Can you call Bayside and find out if the husband is conscious? I'd like to interview him as soon as possible."

His phone rang in his pocket. Seeing the twelve-digit satellite number, he accepted the call.

"You got it," she said as Tanner put his phone to his ear.

"Detective Mulholland." He stepped sideways around the CSI member who was bagging the casing beside the blond woman's body, then moved into the hall.

"Hello?" A gruff male voice came through the call followed by static.

"This is Detective Mullholland from Seattle Homicide," Tanner repeated. "Is this George Waska?"

"Yeah. I got your message." His voice was gravelly, and deeper than his son's, but Tanner could hear the hint of similarity in the two men's voices.

"Thanks for returning my call." As another crime scene investigator moved down the hallway, Tanner stepped aside, careful not to touch the wall with his back. "Like I said, I'm investigating a connection with the recent murders in Tok and some of my other homicide cases. You've heard about the recent murders in your town?"

"Just found out today about the second one. I think you've got the wrong Waska. You should be talking to my son, not me. I'm retired."

"I spoke with him already, and your son said these recent murders in Tok might be related to a couple that happened there in the nineties."

The call went quiet. Tanner checked to make sure they were still connected.

"I'm not sure these cases are any of your business. Where did you say you're calling from again? Seattle?"

"That's ri—

"Wait. You the one who solved the Teacher Killer murders?"

Tanner glanced at the crime scene through the opened bedroom doorway. He needed to get back to his present investigation. "I am."

"You know his widow is dating my son? Is that why you think there's a connection to your cases? I thought The Teacher Killer was dead."

Tanner moved his gum to the other side of his mouth. *I thought so too.*

"Sergeant Waska sent me the casefiles of the two unsolved Tok murders from the nineties, but I wanted to get your take on them."

"My take? Humph." Static muffled George's voice. "Like whether I believe Karl Sadler's fairy tale accusing Dane of leaving the lake where Erica Lavine's body was dumped two days after she went missing?"

Tanner spotted Pete, a Seattle medical examiner, coming up the stairs, carrying the duffel bag he brought to every scene.

"Do you?" Tanner asked George.

He nodded to Pete when the examiner reached the top of the stairs. Pete returned Tanner's nod before striding toward the body lying inside the bedroom doorway. From the way Pete's wavy hair stuck up in the back, Tanner guessed he'd already been asleep when he got the call.

A staticky scoff came through the phone speaker. "It was bull—. We— knew it. Karl came forward right after I fired him for drinking on the job. I have no doubt he made it up out of revenge. Except the part about him being four beers in before late afternoon. That I believe. If Karl *did* see someone leaving the lake that day, it wasn't Dane. Those two murders— a long time ago. Whoever was responsible is no longer in this town any— I'm sure of it. That killer had to have moved on. They're possibly in prison now for a different killing. Personally, I like to think they're dead."

A crime scene investigator emerged from the bedroom carrying two evidence bags with a pistol inside of each.

"Several ----- in ---- had ---- same kind of vehicle that Karl said he saw," George continued, their call breaking up.

Tanner plugged his other ear with his finger, straining to hear George.

"But no other ---- ----- searched. Hell, even ------ had one."

Tanner pressed his phone harder against his ear. "Who had one?"

Static filled the call before it went dead. Tanner checked his screen. *Call dropped.* Tanner swore. He was about to call George back when his sergeant emerged from the bedroom.

"You have to hurry if you want to speak to the husband," she said, marching toward Tanner. "He's conscious, but they're taking him into surgery. You'll need to leave now to have a chance at interviewing him tonight."

Tanner lowered his phone. "Thanks, I will. Can you ask Neil to start interviewing the neighbors? Find out if anyone saw the wife's car arrive and her come into the house? I'll check in with him as soon as I speak with the husband."

"You got it."

Tanner started down the stairs as his sergeant returned to the bedroom crime scene. When he got to the first floor, he redialed George. It went straight to voicemail, which played an automated message. *The voicemail box of the person you are calling is full. Please try again later.*

When Tanner crossed the street to his Fusion, the neighbors

were no longer outside. Tanner climbed behind the wheel, replaying what George had said over the static of the call. *Even— had one.*

Great time for the call to cut out.

Did George think it was a name Tanner would've recognized? As he held in the button to start his engine, he envisioned the short list of suspect names on the case files Dane had sent over.

Bayside Hospital was fifteen minutes away. Ten if he went lights and siren. Tanner flipped the switch on his dash to activate his Fusion's lights and siren and peeled out onto the neighborhood street.

CHAPTER THIRTY-ONE

Cameron spotted Dane's cabin when she came around the bend in the narrow road that wound around Hunt Lake. Disappointed to see the unlit windows and no SUV in the drive, she drove past and pulled to a stop in front of George's cabin next door.

On the hour drive to the lake, a thousand questions had swarmed in her mind. But maybe George could shed a light on who Dane suspected in the new murders, and why he was being so secretive. According to Dane, his father knew more about the old cases than anyone.

A look of surprise washed over George's face when he opened the door. ""Cameron. What are you doing here?" He glanced behind her at his son's neighboring cabin. "Is Dane with you?"

"No. He's not answering his phone. Nelson was looking for him earlier too. I suppose he could've gone out of cell range investigating Sienna's murder, but I thought maybe he'd come up here."

"I haven't seen him." George opened the door wider. "But come in. You know, for a second, I thought you'd come to finish my dental appointment. And if that were the case, I'd have to send you home."

George winked as she stepped inside his cabin, which was dimly lit by a kerosene lamp and the flames flickering from his wood stove. The layout of his cabin was very similar to Dane's, only bigger. George motioned toward his couch facing the window. She took a seat and in the waning daylight, she could make out a bald eagle land on George's floating dock. She stared at the view as George sank onto the other side of the couch. From what Dane had said, her burning questions could be a sensitive topic for George, but she needed to ask anyway.

"What did Dane come to talk to you about after Madison Youngblood's murder?"

George lifted his eyebrows. His expression hardened, confirming her suspicion that it was still a sore subject for him.

"I would've preferred another dental visit if I'd known you came to talk about that."

"I'm sorry. Dane—

George waved his hand through the air. "It's fine. Dane wanted my take on whether it could be related to two unsolved murders from Tok in the nineties. I obsessed over those cases and kept a notebook on the investigations for many years." He turned to face her. "A detective from Seattle actually just called me asking about those murders."

Cameron straightened. "Tanner?"

"Mulholland, I think he said. You know him?"

"I do." Cameron sank against the couch, glad that Tanner was at least looking into those cold cases. But it still didn't answer her questions about Dane. "What did he ask you?"

"He wanted to know if I thought the new murders could be the same killer from the two in the nineties. I told him I didn't think so."

Because it was John. "Why's that?"

"For one thing, they'd be stupid to come back and kill again in Tok after all these years of not being caught. I told the detective that my guess is the killer moved on to somewhere else. He's probably in prison for other crimes, or dead. My gut says these new killings are a sick copycat of those old cases."

Cameron studied George's profile in the glow from the fire, struck by how similar his features were to his son's.

"Who did *you* suspect back then?"

George stared straight ahead. After a minute, he turned toward her, his face somber. "It wasn't Dane if that's what you're asking. Or me. I'm sure you've heard the rumors. Everyone talks in a small town like Tok, especially when they're nervous about getting their teeth drilled."

"Nelson told me."

George shook his head. "Karl was a drunk, even then. He made that statement right after I fired him for drinking on the job. That I believe."

His gaze returned to the window, watching the eagle fly toward the darkening tree line on the far side of the lake. "To answer your question, I thought it was an out of towner. Still do. Someone in law enforcement, or who had at least been at one point."

"Dane told me the other night that he suspects someone in these new murders. But he wouldn't tell me who. Did he tell you who it was?"

George looked surprised. "That's news to me. When he came up here after Madison's murder, he didn't know what to think. That's why he asked for all my notes on the old cases." He motioned to a cardboard box near the wood stove. "Luckily it wasn't too hard to find."

Cameron stared at the box, her thoughts spinning.

"Why all the questions?" George asked.

She debated telling him about Dane's unexplained absence the morning of Sienna's disappearance. And how he lied about being here with George.

"I'm just worried about Dane," she finally said. *And John.*

"I know it might be hard to trust after your late husband," George said, as if reading her thoughts, "but if Dane's keeping something from you regarding the investigation, he has a good reason." George sat tall and placed his hands on his knees. "Are you hungry? I haven't had dinner yet. You want to stay for some lake trout?"

Cameron looked out at the night beyond the window, exhaustion settling over her from her lack of sleep over the last few days. "Thanks for the offer, but I should be getting back."

George stood from his couch. "Another time then."

Cameron nodded. She glanced at the opened box in front of the fire as she followed George to the door. Atop the stack of notebooks piled inside were some printed photographs. Her gaze caught on one of the photos, reflecting the flickering light from the fire.

She paused to look at the image. "Is that you or Dane?"

George followed her gaze and smiled. "Me. That was nearly thirty years ago."

Cameron studied the photo, amazed at how much Dane looked like his father. If they'd been the same age, it would be hard to tell the father and son apart. Cameron took one last look at the photo, which captured George standing next to a man with graying hair in front of a white SUV. There was something familiar about the older man in the photo with George, but Cameron didn't recognize him.

She considered asking George, then decided against it. She'd pried enough for one night.

"Try not worry about these new murders," George said after Cameron stepped outside. "Dane's a good investigator, and he's got good instincts. I'm confident that he'll find who's behind this."

Cameron forced a smile before turning for her truck. She hoped George was right.

CHAPTER THIRTY-TWO

Cameron woke to headlight beams shining through her window. She sat up on her couch. Seeing her empty wineglass beside the half empty bottle of merlot reminded her of all the nights in the months following John's alleged fatal bear attack that she'd consumed a whole bottle by herself to go to sleep.

When she'd returned home from George's cabin the night before, Dane's drive had still been empty. Then, after her call had gone straight to voicemail, she'd opened a bottle of wine and tried to reassure herself that George was right. Dane had to have a good explanation for lying to Nelson about his whereabouts the morning of Sienna's disappearance. But none of the reasons she could come up with were good. Before turning out the light, she'd run another internet search to see if human remains near Eagle had been identified, but there'd been no updates. Sleep hadn't come easily after that.

Cameron stood and pulled the drapes aside to peer outside at the pair of headlights moving slowly down Dane's driveway, then checked the time on her phone. It was after midnight and Dane still hadn't returned her call. But finally, he was home, and she could ask him why he lied to Nelson about going to see his father.

She slipped on a pair of flip flops beside her door before going outside and marching down her porch steps, heading toward Dane's SUV as it braked three-quarters down his driveway. She folded her arms from the temperature drop that came with the setting sun, wishing she'd put on warmer shoes, as she crossed the grass, stiff from a light frost, between their properties.

The SUV's engine idled as she strode toward the vehicle. *What is Dane doing?*

She reached Dane's gravel drive, squinting from the strobe of the headlights piercing the darkness to illuminate her face. As she made for his driver's door, Dane still hadn't turned off his engine. Seeing the vehicle's license plate, she stopped short.

She froze in the middle of the drive, staring at the civilian plate. Her heart beat into her throat as she lifted her gaze and strained to make out the driver. But all she could see beyond the windshield was darkness.

The SUV's engine revved, its tires spinning on the gravel before it sped toward her. Cameron gasped, staring into the approaching beams before spinning on her heels to run. She cut to her right, toward her house, the crunch of the tires growing louder. She shot a glance over her shoulder as she ran, seeing the SUV soar off the gravel path and follow her onto the grass.

Her ankle rolled on the uneven ground. Pain soared up the side of her foot as it twisted off the flimsy strap of her flip flop. A cry of pain escaped her throat.

She started to go right around a spruce tree, but seeing there was room on that side for the SUV to follow, she darted to her left instead. Ignoring the pain in her ankle, she pivoted around the tree trunk, the heat from the vehicle's engine closing in on the back of her legs.

The driver floored the gas and swerved to avoid the tree, sending Cameron flying over its hood. She rolled backward as the SUV ran over a bump in the lawn and slammed against the windshield. The driver braked hard, sending her rolling off the hood onto the grass.

The SUV idled as she struggled to her feet in the blinding beams. No sooner had she stood when the engine roared. She didn't need to turn around to know that the grill was headed straight for her. She sprinted across her front yard, lit up by the SUV chasing after her.

When she neared the front of her house, the headlights turned off. Cameron instinctively cast a look behind her without slowing down. In the dim glow of her porch lamp, she made out the SUV only a few feet behind her, the driver's face indistinguishable in the shadows.

She pumped her legs harder when she turned back toward her house—only seconds before she smacked straight into a tree. The night blurred in her vision as she collapsed to the ground.

Cameron lay on her back, facing the stars. The soft click of the driver's door opening and closing drifted over the grass. A branch cracked beneath her assailant's shoe as they crept toward her. Cameron blinked, trying to clear her foggy vision as the ground spun.

She fought to sit up, but her body wouldn't respond to her commands. The footsteps came closer, and she craned her neck to see her attacker's face. Cameron's head swam, and she tried to focus on the driver as he approached, but as the distance shrank between them, he blurred out. She closed her eyes and opened them again, trying to focus. The broad figure knelt over her. He looked male, but the hood over his head cast a shadow over his face.

Cameron scooted back on the grass, forehead throbbing as fuzzy stars impeded her vision. The figure grasped her upper arm, completely encircling it in his grip. He whirled her onto her stomach in one strong motion and pressed her face into the ground.

Cameron screamed, blades of grass entering her mouth as the man drove his knee into her lower back. Cameron thrust her elbow into the man's ribs. He grunted and gripped her arm, squeezing it to the bone as he twisted her hands together behind her. Then the cold metal of a handcuff dug into her wrist.

Her heart pounded against the ground as she thrashed beneath the weight of the man's knee on her back, but the handcuffs made it impossible to put up much of a fight. She pushed her knee into the ground and twisted her torso to push her attacker off. But she hardly moved under the pressure of his body on hers.

The man pulled her hair away from her cheek and leaned his face toward hers, close enough for her to feel the heat of his breath. She stared at the shadow of his face beneath the hood as he sat up and raised a fist in the air.

There was something vaguely familiar about his touch, but she couldn't quite place it.

"John?"

She realized what he was about to do as his arm came down with force against the side of her skull. *This is it. I'm going to die.* Cameron's face hit the ground from the impact of the blow seconds before a numbing darkness overtook her.

CHAPTER THIRTY-THREE

"Cameron! Can you hear me? Cameron!"

Cameron opened her eyes to the male voice. Her mind flooded with the attack. Feeling the cold ground beneath her and seeing the dark figure hovering over her made a scream erupt from her mouth. She tried to push him away, but her hands were still bound by the handcuffs behind her back.

"Cameron, it's okay!" The man raised his palms in the air. "It's me, Dane." He lowered his hands to her shoulders and bowed his head. "Thank God, you're alive. I—" His voice cracked. "I saw you lying here in the ditch on my way home. At first I thought…"

He lifted his head, and Cameron's gaze darted toward the purr of his SUV's engine parked in his drive. Her eyes adjusted to the dim light, and she recognized Dane's pronounced cheekbones in the glow of his taillights. His eyes were wide with worry, and he still wore his trooper uniform.

He sat up and assessed her head before surveying her lower body. "Are you hurt?"

When she tried to sit up, a painful pulsation shot through her head. Cameron winced, suddenly aware of the ache in her ankle.

"Easy."

She wondered how long she'd been lying here, alongside the road in front of her house. The man must've dragged her here after she passed out. Her assailant left her alive. *But why?*

"Where were you?" Cameron's gaze settled on the yellow badge adhered to the top corner of his vest while Dane dug out his phone from the pocket below.

"It's okay. You just lay still," Dane coaxed, rubbing her arm.

She rested her head on the ground as Dane lifted his phone to his ear. She studied him, clawing at her memory to recall what her attacker looked like. He was roughly the same size as Dane—and John. Both were broad shouldered and close to six feet tall.

She had a sudden instinct to run away from him. But she knew that even if she managed to stand up, she wouldn't get far. Recalling the man's hooded sweatshirt and civilian SUV, Cameron felt some of the tension ease from her body.

Cameron's eyelids grew heavy as Dane lifted his phone to his ear and called for an ambulance. She was so tired.

"Cameron! Stay with me!"

She managed to open her eyes for a moment, seeing the flush of concern on Dane's face, before her eyelids fluttered closed. She needed to sleep.

Dane gripped her shoulder. "Cameron! I need you to stay awake until the ambulance gets here."

Her breathing slowed. She heard him yell her name again, but his voice sounded distant. She succumbed to her overwhelming exhaustion as his voice faded from her mind.

Cameron woke to a soft, rhythmic beeping above her head. Her ankle throbbed. She was lying in a hospital bed with an IV in her hand and a blood pressure cuff wrapped around her other arm. Daylight streamed through the window behind where Valerie sat. Outside, Cameron recognized the parking lot and sign for the Tok Medical Center. From the small size of the room, Cameron guessed she was in the ER.

Valerie stood from her chair when Cameron's eyes met hers. There were bags beneath the motel owner's red eyes. Valerie's normally neat, low ponytail was loose and off to one side. A few short, gray strands fell around her face. Like always, she wore a faded Howling Wolf Motel t-shirt. As Valerie crossed the room, it struck Cameron that she'd never seen her wear anything else.

"Thank God you're okay." Valerie clasped her dry hand around Cameron's. "You scared the shit out of me, my dear." Her expression looked cross before softening. "I couldn't handle losing you too." Worry lines spread across Valerie's forehead as she studied Cameron. "How's your head? The nurse said you have a concussion."

Cameron felt the tender bulge on the left side of her scalp. She winced. "I've been better."

Valerie reached for a remote attached to a cord on the edge of her bed and pressed a button. "Your nurse wanted me to call her when you woke up."

Cameron sat up. "My dental practice." The beeping quickened on her monitor along with her heart rate. She'd already lost one dental practice. She wasn't losing another. "My patients. I have appointments. I—"

"Don't worry about that, dear. I called your office and told them you wouldn't be in today. And likely not the rest of the week, based on what your nurse told me."

Cameron sank against her hospital pillow. "Thank you."

Valerie's face turned somber as she perched on the edge of Cameron's bed. She leaned toward Cameron, her voice low. "Did you see the face of the man who did this to you?"

Cameron envisioned the outline of her attacker, his face concealed beneath the shadows of his hood. "I'm sorry. But no."

Valerie patted her hand, but there was no mistaking the disappointment on her face.

"That's okay," she said. "I'm just glad you're okay."

The curtain to her room flung open. "Oh, good. You're awake." A middle-aged brunette wearing navy blue scrubs strode into the small space, stopping beside Cameron's bed. "How are you feeling? In any pain?" She looked from Cameron to the cardiac monitor mounted on the wall.

"A little."

"Your ankle or your head?"

"Um." Her mouth was dry. "Both."

"Can you tell me your name and date of birth?"

"Cameron Prescott."

A crease formed between the nurse's eyebrows.

"I mean, Jenkins. July 8, 1986."

"Excellent. And do you know where you are right now?"

Cameron glanced out the window. "The Tok Medical Center."

"Good." The nurse bent over and pressed a button on Cameron's IV pump. "Can you rate your pain on a scale of one to ten?"

"Five to six."

"Okay, I can get you something for that." She withdrew a pen light from her pocket and held up one of her hands. Cameron saw that her name badge that hung from her neck read *Cheri*. "Do me a favor and look toward me." She shielded one of Cameron's eyes, then the other as she shone the light into each pupil. "Great." She tucked the pen back into her pocket. "You were awake when you first got here. Do you remember that?"

Cameron had a fuzzy recollection of being wheeled down a hallway on a stretcher. "Kind of."

The nurse nodded. "It's normal to have some memory lapse or fogginess with a concussion. Do you recall what happened before that?"

Cameron's mind flashed to almost being mowed over by the SUV, and she drew in a sharp breath. Then being chased through her front yard by the bright headlight beams. Her saying John's name as her assailant raised his fist to deliver what she'd thought was going to be a fatal blow. "I remember passing out in the ditch after Dane found me." She turned to Valerie, who'd gotten up from her bed. "Is he here?"

Valerie's expression darkened. She shook her head.

Before Cameron could ask where he was, the nurse placed her hand lightly on the blanket over Cameron's knee. "I'll be right back with something for your pain. And I'll let Dr. Patel know you're awake. He'll want to examine you again, and we'll need to make sure you can get up without falling. But if all goes well, you should be able to go home in the next couple of hours." She paused halfway to the door. "Do you have someone who can stay with you?"

"My boyfriend—"

"I can," Valerie said.

Cheri looked between them before turning for the curtain. Cameron studied Valerie's troubled gaze.

"Where's Da—"

When Cheri swung open the curtain, Nelson appeared in the doorway. "Hey, Cameron."

Trooper Marissa Downing, a female trooper Cameron had met but didn't know well stood at Nelson's side.

"You feeling up for some questions?" Nelson asked.

"Yeah," Cameron said.

"Not for too long though," Cheri said to Nelson and Downing. "She just woke up and needs to rest before she goes home. I don't want her getting worked up."

"You got it," Nelson said before entering the room.

Cheri disappeared behind the curtain as Downing followed Nelson into the room, which felt like it was shrinking with the two troopers' presence.

Cameron turned back to Valerie. "Where's Dane?"

Valerie shot Nelson a wary gaze. "I'll let him tell you, dear."

Cameron's throat tightened. *Tell me what?*

"I need to call my sister." Valerie started to move past the troopers toward the curtain but stopped in front of Nelson. She lifted her eyes to his. "Promise me you'll find the *real* person responsible for this."

Cameron scooted up in bed, looking between the troopers as Valerie stepped out of the room. "What is she talking about? Where's Dane?"

CHAPTER THIRTY-FOUR

Nelson stepped closer to Cameron's hospital bed, tossing a glance at Trooper Downing. "He's been arrested, Cameron."

Pain stabbed the side of her skull when Cameron sat up. "What? Why?"

Nelson frowned. "The handcuffs you were bound with when Sergeant Waska found you turned out to be his."

Cameron gaped at the trooper in disbelief. "How can you be sure?"

"They were engraved with his badge number. We all do that so that we can get our own cuffs back after we use them. Waska still had one pair on his duty belt, but he was missing his backup pair—the cuffs that were on your wrists. He claimed that he thought he misplaced his backup pair a few of days ago but hadn't reported them missing yet, saying he thought they would turn up."

The moment when her attacker's face was only inches from hers flashed in her mind. She sensed something familiar about him but strained to remember what it was. She'd said John's name, but she wasn't sure that it was him. He had no scent, and she distinctly remembered the smell of Dane's aftershave when he found her in the ditch.

"It wasn't Dane. I'm sure of it." She wasn't sure whether she added the last part for the troopers' reassurance or her own.

Nelson and Downing exchanged a look that told Cameron they were unconvinced.

Cameron gaped at them. "You don't really believe he did this, right?"

"The emergency responders said that you claimed it was an SUV that tried to mow you down before you were attacked."

"Yes, but it wasn't Dane's. It had a civilian plate, although… I can't remember the number. Only that it was Alaskan, and it wasn't government issued. Dane found me in the ditch. He helped me."

Nelson put his hands on his hips. "I know this is a tough thing to swallow, but those handcuffs *belonged* to Sergeant Waska. You're probably already aware of this, but his father owns a black Ford Expedition. And last night, after I interviewed Sergeant Waska at the station, he went up to see his dad at Hunt Lake. George confirmed it this morning, saying he fell asleep while his son was still there." Nelson pressed his lips together and glanced out the window before returning his gaze to Cameron's. "There was enough time from when Sergeant Waska left the station for him to have taken his dad's SUV, attacked you, and then come back in his trooper vehicle when he claimed to have found you on the side of the road."

Cameron furrowed her brows. "No. I don't believe it. Can you stop calling him *Sergeant Waska?* He's your friend, not some suspect!"

Nelson raised his hand. "We can do this another time if it's too much for you right now, considering your injuries."

Cameron shook her head. "No, it's fine." She took a deep

breath. "I'm fine. I went to see George last night too. I didn't leave until nightfall, and I didn't pass any cars until I got within a few miles of town. So, Dane couldn't have gotten to George's until after ten." Cameron swallowed, recalling the time when she'd woken up on her couch from the headlights shining through her window. It had been after twelve-thirty. Nelson was right. There would've been enough time for Dane to visit his dad and return in his father's SUV. But that didn't make him guilty.

"Did you check George's Expedition for damage? I flew onto the hood of the vehicle that attacked me. It might've left a dent."

Nelson nodded. "We did. And there was no visible damage to the vehicle."

"Why would Dane call 911 and leave his own handcuffs on me? It doesn't make sense."

"Maybe he thought we'd believe they'd been stolen. I'd like to ask him." Nelson folded his arms and shot a look at his cohort. "But he's gotten a lawyer now and is refusing to speak to us anymore without him."

Cameron looked between the two troopers, surprised that Dane had gotten an attorney. But murder was a serious charge. A phrase John used to say popped into her mind. *Getting an attorney doesn't make someone guilty. It makes them smart.*

"There was something familiar about the man who attacked me," she added.

Nelson raised his eyebrows.

"But it wasn't Dane!"

"Did you see his face? Anything that could help us identify who attacked you?"

Cameron let out the breath she'd been holding, feeling her hope deflate along with her lungs. "No."

Nelson withdrew a small notebook from his vest pocket. "What about height and build?"

"He was around three to four inches taller than me. So about six feet tall."

When Nelson lifted his gaze from his notebook, his counterpart shot him a look. Cameron knew what they were thinking—Dane was six foot one.

She looked between the two troopers, debating whether to tell them about the possibility of John still being alive. But how would she explain that? Remembering the remains that had been found north of Eagle, and the likelihood John was dead, made her suddenly queasy. She closed her eyes, feeling the bed spin beneath her.

Nelson rushed to her side, steadying her as she swayed toward the edge of the bed.

"Careful," he said, helping her lean back against the pillow.

"Wait, did you say you were interviewing Dane last night?" She searched Nelson's face. "Why?"

The curtain flung open, and Cheri appeared in the doorway, her lips pursed, eyes narrowed. She shot a look of disapproval at Nelson.

"I told you she shouldn't get worked up." Cheri marched across the small space, glaring at Nelson. Her face softened as she extended a medicine cup toward Cameron. "I brought you an oxycodone for your pain."

Cheri checked the ID band around Cameron's wrist. "Can you verify your name and date of birth for me again?"

When Cameron was finished, Cheri turned to the two troopers. "Her heart rate is up, and your questions are clearly causing her distress. She needs to rest with minimal stimuli. You two need to leave."

"It's okay." Cameron held up her hand. She studied the look on Nelson's face, needing to know why he was interviewing Dane yesterday. "I'll be calm," Cameron assured her nurse. "I'd like to get answers to a few more questions before they go."

Cheri crossed her arms and lifted her gaze to the monitor mounted on the wall above Cameron's bed. "I'll give you a few more minutes." She turned to the troopers. "But I don't want you to agitate her. And then she needs to rest."

Nelson nodded. "You got it."

Nelson waited until Cheri left them alone to speak. He glanced at the closed curtain and lowered his voice. "Some evidence came up linking Dane to Sienna's murder."

Cameron's stomach churned. She glanced at Trooper Downing. The woman's somber expression made Cameron feel like she might throw up. "What evidence?"

Nelson exhaled through his mouth. "The Fairbanks medical examiner found Dane's lucky trout fly tangled in Sienna's hair."

The room spun. Cameron grabbed the bedrail and pressed her spine against the upright mattress.

"How can you be sure that it's Dane's?"

"I recognized it when the ME sent over a photograph. The hook had been removed, and I've seen Sergeant Waska, *Dane,* carry it for the last twenty years. I went to Fairbanks yesterday and checked it out of evidence to show him. I was hoping he'd say it had been missing for awhile or have some kind of explanation. But he didn't. While he denied knowing how it got entangled in Sienna's hair, he confirmed that it's his."

No. It can't be. Cameron gripped the bedrail tighter as the room continued to spin, remembering when she gave it back to Dane the morning after Madison's murder. Her temple throbbed, and she lifted her hand to the side of her head.

"When I spoke with Dane's father about Dane's whereabouts last night, George also denied that Dane visited him on the morning Sienna was reported missing," Nelson said. "Which Dane lied to me about. So far, Dane is refusing to account for his whereabouts that morning."

Goosebumps prickled her arms, and the temperature of the room felt like it dropped several degrees. "So was Dane arrested on suspicion of attacking me or killing Sienna?"

Looking down at Cameron, Trooper Downing folded her arms. "Both. He's going to be arraigned for a bail hearing tomorrow."

Cameron envisioned the fear in Dane's eyes when he'd roused her in the ditch. No alibi and access to his dad's SUV when she'd been attacked. Had his panic when he'd found her been an act?

Nelson rested his hand on the bedrail above Cameron's hand. "George also told me that he saw you at your dental office yesterday. And about your visit last night." His eyes were laced with suspicion when they pierced hers. "You knew Dane lied about going to see George that morning, didn't you? But you didn't say anything."

Cameron stared back at him.

"What else aren't you telling me, Cameron?"

Her monitor alarmed on the wall behind her, making Cameron jump. The curtain swung open with a screech.

"Okay, that's enough." Cheri pointed to the troopers before gesturing to the open doorway. "Cameron's heart rate is spiking again. You two need to leave so my patient can rest." She crossed the room and reached over Cameron's head to silence the beeping.

"Wait!" Cameron sat up when Nelson and Downing turned for the door. "Dane told me that he had a suspect in these new murders." She squeezed her eyes shut, trying to remember exactly what he'd said. "But he couldn't tell me who. But he said he should know for sure soon. He seemed confident that he knew who killed Madison and Sienna."

The room blurred when Cameron opened her eyes. She blinked to clear her vision. Feeling lightheaded, she brought a hand to her forehead.

Nelson spun around and came to the edge of her bed. Her vision cleared enough to see that his eyes were fueled with intensity when they locked with hers. A crease formed between his eyebrows. "What exactly did he tell you? Did he give you a name? Who was he looking into?"

"I don't know!" Her head pounded. "That's all he said. He wouldn't tell me any more, which makes me think it was someone we all know." She thought of Karl and how he accused Dane all those years ago. "What about—"

"That's enough!" Cheri extended her arm toward the door. "Her blood pressure is climbing now too. You guys need to go. *Now.*"

Nelson raised his palms in the air. "We're going."

He backed away from her bedside but paused before following his colleague out of the room. Ignoring Cheri's disapproving stare, he met Cameron's gaze.

"Dane could be out on bail tomorrow. If he is, I think you should keep your distance for the time being." He started through the door before looking over his shoulder. "You should know as well as anyone that you need to be careful who you trust."

CHAPTER THIRTY-FIVE

Cameron closed her bedroom door behind her before dialing Tanner. Even though it had been several hours since Nelson had broken the news, her mind still reeled over Dane's arrest. As Cameron put the phone to her ear, she could hear Valerie in the kitchen on the other side of the wall cleaning up the dinner they were both too distraught to eat. The motel owner insisted on bringing her home from the hospital and spending the night.

Cameron looked down at the faded Howling Wolf Motel t-shirt and relaxed fit Levi's Valerie had loaned her to wear home from the hospital since her clothes had been taken for evidence. They were a far cry from the designer jeans and Nordstrom tops that Cameron brought with her from her old life in Seattle.

Tanner's phone rang four times before going to voicemail.

Cameron swore and sighed into the phone. "Tanner, it's Cameron. I need to talk to you. Dane's been arrested in Sienna's murder, and I think he's been framed." Right before calling, she'd searched but didn't find any updated news on the unidentified remains that had been discovered outside of Eagle. But it was possible Tanner had gotten word before the media. "Dane had a lead on a suspect, but he wouldn't tell me who. I need your help. I'm not sure who else I can trust."

She hung up. Last night's attack felt like too much to leave on a voicemail.

Cameron set her phone on her bedside table beside her gun and opened her bedroom door. She found Valerie sitting on her living room couch, surprised to see her friend's hunting rifle propped beside it, although, after everything that had happened lately, Cameron knew she shouldn't be surprised.

She hobbled into the living room, careful not to put too much pressure on her injured ankle. Cheri had tried to send her home with crutches, but she'd refused. It was only a light sprain. She dropped onto the other end of the couch, feeling the room sway. The doctor said that due to her concussion, she could expect to have dizziness, trouble with balance, memory problems, blurred vision, and even confusion for up to a week.

Valerie lifted the steaming mug in her hands. "It's earl grey. You want a cup?"

"No, thanks. You don't have to stay tonight. I'll be fine. You should go be with your sister."

Valerie shook her head. "She's gone back to Anchorage." Her gaze traveled to the edge of the room. "I don't think she'll ever forgive me for what happened to Sienna. And I don't blame her." She cleared her throat. "I don't think I'll ever forgive myself."

Cameron's heart ached to comfort the woman she'd grown close to the last several months. "It's not your fault."

Cameron's words lingered in the air as they sat in silence for a few moments.

"It's not Dane, Val," Cameron finally said.

"I know." Valerie's voice was calm. "I never thought it was, not even back then."

Cameron turned to her. "Who *did* you think it was back then?"

"Karl, for a while." Valerie slid her elbow onto the back of the couch. "He was fired from being a trooper right after the murders. At the time, I wondered if it was because there was some evidence against him. But he proved to be too much of a drunk. If he were guilty, Karl would've spilled his guts by now some night while drunk at the bar. There's no way he could keep it to himself all these years."

"What about now?"

Valerie brought her gaze to Cameron's. "I don't think the person who killed Madison and Sienna is the same one who killed those two women here in the nineties."

Cameron's stomach sank, thinking of John. "Why's that?"

Valerie shrugged. "Gut feeling, I guess." She leaned over and patted Cameron's knee. "You should get some rest."

Cameron stifled a yawn, exhausted. Her head felt fuzzy, and she wasn't sure if it was from the pain medication they'd given her at the medical center or from the blow to her head. Her thoughts drifted to Dane, spending the night in jail, and the panic she'd seen in his eyes last night when he found her in the ditch.

She leaned her head against the couch, recalling the grunt her attacker made when she elbowed him. She was certain it wasn't Dane but frustrated she couldn't pinpoint the man's identity. Valerie was right. She needed to rest. Maybe some sleep would help clear her mind.

She pushed herself up from the couch. "I think I'll turn in." She spun to face Valerie. "Do you want to sleep in my bed? I feel bad to put you on the couch."

Valerie pulled the wool blanket off the back of the sofa. "I can sleep anywhere. You don't worry, honey." She gestured to the rifle leaning against the side of the couch's armrest. "And I want you to sleep soundly. No one's getting through that door tonight without taking a bullet in their chest."

Cameron paused, shifting her weight onto her uninjured leg and glancing at Valerie's rifle. "Just make sure they're a hostile intruder before you shoot."

Valerie stretched her legs over the couch cushions, draping the blanket over them. "Like I said dear, you don't worry about a thing. I may not have protected Sienna like I should've, but I'm sure as hell not going to allow anything to happen to you tonight."

Cameron felt a faint smile reach her lips. She didn't doubt Valerie would stop anyone who tried to come inside. Even John likely wouldn't stand a chance against the sixty-year-old wolf hunter.

"Thanks for staying."

"You're welcome, dear. Goodnight."

When Cameron reached her room, her phone lit up next to her bed. She swiped it off the bedside table.

Tanner.

"Hey, did you listen to my voicemail?"

"Hi, Cameron. Yes, I just did. What evidence led to arrest Dane?"

Cameron launched into everything that had happened since last night, talking fast: Dane's trout fly found in Sienna's hair, last night's attack near her house and Dane's lack of alibi when it happened, and finally, Dane's arrest after his handcuffs were found on Cameron's wrists.

"Whoa, slow down." Tanner said. "Did you see who attacked you last night?"

"No. There was something familiar about him, and it's driving me crazy that I can't place what it is. It was a man, I'm certain. And he was about six feet tall." She perched on the edge of her bed as the floor shifted beneath her feet.

"So, it's *possible* it could've been Dane?"

Cameron straightened in defense. "No, that's not what I'm saying. I feel like I knew him, but I can't explain why. He was around the same height as John, and yes, Dane." *And Dane's father and Trooper Nelson. Even Karl was only an inch or two under six feet.* "But Dane suspected someone in these new murders, and I think he was close to proving it. On the morning of Sienna's disappearance, Dane said that he'd gone to see his dad. But it was a lie. I'm wondering if that's because Dane doesn't want anyone to know who he suspects in these new murders. Look, I know how this must sound, but I think Dane suspected someone in this town—someone I know—and he didn't want to risk me saying anything. Or put me in danger." Although, it was too late for that now. "I need you to find out."

"So, you think it was John or you don't?"

"I don't know!" She brought a hand to her temple, trying to soothe the dull ache on the side of her head. "I have a concussion, and I'm struggling to remember all the details. "Do you have an ID yet on those remains?"

"No, not yet. I'm still waiting to hear."

"There's an older man who lives here, and he was a trooper at the time of the nineties murders. Karl Sadler. He's too drunk most of the time to be capable of anything now, but the other day he had a moment where he seemed strangely sober. Dane's father was also a suspect." Cameron ran a hand through her hair. If George was guilty, it could explain why Dane had been so secretive about it. "Trooper Nelson was also working here at the time of the old murders." She gasped. "Shit. I told Nelson today that Dane suspected someone. What if it was him?"

"Cameron, I think you need to rest. I've already been looking into the old cases. I'll keep trying, but there's not a lot more I can do from here."

"Then you should come back up here."

"I can't. I'm wrapping up a new homicide case. Are you at home? Are you safe?"

She glanced at her pistol on her bedside table. "I have a friend staying with me tonight. I'll be fine."

"I'll call you as soon as I hear about the ID of those remains. Or if I learn anything else. In the meantime, I think you should get some rest."

"I will. Goodnight, Tanner."

After ending the call, she stepped out into her living room and found Valerie asleep on the couch, snoring lightly with her rifle propped beside her.

Cameron padded across the room and double checked that her doors were locked before returning to her bedroom. She mentally replayed the sound her attacker made when she elbowed him the ribs. *Why can't I place who it was?*

Frustrated, she ejected the magazine in her 9mm, making sure it was loaded before she flicked off the lights and climbed into her bed.

Her mind drifted to Dane, sleeping in a jail cell. How had her attacker gotten Dane's handcuffs in the first place? Unless…

Have I fallen for another monster? Am I too blind to see what's right in front of me?

She closed her eyes, deciding that Tanner was right. She needed to rest. Hopefully, her mind would be clearer tomorrow.

She drifted to sleep within minutes and dreamt of John.

CHAPTER THIRTY-SIX

Cameron waved goodbye to Valerie from her front porch, watching as her friend backed her Subaru out of Cameron's long drive. It had taken some convincing that morning to assure Valerie that she would be fine on her own. Cameron knew that Valerie needed to get back to work at the motel, especially since she didn't have Sienna to help her.

Yesterday's sun was hidden behind a patch of gray clouds. Cameron wrapped her sweater tighter around her waist before going inside, spotting the light covering of frost that covered the shaded corner of her porch. The temperature had dropped dramatically in the last few days. She recalled Dane telling her that Tok often got its first snowfall of the season in September. Sometimes, even in August, which still had a few days. Over breakfast, Valerie had told her there was a winter storm warning for their area starting tonight. Even though they were still days from September, Tok was expected to get several inches of snow overnight, along with over fifty-mile-an-hour winds.

She moved past Valerie's rifle leaning against the wall that the motel owner had insisted on leaving with Cameron for protection.

"I already keep a pistol in my bedroom," Cameron had told her. "I don't want to take yours."

At that, Valerie had laughed. "Honey, I have several more at my place. Plus, this is my lucky shooter. It's what I shot that beautiful beast that's mounted in my motel office with. Keep it for now. I'll feel better knowing it's here with you."

Cameron glanced at the rifle as she lifted her empty plate off the kitchen table. Valerie had waited to make sure Cameron could keep down the eggs and toast she'd made for breakfast before agreeing to leave, then made Cameron promise to call her at the motel if she needed anything.

Cameron glanced at the time on her stove, surprised to see it was nearly eleven. She'd slept in later than she had in years. But having a concussion could do that to someone. When she'd woken this morning, she had a text from Nelson saying that Dane's bail hearing had been set for 1:00 p.m. at the Tok District Court.

She set her plate in the sink before returning to the table to retrieve the empty coffee mugs, thinking of Valerie's offer to drive her to Dane's hearing. She hadn't decided whether she would go.

Movement out the window caught her eye. Cameron froze as she watched a state trooper SUV pull to a stop in front of Dane's house. *Had Dane gotten released early?* A woman stepped out of the SUV, and Cameron recognized Trooper Downing's light brown hair. Her long ponytail blew in the wind as she spoke into her radio and climbed the steps to Dane's front door.

Cameron set down the mugs and moved toward the window. Branches in the trees near Dane's house swayed from the gusts as Trooper Downing crossed Cameron's lawn. She opened her door as the trooper ascended her porch steps. Trooper Downing's frown sent a ripple of apprehension down Cameron's torso.

"Hi, Cameron. I'm looking for Sergeant Waska. Have you seen him?"

"Isn't he still under arrest? I thought his bail hearing wasn't until one."

The trooper sighed. "He got his hearing moved up and posted bail." She put her hands on her hips as her gaze drifted to Dane's house.

Cameron noticed the diamond band on the trooper's ring finger, suddenly remembering what day it was. She and John would've been married for ten years today.

"He must've pulled some strings with the judge. Or had help from someone."

Trooper Downing turned back to Cameron. "So, you haven't heard from him this morning?"

Cameron stared beyond the trooper at the tree in her front lawn that she'd run into when the SUV had chased her. "No."

"Sergeant Waska's attorney promised they would fully cooperate after the sergeant's release and agreed to come to the station and answer some questions. Waska told his lawyer he was going to run home and change first, but we've been waiting nearly an hour for him to show." She glanced around Cameron's yard. "All right. Call us if you hear from him." She pulled a business card out of her vest pocket. "Here's my number in case you can't get ahold of Nelson."

Cameron accepted the card as the trooper looked beyond Cameron into her house.

"You here all by yourself? I thought Valerie was staying with you."

"She was, but she had to go work at the motel this morning."

The trooper's expression turned to concern. "You going to be okay alone?"

"Yeah, fine."

Tropper Downing stepped back. "Keep your doors locked. And call if you see Sergeant Waska." She surveyed the woods that surrounded Cameron's property. "Or if you see anything suspicious."

"I will."

She locked the door as the trooper strode back to her SUV, knowing the deadbolt wouldn't do any good to keep out whoever had attacked her. If they wanted to break in, they would. She leaned against her door before grabbing her phone off the counter. She dialed Dane. It rang only once before going to voicemail.

"Hey, it's Cameron. Trooper Downing was just here looking for you. Call me when you get this."

She sent him a text after hanging up. *Call me.*

She glanced out the window, watching the trooper's SUV backing out of Dane's drive. Dane couldn't have been the one to attack her. He had to have been framed.

Then where is he?

She searched the kitchen for Valerie's plate and realized that Valerie must've loaded hers into the dishwasher before she left. She stared out the window at the limbs of the spruce trees swaying in the wind as she rinsed the coffee mugs she'd set in the sink earlier, thinking about all the evidence stacking up against Dane. She thought this time would be different. That she'd finally found a man she could trust.

Her throat tightened as her gaze traveled to the spot in front of her house where she fought with her attacker—and lost. But he'd left her alive. *Why?*

She relived the moment when she woke to Dane hovering over her. The panic she'd seen in his eyes. Had he taken his father's SUV like Nelson proposed, attacked her, then gone back to George's cabin to switch vehicles before returning to play the role of her savior?

Her stomach churned as she pressed the palm of her empty hand against the edge of the counter and closed her eyes, trying to force her mind to recall what was familiar about the man who'd tried to run her down the night before last. She strained to envision his face. *Was it Dane? John? Someone else?* All she could remember was the deep shadow beneath the man's hood.

Frustrated, she opened her eyes. She caught the reflection of her short, dyed red hair in the kitchen window as she ran water over the plate. A lump formed in her throat at the memory of cutting out her blond hair extensions with her kitchen shears and coloring her hair in her upstairs bathroom in her home in Seattle to keep from being recognized as The Teacher Killer's wife.

She opened the dishwasher and slid out the lower rack. Maybe she really did emit some kind of signal that attracted wolves like Miles, and John, and… No, she wasn't ready to say Dane.

But if she did exude something, was there a way for her to change enough to keep them away?

Cameron dried her hands on her jeans and turned from the sink. As she made her way to her room, she regarded the locked deadbolt on her front door. If her attacker *did* come back for her, she'd be ready. She swiped her pistol off the bedside table, slid it into the holster that Dane had gotten her for her birthday, and clipped it to the waistband of her jeans.

When she returned to the kitchen, her fingers trembled as she set the empty coffee mugs upside down in the dishwasher's top rack, envisioning Dane's trout fly entangled in Sienna's long blond hair. What scared her even more than the idea of Dane being a killer was that she could've let herself down again—could have opened her arms to yet another man who preyed on women. Another monster.

She thrust the thought from her mind. The killer had to have taken Dane's trout fly from Dane's home, along with his handcuffs, and planted it in Sienna's hair.

Cameron bent forward to close the dishwasher door.

She gasped, suddenly remembering. Her attacker's *hands.* They were calloused. Rough.

She closed her eyes as she mentally relived the moment the other night at Dane's house when his smooth palm rubbed against hers. *It couldn't have been Dane who attacked me.*

Cameron recalled John getting calluses on his hands after staying at his Washington hunting cabin, chopping wood with an axe for a few days in a row. And after she'd plunged the knife into his torso last February when she last saw him, and he'd grabbed her wrist, his grip had felt like sandpaper.

She pressed her hand against her butcher block counter and stared out her kitchen window, her heart beating into her throat. Those remains found in Eagle couldn't be John. *John is alive. And he's here. A predator stalking his prey.*

Cameron straightened, closing the dishwasher with a clang. But John had made a miscalculation if he thought she'd go down without a fight.

CHAPTER THIRTY-SEVEN

Tanner checked the time on his laptop as he officially marked Megan Wallis the verified suspect in the first-degree murder of Natalie Thomas and attempted murder of her husband, Justin Wallis. His leg jiggled from his lack of sleep and four cups of coffee he'd consumed earlier that morning.

The night before, he'd made it to Bayside before the husband was taken into surgery. He was conscious and gave Tanner the same account he'd given to the 911 dispatcher and first responders: his wife had come into his girlfriend's bedroom with a gun. Upon seeing them in bed together, she started shooting, killing his girlfriend before he returned fire with the pistol he'd bought Natalie for her birthday. His wife managed to fire two shots into his chest before he killed her.

The husband was now in stable condition. Ballistics confirmed his account, along with a witness—a neighbor walking her dog—who spotted his wife's Audi pull to the curb right after her husband and Natalie parked in her drive.

Tanner withdrew a stick of gum from his pocket and folded it into his mouth, thinking Megan Wallis had to have known she'd been seen. Tanner guessed she was too enraged to care. She'd even used a gun she'd bought and registered in her own name three weeks earlier.

His phone vibrated in his suit jacket pocket, pulling him from his thoughts. It was the Fairbanks detective, Morton.

"Hey, Morton."

"Hi, Mulholland. We just got an ID on those male remains that were found north of Eagle. It was the body of a sixty-eight-year-old Canadian man from Forty Mile, just on the other side of the border. He lived alone, no family, and no one reported him missing. Looks like he'd been traveling up the frozen river on his snowmobile when he had a heart attack."

Tanner sat forward, his warrant sliding off his lap onto the floor. John could be alive.

"I'm also calling because I got the expedited results back from the DNA on the bear trap I submitted."

"Already?" Alaska's state crime lab must not have been as backlogged as Washington's.

"Yep. And that *is* a match to John Prescott."

Tanner stared at the floor.

"You still there?" Detective Morton asked.

"Yeah." Tanner felt his coffee rise to the top of his throat. He swallowed. "Thanks for letting me know. Let's not release anything to the media yet. In case he's alive, I don't want to tip off Prescott that we know."

"You got it. But I should release something to our law enforcement up here. If there's a possibility that Prescott is out there, they need to know."

"I understand," Tanner said. "We also need to go back to that cabin and do a more thorough search for Prescott's body. We'll need a search team and cadaver dogs. And I want to be there."

Tanner glanced at the closed door to Judge Hopkins' chamber. "Can you arrange the search if I fly up tomorrow?"

"Weather dependent, I could probably organize it within this next week, given the severity of Prescott's crimes. There's a winter storm warning in effect starting tonight, but it's supposed to hit south of here and will likely blow over in a few days."

"Winter storm? It's not even September."

Morton chuckled. "This is Alaska. Anyway, I'll keep you updated on when we can arrange the search. Then you can book your flight once I get everything approved and organized."

Tanner thanked Morton and hung up. His pulse quickened. Cameron could be right. And if Prescott was in Tok, he needed to warn her. He grabbed the skull bobblehead off the edge of his desk and set it in front of Detective Tess Richards, who worked in the cubicle across from him next to her partner, Ben Suarez.

"You're up," Tanner said when Richards lifted her head toward the bobbling skull.

"That was fast," she said, turning to her partner. "I was hoping we'd at least get through the weekend first."

Tanner reached for his phone to call Cameron as it vibrated in his pocket. *Incoming call. Cameron.*

"Hi, Cameron. I was about to call—"

"It's John. He's alive." She sounded breathy.

"How did you—"

"His hands were callused. The man who attacked me—it just came back to me. They were just like John's. I knew there was something familiar about him, but I couldn't place it until now." She talked fast, like the night almost a year ago when she suspected her husband was still alive and had killed Bethany Long in Tok. "John was the one who attacked me the other night—not Dane. His hands felt exactly like they did when—" She paused, and for a moment he thought the call dropped. Then she exhaled into the receiver "—I saw him last. The body found north of Eagle can't be John."

Tanner pinched the bridge of his nose. "It's not. I just got a call from a Fairbanks detective this morning. They were the remains of a sixty-eight-year-old Canadian man." He pulled out his chair. "Where are you? Are you safe?"

"I'm at home. And I'm armed."

"Are you alone?"

"Yes, but I'm fine. Don't worry. I've handled John before."

Tanner remained quiet, knowing that was likely the closest she'd ever get to admitting to whatever she did to John at that remote cabin.

"But you need to come up here. Now."

Tanner's gaze fell to the signed warrant on his desk. He had no arrest to make since the killer was already deceased.

"Dane posted bail this morning," Cameron added. "And no one seems to know where he is. One of the troopers was just here looking for him."

Laughter erupted from the adjacent cubicle, startling Tanner. Suarez was jiggling the bobblehead over Richards' head. Tanner turned around, facing his desk.

"Please, Tanner," Cameron continued. "I'm not afraid of John, but he has the advantage now. He knows where I am. I feel like a sitting duck in this place. You *know* John killed those two women. And he's coming for me next. I need your help. Plus," she breathed a sigh into the call. "I'm terrified something's happened to Dane."

Tanner opened his laptop. "I'll see if I can get a flight out of SeaTac tonight."

CHAPTER THIRTY-EIGHT

Cameron paced back and forth on her living room floor. She should've known those remains wouldn't be John's. *I should've trusted my instincts.* She'd known it in her gut this whole time. Her phone was still in her hand from her phone call with Tanner, so she called Dane again. It went to voicemail. She hung up.

Where are you, Dane?

The floor swayed. She set her phone on the kitchen counter and brought a hand to her throbbing head. Her hand fell to her gun as she spun to look out her front window. It was late afternoon, several hours since Trooper Downing came looking for Dane. Tree branches swayed beside the spot where John had attacked her two nights ago.

Why did he leave me alive?

He had the perfect opportunity to kill her if he wanted. He wanted to taunt her. To watch her suffer while Dane went down for John's murders.

But where is Dane? He had nothing to do with Madison and Sienna's murders—or her attack—she's certain of that now. *So why does he keep disappearing, making himself look suspicious?*

Something slammed against her living room window, causing her to whip around and draw her gun. Her pulse pounded in her ears as she aimed her pistol at the branches that had broken off and blown against the house.

Her chest heaved with each breath as she slowly lowered her weapon. Behind her, her phone rang, giving her a start. She whirled around. It had to be Dane. She reholstered her gun, her heart sinking into her stomach as she stared at the number she didn't recognize.

"Hello?"

"Oh, hi. Dr. Jenkins?"

Cameron pressed her hand atop her counter to steady herself as the room swayed. It felt as if the wind was blowing inside the house.

"Yes?"

"It's Lillian."

"From the Tok Library," she added when Cameron didn't respond.

The library? Cameron sighed, envisioning the petite older woman who volunteered to keep the town's library running. *I do not have time for this right now.*

"I'm calling about a book," Lillian said.

Cameron raised a hand to her pulsating temple, her gaze darting to the thriller on her coffee table. Valerie had recommended it, so she'd checked it out last month and still hadn't finished reading it. She'd never been much of a reader.

"Sorry, um…Lillian, this isn't a good time. I'll return my book in a few days. I'm not feeling well at the moment."

"Oh, no. That's not why I'm calling. I found a book on the library doorstep with a sealed envelope when I arrived. The phone rang right after I got inside, and it was a gentleman saying he'd left it and asked me to give it to you. Sounded like a lovely fellow. He said you two were old friends, but he was eager to get out of town before the storm hit."

Cameron's heart dropped into her stomach.

"Anyway," Lillian continued. "I called your dental practice, but they told me you weren't in today. That you'd had an accident. An attack, actually. I'm so sorry. I hope you're okay."

"Did he give you his name?"

"Oh, yes. Sorry. Miles. Miles Henson."

Cameron's breakfast rose to the back of her throat. Of course, John used the name of her first husband that she'd killed after years of suffering under his abuse. The secret she thought she'd kept from the world. The thing that John had known all along.

She became aware of Lillian saying something but couldn't focus on what it was. Cameron stood tall, fighting the nausea rolling through her like a wave. Movement in Dane's front yard caught her attention, but it was only a branch getting tossed about by the wind.

"Dr. Jenkins?"

Cameron closed her eyes. "I'm sorry, what was that again?"

"I said it's *The Call of the Wild*. Such a great book."

Cameron's eyes opened, recalling the worn-out copy of that classic she'd seen at Miles's cabin, where she thought she'd left John to die.

"I'm going to close down at four today before the storm is set to hit," Lillian said. "This gentlemen seemed very eager to get this book to you. We won't reopen again until Wednesday next week, but I can drop it by your dental practice on my way home."

"No, no. I'll come get it right now." Cameron turned to peer out her font window, willing John to emerge from behind a tree and fight her like a man. Instead of this cowardly game of cat and mouse that left her no choice but to play along.

"Are you sure? I thought you weren't feeling well."

"I'm much better. See you soon." Cameron snatched her truck keys off the kitchen table and pulled a jacket off her coat hanger to pull on over her gun before racing to her truck through the wind.

CHAPTER THIRTY-NINE

When Cameron turned onto the Alaska Highway, rain beat against her windshield. She drove slowly past the trooper station, hoping to see Dane. There was a trooper SUV parked out front, but as Cameron passed, she spotted Trooper Downing getting out.

When she'd pulled out of her driveway, she'd gotten a text from Tanner saying he'd booked a flight arriving in Fairbanks tonight at 6:00 p.m. He likely wouldn't get to Tok until close to midnight with the weather—if he could even make the drive tonight with the storm. But at least he was on his way.

Cameron accelerated as a black truck pulled out of the Wolf Pack Bar parking lot. She recognized Karl behind the wheel, surprised to see him leaving the establishment in the afternoon. His truck normally stayed at the bar until closing when Joan would get one of the other locals to drive him home. But maybe she'd sent him home early today before the storm.

Karl's truck weaved over the center line, and Cameron laid on her horn. She swerved onto the narrow shoulder as Karl continued toward her. His truck jerked back into its own lane seconds before they would've collided, Karl's face showing no reaction to their near miss.

Cameron's heart pounded against her chest when she turned into the library parking lot, empty aside from a black Jeep. A siren wailed from up the road. Cameron turned, relieved to see Trooper Downing's SUV peel out of the trooper station and pull over Karl's truck.

Cameron climbed out and the driver's side door slammed from the wind. Dark storm clouds swirled above, threatening more rain, as Cameron pulled the hood of her jacket over her head. A damp strand of hair blew across her face, and she tucked it behind one ear, shooting a glance at Trooper Downing getting out of her vehicle and approaching Karl's truck now stopped on the side of the highway.

Her concern over Dane's whereabouts was morphing into anger. *Why was he evading the other troopers like this?* He was letting John win by making himself look guilty. Why couldn't he at least return her call?

Where the hell are you, Dane?

Lillian looked up from her paperback from behind the small desk near the library's entrance when Cameron stepped inside. The librarian's eyes brightened, and she set down her book.

"Hi, Dr. Jenkins."

Cameron forced herself to return the woman's smile as if she were picking up a gift from an old friend, not her serial killer husband who'd come back from the dead. "Hi."

Lillian eyed Cameron's hood. "Getting stormy out there?"

"Yeah, starting to." Cameron searched the desk for whatever John had left her.

"Well, here it is." Lillian beamed as she slid a leather-bound book across the desk toward Cameron.

Cameron's stomach churned as she read the title, *The Call of the Wild*, remembering the same book from the bookshelf inside Miles' cabin when she'd gone back inside before leaving John for dead. But this book was new, the title not faded, and the leather not cracked like the copy she'd seen at the remote cabin.

"He left this too." Lillian extended a small, square envelope.

She swallowed, accepting the envelope from Lillian with numb fingers. She tore it open as Lillian looked on with wide-eyed interest.

Cameron slid the greeting card out from the envelope. Hearts floated around the heads of a male and female deer on the front of the card. *Deerly Beloved* was printed in cursive at the top. Her heart thudded against her chest when she opened it.

Happy Anniversary, Deerest was printed on the inside of the greeting card. Below, in black ink, it was signed with a *J*.

Cameron closed her eyes, recalling her last anniversary. John created an elaborate scavenger hunt for her. He'd written his clues on index cards, leading her to the trail of gifts he'd left in various rooms of their Seattle home: two dozen roses in the kitchen, a box of her favorite chocolates and a bottle of champagne on top of their baby grand, a pair of Manolo Blahnik pumps on the stairs. His grand finale had been in her bedroom nightstand. He'd always gone over the top for birthdays and holidays, but last year he outdid them all.

She opened her eyes and stared at the card, her vision blurring as rage simmered inside her veins.

"You okay?" Lillian asked.

Cameron blinked, tearing her gaze from the card.

Cameron grabbed the book, flipping through its pages for another message from John. But there was no writing inside. *What now?* she thought, aware of the weight of her pistol on her hip. Was she supposed to go home and wait for John to make his next move? There was no way she was going to let John remain in control.

"Dr. Jenkins? You look like you've seen a ghost."

She flipped John's card over, making sure he hadn't scrawled something on the back. But it was blank. The room swayed, and Cameon staggered backward. Lillian jumped from her chair and rounded the desk.

"Oh! Let me help you!"

Cameron felt the librarian's petite arm wrap around her waist.

"Here, you need to sit down." Lillian led her around the desk.

Cameron blinked to clear her vision as she plopped into the librarian's chair.

"I should take you to the medical center." Lillian's brows were furrowed with concern. "You're not well."

Cameron waved her hand through the air. "I'm fine. I just need to go home."

Lillian frowned. "All right, but I'm driving you. First, let me get you some water." She pointed at Cameron as she backed away. "Don't you fall off that chair while I'm gone."

She stared at the inside of the card, and the letters blurred again as Cameron's blood boiled with anger. She'd failed to kill John, and two more women were dead. Now, he was taunting her for enjoyment while ruining Dane's life—or worse—before her evil husband made his final move. The floor shifted as the horrific possibility of why Dane was missing entered her mind.

Had John already killed him?

CHAPTER FORTY

"For those traveling on Alaska Airlines Flight 875 to Fairbanks, we are ready to begin our boarding process, starting with our gold medallion members, first-class passengers, active-duty military, and any passengers requiring additional assistance with boarding."

Tanner stayed in his seat in the waiting area at the SeaTac terminal, connecting his laptop to the virtual private network provided by Seattle PD. Passengers slowly ambled by his seat, lining up at the gate.

John Prescott may have killed Madison Youngblood and Sienna Lovell, but he didn't kill Amy Clarke and Erica Lavine in the 1990s. Prescott had been a UW student with near perfect attendance during the time of their deaths. Tanner knew from his extensive investigation into John Prescott that Prescott had also been a high jumper in college. On the day Amy Clarke was murdered, Prescott had been at a state championship in Olympia.

Tanner pulled up a database to search Alaska's vehicle registration history, his hip feeling naked without his gun that he'd had to pack in his checked bag. George Waska had been right.

Those cases weren't Tanner's jurisdiction. But after his call with the retired sergeant, something gnawed at him. He hadn't had time to check until now.

"We would now like to welcome those passengers seated in zones A and B to board Flight 875 to Fairbanks."

Tanner narrowed his search to vehicles registered in the state in 1995 and typed a name into the search bar beside the year. There were two vehicles registered under that name. The first was a 1989 black F150. Tanner stared at the second result as another boarding announcement was made.

It was a 1993 white Mazda Navajo. Tanner copied the vehicle description and pasted it into his Internet search bar, unable to picture what the vehicle looked like. His jaw fell slack at the image that appeared at the top of his search results. The white SUV looked strikingly similar to a Ford Explorer, aside from the small Mazda logo on the grill.

Tanner's pulse quickened, now able to fill in the blank from what George Waska had told him on their patchy phone call when he argued that Dane wasn't the only one in town with a white SUV: Even *Trooper Nelson* had one. Tanner stared at the image of the Mazda, vaguely aware of another boarding announcement drifting through the boarding area.

More passengers got up from their seats around the gate as Tanner searched for Trooper Patrick Nelson's driver's license photo. Tanner enlarged the photo. The trooper's brown hair, lightly peppered with gray, wasn't as dark as Dane Waska's. He was five foot eleven with blue eyes.

"Flight 875 to Fairbanks is now boarding all rows for an on-time departure to Fairbanks. The doors will close in five minutes."

Tanner lifted his gaze from his laptop, seeing he was the only one remaining seated at the gate. The last passenger in line scanned their boarding pass with the gate agent and disappeared inside the jetway. Tanner scrambled to his feet, closing his laptop and tucking it inside his bag.

He slung his bag over his shoulder and loaded his boarding pass on his phone as he made for the gate agent. It had been a nearly full flight when he booked his ticket a few hours ago, leaving his only option a middle seat toward the back. He wasn't looking forward to it.

The gate agent met his gaze after he scanned his virtual ticket. "Have a nice flight."

"Thank you." Tanner responded on autopilot, his mind reeling as he strode down the sloped jetway, considering the ramifications if Karl Sadler's witness statement was legitimate—or at least as accurate as Sadler's recollection a few months later after having had a few beers.

Tanner stepped over the threshold, greeted by a flight attendant before he moved down the narrow aisleway of the full aircraft. Tanner paused when he got to his row. The overhead bin was completely full of carry-ons. He glanced around the surrounding bins, realizing he would have to stuff his bag beneath the seat in front of him, where he'd already be pressed for legroom. The twenty-something guy in the aisle seat tore his eyes from his seatback screen and looked up at Tanner.

Tanner pointed to the empty seat beside him. "That's my seat."

The guy let out an audible sigh and removed his headphones from his ears before standing.

"Thanks," Tanner said.

The young man offered no response as Tanner slid into the middle seat beside a blond woman around Cameron's age. After glancing at his left hand, bare of a wedding ring, she flashed Tanner a warm smile.

"Hi," she said.

"Hi." Tanner gave her a polite nod before shoving his carry-on beneath the seat and turning straight ahead.

He pressed his lower back against his seat cushion, which did nothing to keep his knees from digging into the seat in front of him.

A female voice came through the Intercom. "Ladies and gentlemen, welcome aboard Alaska Airlines flight 875 with nonstop service to Fairbanks. We appreciate your full attention for the next few moments as we give you a brief safety announcement. Please refer to safety cards in your seatback pocket."

The announcement continued as Tanner reflected on Trooper Nelson's driver's license photo. Sergeant Waska and Trooper Nelson weren't twins by any means. But not only did Nelson have a nearly identical vehicle, but an inebriated witness could've easily mistaken him for Dane Waska.

CHAPTER FORTY-ONE

Rain mixed with hail pelted against her windshield when Cameron climbed out of her truck. She looked up before pulling her hood over her head. Dark gray storm clouds now fully covered the sky. After their seemingly endless days of sun, the strange darkness made it feel late.

Lillian rolled down the window of her Jeep after braking to a stop in Cameron's drive. "You sure you're all right to be alone?"

"I'll be fine," Cameron said.

Not wanting to leave her truck at the library, she convinced Lillian she was well enough to drive herself home. Reluctantly, Lillian conceded but insisted on following Cameron home.

Lillian looked unconvinced. "Maybe I should call someone to stay with you. You almost passed out back at the library."

She looked beyond the librarian at Dane's empty driveway next door, sliding her hand over John's card in her jacket pocket. *What if Dane's disappearance isn't voluntary?*

"Really," Cameron added. "I'm feeling better. Thanks for following me home."

"Don't forget this!" Lillian called, extending *The Call of the*

Wild out her window when Cameron started toward her house. “You left it behind.”

“Thanks,” Cameron moved against the wind and accepted the book before turning for her home. She took quick steps up her porch as small beads of hail struck the top of her hood.

Lillian kept her Jeep idling until Cameron reached the top step. She gave the librarian a wave before going inside, realizing she’d left in such a rush that she’d forgotten to lock her front door. A simple lock wouldn’t deter John, but she berated herself for being so careless, wondering if her concussion was to blame. She dropped the book on her kitchen table, repressing the shudder as she envisioned John walking to the library in broad daylight, leaving the book on the stoop.

She scanned the main living space of her empty house, searching for a sign John had been there while she was gone. But everything in her place looked as it always did—the cable knit throw pillows arranged by the bay window, the thriller she’d checked out from the library last month but hadn’t read lying in the same place she’d left it on the coffee table, and Valerie’s rifle against the wall by the front door. The framed photograph next to the coat rack, of a moose walking down the Alaska Highway in the middle of Tok, had been left by the previous owner, and right now, it seemed to be mocking her. What was she thinking, coming out here to the middle of nowhere? Away from the six-minute response time of ambulances and police of Seattle. She felt desperately alone.

She imagined John jumping out from behind her couch then thrust the thought from her mind, refusing to let him get to her. She turned from the living room, having no intention of playing into his hand.

She checked her phone. Still nothing from Dane. She started to call him again but tried George instead. Maybe Dane had gone to see his father about his arrest. But George's phone went straight to voicemail. She tossed her phone on the table beside the Jack London novel, understanding Dane's frustration over his father not keeping his satellite phone charged when Dane needed to get hold of him.

She felt chilled from her short time outside—and John's anniversary gift—and made for the kitchen. She reached for her kettle and filled it with water before turning on the stove.

An involuntary shiver coursed through her upper body as she imagined John standing in this very spot after he'd attacked her outside, assessing the new home she'd made for herself. She glanced at the book on her kitchen table. *If he wanted to play games, why didn't John leave the book and the card here that night?*

Knowing John now, he probably wanted to strike a nerve on their anniversary. A memory of one of their last celebrations together ran through her mind.

She'd smiled at John's last clue that he'd left beside her shoebox as she ascended the stairs, passing the abstract painting she'd fallen in love with in a gallery in Chelsea on their trip to New York a few years back. She shook her head, recalling when John told her he'd bought it for her, and its outrageous price. Slow jazz—John's favorite—played softly throughout the home's speakers. He'd teased her that the next gift was hidden where she would keep a book, if only she were a reader. Unlike Cameron, John was constantly reading something. Every night before going to sleep, he'd tuck his book into the top drawer of his nightstand, too meticulously organized to leave it sitting on top.

In her nightstand drawer, Cameron found a rectangular Tiffany box. She drew in a sharp breath when she opened it to find the gleaming diamond tennis bracelet worth more than her car.

"Do you like it?"

She spun to find John beaming at her, leaning against their bedroom doorway. He hadn't changed from the office and was devastatingly handsome in his navy suit.

"I love it."

"And I love you." He came toward her.

"I love you too, John."

He smiled, his gaze falling toward the bracelet. "Here."

He clasped it onto her wrist and wrapped his arms around her. He hummed as they slow danced to the jazz in their bedroom.

"Happy anniversary," he whispered in her ear.

"I love the gifts, but I don't need all this, John." Cameron pulled him closer and leaned her head against his. "All I need is you."

Cameron crept slowly through her small house, her hand traveling to her holstered pistol. If John had really wanted to mess with her, why hadn't he left her another scavenger hunt, like he'd done for the last several years? Why the cheesy card? Outside, the wind howled, muffling the creaks made by her footsteps on the hardwood. She withdrew her weapon, imagining John holding Dane at gunpoint in her bedroom. And the broad grin that would spread across John's face when she found them.

Pointing the gun with outstretched arms, Cameron moved down the hallway to her room. She kicked open her bedroom door, half-expecting to find Dane's dead body on her bed. She exhaled at her empty, half-made bed.

It was exactly as she'd left it. Her tea kettle whistled. Cameron pivoted, then stopped. Spotting the drawer of her nightstand slightly ajar, she pulled it open. It was empty, as it should be.

Cameron gritted her teeth. Heart racing and head throbbing, she crept back to the kitchen with her gun outstretched.

She envisioned her husband, waiting for her in front of her stove, arms crossed, wearing a crooked, cocky smile. But her kitchen was empty. A billow of steam blew from the screeching kettle's spout. She lowered her gun and flicked off the stove before moving the kettle to another burner to stop the ear-piercing noise.

She whirled around. Had her nightstand drawer been ajar before she left? She squeezed her eyes shut, straining to remember. But she couldn't. Had John been inside her house just now, while she was out? Was that why he left the book at the library instead of here, on her doorstep? If so, John couldn't have gone far. He was probably still here. Lurking. Waiting.

"Where are you, John?" She threw her arms in the air. "Huh?"

Her gaze landed on John's stupid Jack London novel on her kitchen table.

A memory flashed in her mind of her first husband, Miles, watching football on the couch as she crept up behind him, gun in hand. Something snapped inside her the first time he'd laid a hand on her. That first time Miles struck her, she'd been too shocked to fight back. When it kept happening, she'd learned not to—it only made things worse. At first, she planned to leave him. But after learning how useless retraining orders were, especially considering how obsessive Miles had become, she knew she couldn't chance living a life always looking over her shoulder. So, she put an end to his abuse. Forever. When she'd met John, she thought that was all behind her.

She snatched the book off the table and made for the front door. After going outside, she stepped to the edge of her porch and hurled it in the direction of where John had attacked her, as a feral scream erupted from her throat. "And I don't give a shit what you're reading!"

A fog had settled over the ground since she returned from the library, and the rain had turned to snow. She scoured her surrounding property through the bleak haze of white.

"This is *my* house!" She jabbed her chest with the barrel of her pistol. "My house! You don't get to come here and terrorize me. You don't scare me, John!"

She descended her porch steps, her nostrils flaring and chest heaving. She stretched out her arms again, gun gripped tightly, pivoting slowly in 360 degrees.

"You wanna fight me? Come and get me you coward! I'm right here!" Movement on the ground caught her attention, and she spun to spot a fox racing through the bushes.

She lifted her gaze and scanned the surrounding trees emerging from the thickening layer of fog. *John has to be here.* A snowflake landed on her eyelash as a head swiveled in her direction on one of the branches. She blinked it away as the owl's yellow, narrow-set eyes stared back at her, its round head emerging from its camouflage.

On a normal day, she would've admired the beautiful creature. It was the first time she'd seen one in the wild, and it looked identical to the wood carving in Dane's house. She wondered if perhaps John was hiding there, but then rethought, turning to her own house again.

I didn't check the bathroom. She ran inside and edged toward the back of her house, gun covering every corner. She swung the ajar door open with her free hand and swiped her gun through the air at the empty bathroom. Then she sank onto the toilet lid and ran a hand through her hair, wet from the snow.

She pinched the bridge of her nose when a sharp rap sounded on her front door. Her head shot up. She leapt to her feet, training the barrel of her pistol toward the sound as she emerged from the bathroom.

Spotting the man's brown hair through her front window, she slid her finger onto the trigger. *John.* The man stepped in front of the window. Seeing his trooper uniform, and the SUV parked in her drive, Cameron exhaled, lowering her gun.

It was Trooper Nelson, not John. The storm must've muffled the sound of him pulling up her drive. She holstered her gun and took a deep breath as she moved to let him in. Hopefully the trooper had heard something from Dane.

CHAPTER FORTY-TWO

The cabin lights dimmed. Tanner folded a fresh stick of gum into his mouth, still thinking about Trooper Nelson.

"At this time, please ensure that all tray tables and seatbacks are in their upright position. It is a federal regulation that all cellular and electronic devices should be turned to airplane mode. We will be moving through the cabin to conduct our final safety check prior to departure. Thank you for choosing to fly with Alaska Airlines."

The plane braked to a stop as they lined up for the runway. Tanner turned the details over in his mind. The Ford Explorer that Karl claimed to have seen was a much more common vehicle than Nelson's Mazda Navajo, which was only made for a few years. It seemed likely that Karl could've mistaken the Navajo for the more common vehicle. Especially after four beers.

A tall, dark-haired flight attendant moved down the aisle, her head swaying side to side as she scanned each row. Tanner's phone rang in his pocket as the plane rolled forward. The flight attendant's gaze darted toward Tanner, her eyes narrowing. The ringing grew louder as Tanner pulled out his phone. Several heads turned in his direction.

It was the Alaska State Crime Lab. They were probably calling with the DNA match from the blood on the bear trap, not realizing Detective Morton had already told him the results. But it was possible they got a different match from the blood *inside* the cabin. Possibly to Cameron. The flight attendant frowned, quickening her pace toward Tanner's row as he lifted the device to his ear.

"Detective Mulholland."

"Hi, detective," a woman said. "I'm a technician calling from the Alaska State Crime Lab with a DNA match on a sample that was recently submitted to us."

Tanner glanced at the flight attendant whose eyes remained on him while she swiftly marched down the aisle, lips pursed.

"Is this from the sample obtained from the bear trap? Detective Morton already called me about that."

"No, this sample was submitted last week by Alaska State Trooper Dane Waska."

Tanner sat tall, confused. Why was she calling him with a result submitted by Sergeant Waska?

"It came back a match to evidence Waska submitted for testing from a female murder victim found in the woods in the Chena Rivers State Park, outside of Fairbanks, in 1999. We expedited the submission sample due to the sensitivity of the identity of who we were testing."

The flight attendant reached Tanner's row. "Sir, you need to get off your phone." Her firm voice was laced with irritation.

"One second." Tanner raised his finger in the air toward the attendant before addressing the woman on the other end of the call. "I'm sorry but shouldn't you be calling Sergeant Waska?"

"I did," she said. "But he didn't answer. And he requested that I notify you if I couldn't get ahold of him."

Tanner thought of Cameron's concern over Dane's recent disappearance after his bail hearing.

"*Sir!* Excuse me!" The attendant said, raising her voice and leaning over the man in the aisle seat to bring her face closer to Tanner's. "You need to get off your phone. You're violating a federal regulation."

A male voice came through the overhead speakers. "Flight attendants, please be seated for takeoff."

The technician on the other end of the call said something Tanner couldn't understand amid the flight attendant's shouts and overhead pilot announcement.

The guy in the aisle seat tapped Tanner with the outside of his hand. "Come on, dude. Do what she says."

"Detective? Are you still there?" the crime lab technician said.

Tanner pressed his finger to his other ear as another flight attendant rushed toward them from the front of the plane. "I'm sorry," he said. "Could you repeat that?"

The flight attendant kept yelling at him. Tanner looked down at his lap.

"I said the DNA sample wasn't a match to the profile Sergeant Waska recently submitted, but it we did get a familial hit for another case. It came back a direct familial match to John Prescott, The Teacher Killer. The profile is male, so it's likely his father."

"*Sir!*"

The guy beside him tapped Tanner again. "Dude."

"I got it, thank you," Tanner said into his phone. "I have to go."

"We will have to return to the gate if you won't comply."

The second flight attendant reached them when Tanner

lowered his phone. She was a head shorter and a few decades older than her cohort, who glared at Tanner.

The older attendant looked between Tanner and the tall brunette. "Is there a problem, sir?"

Tanner lifted a palm into the air, his mind still spinning from the phone call. *Louie Prescott, John Prescott's father, murdered a woman in 1999 in Alaska, only a few years after the Tok murders.* "Shit," he said. "I mean no problem. I'm putting it on airplane mode."

Frowning, the taller flight attendant crossed her arms, eyes glued to Tanner, as her colleague returned to the front of the plane. She waited until Tanner slipped his phone into his pocket before making a move for the back of the plane, shooting him a final glare of annoyance.

The plane turned onto the runway. Tanner stared at the screen on the seatback in front of him, wishing he'd asked the crime lab technician whose DNA profile Waska had submitted for testing, the one that hadn't been a match. What had she meant by *the sensitivity of the identity?* That it was a trooper? Had Waska suspected Nelson in the Tok murders? And now Waska had been arrested for murder.

He reached into his pocket. He needed to find out whose DNA Waska submitted to the crime lab, and why. The drone from the engines filled the fuselage as the aircraft accelerated, propelling Tanner against the back of his seat.

The guy beside him motioned to Tanner's phone in his hand. "If you make another call, I'm calling the flight attendants and getting you kicked off the flight."

"It's too late for that," Tanner said seconds before the nose lifted off the runway. He still had a signal after taking his phone off airplane mode, but he would lose it any minute. He typed a quick text to Detective Morton, hoping he received it before

Tanner lost service. *DNA came back a match to John Prescott's father from 1999 Fairbanks murder. Call AK State Crime Lab. State Trooper Sergeant Dane Waska submitted a different DNA profile to be tested. Need to find out who it was.*

He sent the text, waiting to make sure it sent.

"Are you texting?" the guy asked, peering at Tanner's phone.

The woman in the window seat leaned forward. "Let him be."

Tanner gave her a smile before turning to the guy on his left. "Don't worry about it."

The plane dipped to the side, giving Tanner a view of Elliott Bay—and the SPD headquarters—as they flew over Puget Sound.

"Whatever, man." The twenty-something guy adjusted his headphones and refocused his attention on the movie playing on his seatback screen.

A million thoughts ran through Tanner's head as he peered at the gray-blue water below. The news that Louie Prescott had murdered a woman outside of Fairbanks in the late nineties was huge, but so was the fact that Trooper Nelson had a nearly identical vehicle to what Karl Sadler allegedly saw leaving the lake where Erica Lavine's body was dumped.

"Ladies and gentlemen," a female voice came through the loudspeaker. "We are experiencing some technical difficulties with our inflight Wi-Fi but are working to fix it and will let you know if and when it becomes available during the flight."

Tanner eyed the flight tracker on his seatback screen. Three hours and fifty-two minutes to Fairbanks. He tapped his foot against the floor, willing the flight to move faster and hating the sense of helplessness he felt at being stuck on the flight with no way to communicate.

He believed now that Sergeant Waska had been framed. But by Prescott or Nelson? And which of them was responsible for the two recent killings?

CHAPTER FORTY-THREE

A GUST OF wind whipped into Cameron's house when she opened the door, rattling the framed photograph of the moose.

"Hey." Nelson's gaze fell to her hand. "What's with the gun?"

"I thought you were someone else."

Another gust accosted them, blowing a curtain through the open doorway.

"You want to come inside?" she asked.

He nodded. She stepped aside to allow him in, then pushed the door shut against the wind.

"I came by to see if Dane had come home, but I see his car still isn't here. Have you heard from him?"

She shook her head, her mind still on John. "No."

"I also wanted to ask you a couple of questions. You mind if we sit down?" He nodded toward the weapon in her hand. "Without the gun?"

Cameron scanned the surrounding space. *John's not here. At least not inside.*

"Sure, but I'm keeping the gun." She holstered her firearm and motioned to the kitchen table as an image of John lurking behind a tree with a rifle trained on her house assaulted her thoughts. If they sat in front of the window, she and Nelson would be sitting ducks.

"Actually, how about the living room?"

"Sure, thanks." Nelson eyed her curiously before following her into the adjacent room. He lowered himself onto her couch in the same spot where Tanner had sat a week ago. "I understand you're probably still pretty shaken after what happened."

Cameron sank into a chair across from him, debating whether to tell him about John. Tanner was still several hours away, if he could even make it here tonight with the storm.

"Do you remember anything else from that night?"

"Dane didn't do this." She met Nelson's gaze. "He's not a killer."

Nelson shifted in his seat. "I'd like to believe that too. But I can't argue with the evidence. And I'm afraid his disappearing act after promising to cooperate with us isn't helping his case."

"He had calluses. On his hands."

Nelson's eyes widened. "Are you sure? How do you know?"

There was a perceptible skepticism in his voice, as if he suspected her of making it up to throw suspicion off Dane.

She pursed her lips. "I didn't imagine it! Before I got knocked out, he handcuffed me. His hands were rough, like sandpaper, when they wrapped around my wrists."

"Okay. I believe you." Nelson turned pensive. "Although, that doesn't prove it wasn't Dane."

"Yes, it does! I touched Dane's hands the night before and his palms were smooth. I know what his hands feel like. This wasn't him!" *Why can't he believe me?*

Nelson lifted a hand at her shout. "Look, I know you might want to protect him. And I'm sure it's hard for you to accept that Dane did this, especially after…well, what you've been through."

Cameron straightened. "You mean marrying a serial killer?"

Nelson leaned forward, resting his elbows on his knees while ignoring her question. "If you know where Waska is, you should tell me. He isn't who we thought he was. He's dangerous, Cameron."

"I know who attacked me. And I know who killed Madison and Sienna. It wasn't Dane."

Nelson shook his head in disbelief. "We already arrested Dane. The evidence—"

"It was John. My husband."

Nelson rocked back against the couch, his brows knitting together.

"The Teacher Killer," Cameron added.

She could tell by Nelson's expression that he didn't believe her. *He thinks I'm losing it.*

"He's dead, Cameron."

"No, Nelson. He's not." She put her hands on her knees and launched into what happened last winter as concisely as she could.

Nelson listened intently, but she couldn't tell whether he believed her.

Her gaze traveled to the window beside the couch. "And then I found him."

"Where?"

She told him about the family cabin belonging to her first husband. "John was still alive when I left him. I was sure he wouldn't be for long." Her eyes fell to her hands in her lap. "But I made a mistake, and now he's here." She lifted her gaze. "There are some things in life you will never know you're capable of until you're faced with it. Killing is one of them."

Nelson looked pensive for a moment. He cleared his throat. "I think your head injury is making it difficult for you to think clearly right now."

Cameron gaped at him. "I *am* thinking clearly. You don't believe me? Ask Dane, he—"

Cameron stopped, remembering that Nelson couldn't ask Dane. Because Dane had been arrested for murder and was now missing.

"Wait." Cameron stood. "I have proof." She marched into the kitchen, leaving Nelson looking skeptical on her couch.

When she passed the kitchen island, her phone chimed with a new text message.

Dane.

Her pulse raced, and a heavy sense of dread came over her when she saw it was an image. She opened the message. Her lungs froze as she stared at George Waska, tied to a chair, his bloodied head hanging to one side. His left eye was swollen, but he grimaced with life. A large bloodstain covered the right shoulder of his shirt. Zooming in, Cameron could see he'd been shot.

Bubbles appeared below the image. Cameron's hand flew to her mouth as she read the message.

Come to my lake cabin. NOW. NO COPS – or I'll be a dead man, and my father will too.

CHAPTER FORTY-FOUR

"EVERYTHING OKAY?"

Cameron jumped from Nelson's voice. She spun to find him only a foot behind her. She put a hand over her heart.

"You scared me."

Nelson's steely gaze followed her phone that she dropped to her side. "You get a message from someone?"

Cameron took a step back from Nelson's proximity to her, but her heel ran into the kitchen island.

"Valerie. She's just checking on me."

She couldn't risk Dane's life—or Nelson's—by involving him now. She pictured the blood seeping from George's skull. John was lying in wait, an expert marksman. She doubted John was even afraid to die at this point. He was out for revenge at all costs.

"What were you going to show me?"

"What?"

Nelson frowned. "You said you had proof that your husband was still alive."

"Oh. That." Cameron lifted her hand to her head. "I think

you were probably right, actually. I'm feeling dizzy, and I should probably rest. Maybe I'm *not* thinking clearly."

"Yeah, you should. I'm sorry for what you've been through." Nelson placed his hands on his hips. "I think Waska might've gone to his lake cabin." He turned toward the flurry of white beyond the window. "I'm worried about why he's evading us. Makes me wonder if he and his father are in this together. I should go up there, although with this weather I'd probably end up getting stuck at the lake. But I'd never forgive myself if Dane kills again when I could've stopped him."

Cameron's mind raced. If Nelson got to Dane's cabin before she did. John would kill Dane, just like his father. He'd likely kill Nelson too.

Her gun burned against her hip. She couldn't lose Dane. She also couldn't allow John to be taken into custody in the off chance that Nelson lived to arrest him. That wouldn't be justice. After everything he'd done, John couldn't be allowed to live.

"Get some rest." Nelson's hand was warm on her shoulder before he started for the door. "Call me if you hear from Waska."

"I lied."

Nelson turned.

"That wasn't a text from Valerie. It was from Dane. He's at Northway Junction."

"Northway Junction? What's he doing there?"

Cameron shrugged. "Following up on a lead, he said." The town of less than fifty people was an hour southeast, in the opposite direction of Dane's cabin, which would at least buy her some time. "He said he'll be out of cell range soon and staying there for the night," she added.

Nelson's demeanor darkened as came toward her. "Did he say where?"

"No."

Nelson didn't stop until he was less than a foot away from her. His gaze fell to her phone. Cameron tightened her grip on the device, thinking he might rip it from her hand.

He pointed to it instead. "Ask him."

Cameron pressed her lips together before lifting her phone, tilting the screen so Nelson couldn't see as she typed a response to John's message. *OK. I'm coming. Just me.*

"At the medical center, you told me Waska suspected someone in the recent murders. Did he say anything more? Or who it was?"

When she lifted her gaze, Nelson was waiting eagerly for her response. "No."

Nelson stood still, uncomfortably close to her, but her kitchen island blocked her from being able to back up.

"There's no response," Cameron said, checking her phone. "He probably already lost his cell signal."

Outside, the storm looked to be getting worse by the minute. She needed Nelson to leave.

"Call him," he said.

She wasn't about to call John, but she didn't want Nelson growing suspicious if she refused. She tapped Tanner's name in her recent call log and pressed her phone to her ear. He had to be in the air by now.

As she'd hoped, her call went to voicemail. "You've reached Det—

She hung up. "Went to voicemail."

"Okay, I'm heading there now. Call me if he responds." Nelson's gaze shifted to the pistol on her hip before he turned for the door. "Lock this behind me."

Through the window, Cameron watched Nelson's headlights back out of her drive. As soon as he turned onto the main road, Cameron went to her closet and retrieved her white-hooded parka, boots, a hat, and gloves. She grabbed the box of ammo from her kitchen cabinet, along with her sharpest sheathed paring knife from the top drawer.

She slid the knife into the waistband of her jeans with the sinking realization that Dane could already be dead. This could all be just a trap. Her phone chimed on the counter. Another message popped up. *Hurry. Lover boy and his father don't have long.*

Cameron gritted her teeth and swiped the box of ammo off the counter, tucking it under her arm. "Neither do you, John."

She swiped her pair of birdwatching binoculars from her front windowsill before she opened her front door, then paused midway. She spun for the kitchen as the door smacked against the wall from the wind. She spotted what she'd been about to show Nelson and plucked the anniversary card off the counter.

She'd made a mistake last time. She'd left John too soon—while he was still breathing. She wouldn't make that mistake twice.

After tossing the card in the trash, she made for the door, grabbing the butt of Valerie's rifle and slinging it over her shoulder on her way out.

CHAPTER FORTY-FIVE

CAMERON GRIPPED THE steering wheel tighter, her knuckles turning as white as the snow flurries beyond her windshield. She leaned forward, straining to see through the haze. Since turning off the Alaska Highway to the backroad that led to Hunt Lake, her visibility had waned to almost nothing.

She glanced at her speedometer. She was doing only thirty-five miles an hour, but it felt dangerously fast. She eased up on the gas before pressing her foot down, afraid of what John would do if she didn't get there soon. With the storm, it had taken her double the time it normally took to get this far, and she was only halfway there.

The snow came down harder by the minute. If she took too long, she'd get stuck out here in the middle of nowhere without phone service. She always lost service on this road when she'd come to the cabin with Dane. Her signal wouldn't return until she got to Dane's cabin. And even then it was spotty.

It struck her that John would've had to leave the lake and drive this far to be able to send those messages from Dane's phone. She laid her foot on the gas pedal, thinking of Dane at the hands of John. Had John forced Dane on the drive with him? Or Had John already killed him? She pushed the thought from her mind, needing to keep a clear head if she was going to make it to the cabin in one piece.

The passenger side of her truck dipped. Cameron jerked the wheel to the left, realizing she'd driven off the edge of the road. She lifted her foot from the gas, squinting to make out the stretch of road through the heavy snowfall.

Her jaw flexed as she envisioned John mowing down Madison Youngblood with his car, then leaving her body to rot in a ditch on the side of the highway. *This is all my fault. I should never have gone back and stabbed John. I should've left him to the wolves.* Her gaze flicked to the glove compartment, containing her Ruger LCP.

If someone had told her a year ago that she'd be living in Alaska and keeping a gun in her truck along with one in her house, she would've laughed and told them they were crazy. Just like she would have if someone told her that her beloved husband was a serial killer. She made a mental note to grab the compact pistol as a backup when she could free a hand from the wheel.

When she returned her attention to the road, a large blur of dark brown appeared in front of her truck. The massive thing moved, and a pair of eyes reflected in the glow of her headlights. The beast froze as she sped toward it. She slammed on her brakes. Her tires locked, losing traction as her truck fishtailed, sliding sideways toward the brown bear who still stood in the middle of the road.

Cameron swerved to the right. The rear of her truck spun out in the opposite direction. Her headlights illuminated the spruce tree seconds before her truck slammed into its trunk. A metallic screech erupted from her front bumper as her truck whiplashed to a halt and her forehead slammed against the steering wheel.

Her heart thudded against her ribcage as she stared at the snow-covered branches shifting from side to side above her windshield. She threw her truck into reverse, ignoring the throb in her forehead. She stepped on the gas. Her engine revved and her tires spun.

She swore, lifting her foot off the pedal. She closed her eyes, thinking of Dane. If John *hadn't* already killed him, how long would he let Dane live if she didn't show? She pressed her foot gently on the gas until her truck rolled back.

She exhaled against the back of her seat as her truck reversed farther from the tree. Once on the road, she threw her truck into drive, then crawled down the road at ten miles an hour until she was certain the bear was no longer in her path.

The snowfall lifted after a few miles. The road curved to the left and Cameron knew she was getting close. The tree-lined road narrowed as it wound around the lake. Cameron slowed. Keeping one hand on the wheel, she reached into her glove compartment and felt around for her Ruger, sweeping her hand along the inside of the small compartment, swearing when she realized her gun was gone.

When she withdrew her hand, a stiff paper fell from the glove compartment onto the floor. She glanced down, seeing it was a white envelope, the same size as the one John had left at the library.

Her limbs felt suddenly weak. This was different than the last time she'd come for John—when she'd had the element of surprise. And John hadn't taken hostage the man that she loved.

A fallen tree came into view up ahead, completely blocking the road. Cameron slowed to a stop. As her truck idled, she stared at the thick trunk with branches sticking out in all directions. There was no way she could move it. And this was the only access to Dane's cabin, at least by car.

She'd planned to stop a ways before reaching Dane's cabin to avoid announcing her presence right away, but she'd hoped to get closer than this. Judging from the last mile marker she passed, Dane's cabin was still two miles away.

Maybe she'd been wrong not to tell Nelson. Even if she managed to kill John and rescue Dane, how would she get Dane back to her truck if he was injured? But she needed to come alone.

She killed the ignition and lifted the envelope off the floor. She swallowed, not wanting to open it, but feeling compelled to at the same time. The envelope was unsealed, and as she withdrew the card, she recognized the two deer on the front with hearts circling their heads. It was the same card.

A jolt of revulsion traveled down her arms when she opened it. Instead of a *J*, *NICE TRY* was penned in block letters at the bottom of the card.

She tossed the card onto the passenger seat, slinging Valerie's rifle over her shoulder before getting out of the truck. She pulled on her gloves. They were too thin for this kind of weather but would allow her to slide her finger onto her trigger when she needed to. She felt the front pockets of her parka, wishing she'd brought something better than a paring knife now that she didn't have her Ruger, before she unholstered her 9mm from beneath her coat. She climbed over the fallen tree. It was still daylight, and the snowfall had lifted enough for her to make out a path down the road.

As she walked, a strong wind whipped the snow against her face with a biting cold, making her eyes water. She blinked to clear her vision as along either side of the road, tree limbs shook violently. She tightened her grip on her pistol, her fingers going numb beneath her thin gloves.

After twenty minutes the road curved to a sharp right, which meant she'd reached the south side of the lake. She was less than a mile from Dane's cabin. She moved off the road and into the wooded area that lined the lakeshore.

Zigzagging through the trees, she neared the water's edge. A thick layer of fog blanketed the lake. When she strained to see across the water, she made out a faint light coming from George's cabin. The image of the old man tied to his chair, his eye swollen from the beating John had given him, made Cameron want to throw up on the snow. She kept moving, hoping there would still be time to save him.

She retreated into the woods, knowing John could be watching. As she marched through the freshly fallen snow, she readied herself to finish what she'd set out to do last winter—and failed.

All right, John. Here I come.

CHAPTER FORTY-SIX

When Tanner strode out of the Fairbanks airport, Detective Morton stepped out of his unmarked Expedition. The Fairbanks detective stood a few inches shorter than Tanner as the two men shook hands. A light snow fell on Morton's salt and pepper hair as he lifted the trunk for Tanner's bag.

"I thought it was summer up here," Tanner said.

Morton shrugged. "Typically, not until after Labor Day, but it happens on occasion."

Tanner glanced at the slate sky. It was over forty degrees cooler than when he was here last week. "Thanks for picking me up."

He'd gotten a text reply from Morton once he was able to connect to the flight's Wi-Fi. They communicated through email for the rest of the flight. He'd called Cameron twice since he'd landed, but his calls had gone straight to voicemail.

"You're welcome." Morton moved around the front of his car. "I'm afraid you're here a few days early for that search of the cabin. It looks like with the weather, it will likely be Tuesday before we can get a helicopter back there with the search team."

"I'm just glad I was able to get hold of you. And like I said, I need to go to Tok first to find out what the hell's going on there." Tanner climbed into the passenger seat. "Prescott's widow isn't answering her phone. She called me earlier, convinced that Prescott is alive and responsible for the recent murders in Tok—and her attack. And not Waska."

Morton flashed Tanner a look as he pulled out of the airport. "Can you really trust her instincts though? I mean, she did marry a serial killer."

Tanner withdrew a stick of gum from his pocket. "Her prints were on that door handle at the wilderness cabin. We know she was there. And I believe she's the only person who knows with certainty whether Prescott left that cabin alive or dead." Tanner stared at the snow coming down against Morton's windshield, the wipers leaving a wet streak. He recalled the dried blood caked on the bear trap beside the tree, and the smears of blood on the cabin floor.

"You think she hunted down Prescott, put him in that bear trap, and now Prescott's come back for revenge?"

"I think it's a very real possibility at this point, yes. That's why I need to get down there to Tok. Find out the truth. And whatever the hell else is going on." An image of Cameron flashed in his mind. *And before anyone else dies.*

"That was quite the news you gave me today," Morton braked for a red light. "John Prescott's father being a serial killer, killing that woman in Fairbanks, has huge implications. Won't be long before we link his DNA to other cold cases, at least I hope. Give some of those families some closure."

On the flight, Tanner had asked Morton to send him the casefile from the 1999 Fairbanks murder linked to Louie Prescott. The details of her death were strikingly similar to the 1984 Seattle murder of Sally Hickman, but not to any of the Tok killings.

"Were you able to get ahold of the crime lab?"

Tanner held his breath, readying himself to learn who Waska suspected enough in the recent murders to test their DNA.

"They were closed by the time I called. I left a voicemail but won't hear back until tomorrow."

Tanner sank against the seat, unable to hide his disappointment. Had Waska known that Nelson had a nearly identical vehicle to his Ford Explorer back then? He must have. The casefiles from both Tok murders in the nineties stated that no foreign DNA was obtained from either of the victims. If Waska suspected Nelson, he could've been hoping to link him to the unsolved Fairbanks murder in 1999, since it was around the same time as the Tok killings.

But the killer hadn't been Nelson. It had been Louie Prescott.

"I was able to get in touch with one of the Tok troopers like you asked." The light turned green, and Morton sped through the intersection. "She confirmed what Prescott's widow told you. Waska never cooperated after his bail hearing. They still don't know where he is. He's not due back in court until next week, but his disappearance has her concerned."

Tanner tried to call Cameron again but it went directly to voicemail. Her phone being off made Tanner just as concerned for her whereabouts as Waska's. If not more.

"Anyway," Morton flicked on his turn signal. "I told her we would be down to assist with the investigation in the morning."

"Morning?" Tanner glanced at the time on the dash. It was just after 6:30 p.m.

"Well, as long as the storm clears," Morton said, pulling into the parking lot of a Holiday Inn Express. "Tok is getting hit with a winter storm right now. It should be better by tomorrow and isn't supposed to hit up here in Fairbanks, so, if you want to stay here tonight, we can head down first thing in the morning, given the Alaska Highway is clear by then." Morton pulled to a stop in front of the hotel's entrance.

"We can't wait until tomorrow," Tanner said, making no move to get out of the car. "We have no idea of Waska's whereabouts. And if Cameron is right, and John Prescott *is* alive, we've got much bigger problems than Waska being missing."

Morton rested his palm on top of the steering wheel, his gaze troubled. "You think Waska murdered the girl in Tok?"

Tanner had doubted Cameron's suspicions before, when Bethany Long was murdered, and Tanner had believed Prescott was dead. "I'm inclined to trust Cameron's instincts and her certainty that Waska wasn't the one who attacked her the other night. But I can't know for sure. Which is why I need to get there as soon as possible, to find out before anyone else gets killed."

Like Cameron.

"Look, I understand the urgency—especially with the possible chance of Prescott being alive—but we can't risk driving through a snowstorm either. If the storm's as bad as they're predicting, we'll end up in a ditch at best and a head-on with a semi at the worst."

Tanner glanced at the lightly falling snow out the windshield. "Aren't snowstorms your normal up here?"

"Not this time of year. The roads won't get plowed tonight. And the first snowfall of the year is always a mess before it becomes compact and easier to drive on."

In Tanner's periphery, the hotel's automatic doors slid open. Out his side window, he watched an elderly couple walk outside. *I can't stay the night at an airport hotel while Prescott could be alive and free, closing in on Cameron. Not to mention one of the town troopers possibly being a murderer and Waska's unexplained disappearance.*

"I need to get there tonight." Tanner turned to the detective. "Can you drop me at the rental car agency?"

Detective Morton raised his eyebrows. "Did you hear what I said?"

"I don't feel like there's a choice."

Morton cast him a wary look.

"I have to at least try," Tanner added. "I think Waska suspected one of the other Tok troopers in the new killings."

"Who?"

Tanner told him about the white SUV Nelson owned in the nineties, which closely matched the vehicle Karl Sadler saw leaving the lake where Erica Lavine's body was dumped.

"And we also have John Prescott to worry about."

With a sigh, Detective Morton pulled out of the hotel parking lot.

Tanner leaned over the center console to peer out the SUV's rear window. "I thought the airport was back there?"

"If you're going, I'm going." Morton turned onto an onramp for the Robert Mitchell Expressway. "Have you even seen snow before, living in Seattle?" Morton cracked a half grin before turning serious. "But you're right. That town needs help before someone else gets killed—as long as it's not us." He raised his pointer finger in the air as they merged onto the highway. "If it gets treacherous, we're turning back."

Tanner leaned against his seatback, stretching his legs as far as they could go. After his cramped flight, the Expedition's leg room felt first class.

"Deal."

CHAPTER FORTY-SEVEN

Cameron crept through the snowy woods along the west side of Hunt Lake, just far enough from the lakeshore to keep herself hidden. She used the quiet to form her plan of attack. During the drive, she'd been too focused on getting to George's cabin in one piece to think through how she would gain the upper hand against John. With a jolt of panic, she admitted to herself that it was hard to plan her next move when she didn't know exactly what she was walking into.

Wings fluttered overhead. Startled, Cameron froze, aiming her gun toward the sound. A crow flew from the tree, its black form cutting through the haze of white. She exhaled, lowering her weapon.

She kept walking, scanning her periphery in the waning visibility. The snowfall had lifted, but the freezing fog grew thicker by the minute. An image of the rabid wolf pack ascending the hill below Miles's cabin filled her mind.

She suppressed a shudder and pushed the memory aside, the white woods reminding her of the trek she took last winter through the remote wilderness to the cabin where John had been hiding. He'd underestimated her when he'd faked his death, and his narcissistic confidence had been his downfall. If it weren't for her mistake in going back and stabbing him, it would've cost him his life.

She'd miscalculated John too. What he was capable of. His survival skills were extraordinary. She should never have left before making sure he was dead.

John should have known her better by now. If he thought she would surrender without a fight this time, he was dead wrong. The memory of Miles's head flying backward after she shot him flashed in her mind.

When she neared the northwest corner of the lake, she slowed her pace. Her gaze lingered on the spot Karl's plane had skidded to a stop on the ice when she'd landed on the frozen lake with Dane last winter. It had been her first time landing on the ice. She and Dane hardly knew each other then. She pictured him grinning at her after they'd slid to a stop. She'd been terrified they were going to end up in the trees.

When she rounded the north side of the lake, a glow from George's cabin window came into view. John had already taken too much from her. She wasn't about to let anything happen to Dane.

She scanned her periphery for a sign of John before crouching behind a stump and pulling out her binoculars. She lifted them to her eyes, but the visibility was still poor. She lowered the binoculars, unable to spot any sort of movement inside or around George's cabin.

Smoke blew from its chimney into the twilight sky. The fog laden lake and surrounding woods were eerily quiet as she trekked toward the A-frame.

When she reached George's cabin, Dane's came into view next door. Aside from George's Chevy truck and Dane's trooper SUV, there were no other vehicles that she could see.

The front door to George's cabin was propped wide open. Neither of the two cabins had electricity, and they were the only structures on the remote lake. She moved closer and could see the glow from the fire burning inside. The image she'd been sent of George looked to have been taken inside his cabin, not Dane's.

She shot a glance toward Dane's cabin and straightened her pointer finger along the barrel of her pistol, ready to slide it onto the trigger as she approached the open entrance to the warm cabin. Bracing herself for what she would find, Cameron pressed her back against the exterior wall beside the door before pivoting into the doorway, gun outstretched.

Please, let George still be alive.

The small cabin was empty aside from the outline of a man collapsed on the floor in front of the fireplace. Cameron's heart dropped into her stomach as she rushed toward him.

"No, no, no…"

She sank to her knees in the dark pool of blood beside George's head. His mouth was slack and his dark eyes vacant. A sob escaped her throat as she looked away from the bullet hole in his forehead.

"I'm so sorry, George." She bowed her head over the gruff old man she'd come to care for these last several months she'd been dating Dane.

A flash of light from the neighboring cabin caught her eye. She stood and swept her gun around the darkened interior, peering out the window to see a light coming from inside Dane's place.

John.

She looked back at George before going outside. A fresh surge of rage burned inside her chest as she imagined George's final moments at John's hands. She exhaled a puff of white before she crept toward Dane's, sickened at the thought of Dane having to watch his father die. She passed George's snowmobile parked inside his narrow carport, keys dangling from the ignition, and she wished she'd thought to remove them from John's at his cabin. Instead, she'd left him a way of escape.

She tucked behind a tree, bracing herself to face the man she thought she'd left for dead. And the horrific possibilities of what he might've done to Dane.

Until last week, things between her and Dane seemed almost too perfect. She felt a surge of guilt for doubting him. The panic in Dane's eyes when he'd found her in the ditch was real. He hadn't told the whole truth about his marriage, but he wasn't anything like John.

She emerged from behind the tree, grateful she'd worn white, and crouched down before running up the hill to the side of Dane's cabin. John knew she was coming. She couldn't hide her presence for long. He may have already seen her, but she wasn't about to announce herself.

A shadow moved in front of the cabin window. Cameron dropped to her stomach on the snow, pulling the hood of her parka over her red hair. She held her breath as the figure paused behind the glass.

She was almost certain they couldn't see her. A thick, white haze blanketed the ground where she lay. She lifted her pistol toward the window as the silhouette disappeared behind the wall of the cabin.

After pushing herself to her feet, she ducked low and closed the distance to the cabin's rear deck facing the lake. She climbed the few steps and pushed her back against the siding. She slid her finger onto the trigger and peered inside the cabin window beside her. Inside, it was dim. She squinted and drew closer to the glass.

A kerosene lamp was perched on the small table near the side window, but she couldn't make out anyone inside the cabin. She pulled away, leaning her head against the cabin's wood exterior.

She should've known it wouldn't be that easy. She stared in the direction of the lake, which had disappeared beneath a thick layer of frozen fog. She heard a *snap* and turned back toward the window.

"Cameron."

Recognizing the voice, she whirled around with her gun outstretched. She waved her weapon through the fog. A figure materialized through the haze at the bottom of the deck steps. Cameron stood still. It wasn't who she expected.

It was Dane.

CHAPTER FORTY-EIGHT

"CAREFUL, DOC."

A man peeked out from behind Dane, but not the one she'd been expecting. He pressed a compact pistol to her boyfriend's neck with a gloved hand. Her Ruger, the one that went missing from her glove compartment.

"Nelson?" Cameron swung her gun toward the trooper, her equilibrium faltering as she tried to make sense of what was happening.

Nelson tucked behind Dane.

"I don't understand. What are you doing?"

"You shoot me, you shoot Dane," Nelson said.

Cameron stepped closer, seeing the beads of sweat that covered Dane's forehead beneath his dark hairline. He wore his trooper uniform without his vest. Dane grunted through his clenched jaw. His arms were tucked behind him; they had to be bound.

A swarm of questions assaulted her mind.

She thought back to Nelson being at her house, listening to her confession of killing John.

"You really expected to find your dead husband here, didn't

you?" Nelson asked from behind his captive. Dane shifted his weight and cried out in pain. Cameron's gaze fell to his leg, seeing the hole in the thigh of his uniform pants—and the blood that seeped through the dark fabric.

"I have to say, Cameron, that when I overheard you tell Dane in his office that you suspected your husband John had killed Madison, *after I killed her,* I was floored to discover you might even have more secrets than I do."

Cameron felt sickened recalling how she poured out her confession of killing John to Nelson earlier that day at her home, thinking he was there to help her find Dane. She stared at Dane's pale face as Nelson continued.

"I take it you got the book from Lillian at the library?"

Cameron didn't answer, overwhelmed by the implications of Nelson's guilt. And what about John? Did this mean he was dead?

"I thought leaving the book might be a little overkill. But after overhearing you tell Dane how you suspected John was alive, I realized I had the perfect cover to kill again. So, I researched everything I could on him. I watched a TV news interview of your husband's law firm partner after John's alleged bear attack last fall, where he remarked what a huge Jack London fan your husband was. And when I learned that today would be your anniversary, well, I thought it would be fun."

Cameron stared at Nelson's gloved hand, wrapped around the handle of her Ruger. *His woodcarving hobby.* The calluses she felt weren't John's. They were Nelson's. How had she not thought of it before? "You were the one who attacked me."

"Let's go inside, shall we? It's cold out here." Keeping Dane as his shield, Nelson tilted slightly to peer around the back of Dane's head. "But leave your weapons out here. You can start by setting your pistol on the deck. Then the rifle."

Cameron made no move to lower her pistol. Dane grimaced.

She watched the side of Nelson's mouth curl into a smile before his head disappeared behind Dane's.

She thought of George's body growing cold in the cabin next door. She had no intention of surrendering her weapons and playing into Nelson's hand. If she did, Nelson would kill them both.

Cameron watched more color leave Dane's face as he leaned sideways, fighting to keep his balance on one leg. Cameron prepared to shoot Nelson, but somehow, Nelson kept his head protected behind Dane's.

"But it's safe to say the drugs have worn off by now. Your boyfriend's having trouble standing, Cam. Don't make him wait."

"Shoot him, Cameron," Dane said through gritted teeth.

Nelson twisted the barrel of his gun into Dane's neck. Dane winced and threw his head backward into Nelson's. Nelson grunted as Dane staggered to the side, falling against the side of the cabin and leaving Nelson exposed. Cameron aimed her barrel at Nelson's head as he ducked behind Dane again, sliding his arm beneath Dane's armpit to pull Dane upright, using him as a human shield.

"Drop your gun," Nelson barked. "Or I'll put a bullet in his neck right here."

"Shoot him!" Dane yelled.

Behind Dane's head, she saw the edge of Nelson's face uplift to a smile. "You really believed your dead husband was behind this, didn't you?"

Cameron trained her gun on Dane, ready to shoot Nelson the second he exposed himself. Nelson leaned his forehead into the back of Dane's head, giving her no chance at a shot without killing Dane. "I'm going to count to three, Cameron. If you don't drop your weapons, your boyfriend is dead. One. Two."

Cameron steadied her pistol, making no move to lower her arm. "You'll kill him anyway." Behind Dane, she watched

Nelson's demeanor suddenly darken. A chill went through her. He looked completely unhinged.

"Three."

An ear-deafening blast erupted from Nelson's gun.

"Ahhh!" Dane's face writhed in agony as blood poured from the bullet wound in his shoulder, staining his blue shirt crimson.

"Drop your gun, Doc! Or he dies!" Nelson seethed.

A dark patch bloomed on Dane's shirt when Nelson pressed the barrel of her Ruger into the bottom of Dane's jaw.

"Don't do it," Dane sputtered as Cameron slowly lowered her weapon onto the snowy deck. He doubled over with gritted teeth. "He'll kill us both!"

Nelson smiled after Cameron set down the pistol and laid Valerie's rifle beside it on the deck. "I knew we could be civil about this."

Dane stifled a deep grunt.

"Take off your parka," Nelson ordered.

"Why?"

A scoff. "After what you told me about your wilderness hunt for your husband, I'm sure you've got all kinds of other weapons in there. Let me guess: another gun, a knife, and maybe something else less conventional?"

Nelson lifted the gun up to Dane's temple as Cameron unzipped her coat.

"Hurry up!" Nelson screamed.

She tossed her parka onto the deck. Goosebumps formed on her arms as the frigid wind penetrated her thin sweater. She lifted her hands, aware of the small, sheathed knife hidden inside her waistband.

"I'm surprised, doc. You seem to have come a little unprepared." Nelson leaned behind Dane and swung open the cabin's rear door. He shoved Dane through the doorway. Dane stumbled inside before falling to the floor. Dane swore as Nelson trained his gun on Cameron's chest.

"Ladies first."

Cameron stepped into the cabin as Dane struggled to get to his knees with his hands zip tied behind.

"How did you send the texts from Dane's phone when you were with me?" Cameron asked, hoping her question would distract Nelson while she figured out a way to get him out of this.

Cameron realized the answer before Nelson replied.

"I sent the first text before I came inside."

That explained how he had the cell service to send them.

"I sent the others while you were in the kitchen and when you thought I was texting Trooper Downing. George was already dead, and I left Dane here, tied up and sedated with some fentanyl I confiscated from a drug bust a while back."

Dane managed to sit up as Nelson's footsteps sounded on the wood floor behind her.

She locked eyes with Dane as she reached beneath her sweater. It was now or possibly never.

She pivoted as she unsheathed the knife, bringing the blade over her head in one fluid motion. Her eyes trained on Nelson's neck as she spun. She lunged at his throat, preparing to lodge the knife into his carotid.

Nelson raised a fist in defense. Her forearm impacted with his before the blade could draw blood.

"Uhh!" She tightened her grip on the blade's handle as she drove it toward him with all her strength, fighting against the weight of his forearm pushing against hers.

The blade tip drew closer. She felt a surge of hope. Then, out the corner of her eye, she caught a flash of movement seconds before the butt of Nelson's pistol slammed into her temple.

CHAPTER FORTY-NINE

For the last hour, their visibility had been next to nothing. Morton slowed to thirty miles an hour, which still felt too fast on the two-lane highway. They could barely see through the white haze beyond the windshield. The last few pairs of headlights they passed didn't appear in the oncoming lane until they were terrifyingly close.

Each time, Tanner braced himself for a head-on collision. But somehow, the passing trucks all managed to stay in their own lanes.

"Should we turn around?" Tanner's whole body tensed after headlights emerged from the freezing fog seconds before a semi passed in the opposite lane, spraying a blanket of muddied snow that completely covered Morton's windshield.

Tanner gripped his side door while Morton turned the wipers to their fastest speed.

Tanner hated the thought of not getting to Tok tonight, but they wouldn't do any good if they died before they got there.

Morton shook his head. "It's just as bad behind us. We'll be to Tok in a half hour."

At Tanner's horrified expression, Morton cracked a grin. "I'm just kidding," Morton said as he pulled into a snow-covered parking lot. Tanner made out the words "Tok Trooper Station" through the driving snow and breathed a sigh of relief.

"Let's hope this trip was worth risking our lives for," Morton added before getting out of the SUV.

It had grown dark during the last stretch of their drive. Tanner checked his phone. He had returned to full bars but still hadn't heard back from Cameron.

Tanner called her again as he climbed out and followed Morton to the entrance of the station, still in shock they'd made it one piece. Cameron's phone went to voicemail when a trooper who looked no older than thirty let the two men inside. She looked surprised to see them and introduced herself as Trooper Downing, the person who Morton had spoken with earlier. Tanner ended the call without leaving Cameron a message.

"I didn't realize you were coming down here tonight," she said as they trailed her down a short hallway that led to an open area in the middle of the station. "I hope the roads weren't too bad."

Tanner hadn't come to the station on his last visit to Tok. There was a long folding table in the middle of the room. A stack of papers and a coffee sat on top.

"It was fine," Morton lied.

Tanner shot him a look before his gaze traveled to the large whiteboard on the far wall. He recognized the photos of Madison Youngblood and Sienna Lovell adhered to the top of the board. Beneath them was a handwritten timeline of their disappearances and deaths. The wall to the left of the whiteboard was covered with a map of the area.

A second trooper stepped into the room from a rear hallway. He wore a uniform similar to Trooper Downing, only his shirt was tan instead of blue.

Trooper Downing pointed in his direction. "This is Wildlife Trooper Webb."

The wildlife trooper nodded at Tanner and Morton, placing his hands on his hips.

"He was kind enough to come in off duty tonight due to this storm," Downing added, "which has already slammed us with more call outs. Waska's arrest left only me and one other trooper on duty. We have two other troopers, but they both happen to be on vacation. I'm actually surprised you caught either of us here at the station."

"Did you ever find Waska?" Tanner asked.

Downing shook her head. "No. But our other trooper on duty got a tip earlier today that Waska was in Northway Junction—about an hour east of here. He headed up there to see if he could locate Waska, but I haven't heard whether he did. Our radios can be spotty that far out of town, so I likely won't hear whether he found Waska until he's on his way back."

Tanner rolled his gum to the other side of his mouth. "Was that Trooper Nelson?"

She nodded. "Technically, Waska's not due back in court until next Tuesday, so there's not much we can do until then if he chooses to evade us." She pointed a thumb at the wall behind her. "Especially in this weather."

She looked between the two detectives as the wildlife trooper leaned forward, placing his hands on the back of a folding chair.

He peered out the blinds at the snowstorm, then shook his head. "I can't believe you guys drove in this."

"You two couldn't have driven down here just to ask if we found Waska." Trooper Downing crossed her arms. "What's going on?"

Tanner's phone rang and he pulled it out of his coat, a number he didn't recognize with an Alaska area code. Morton shot him a look, and Tanner nodded at him to go ahead. During the drive, they'd agreed they needed to tell the local troopers about their suspicions that John Prescott could still be alive.

Tanner stepped into the adjacent hallway to take the call, hearing Morton launch into what they found at the remote wilderness cabin.

"Detective Mulholland."

"Oh, hi, detective. This is Lisa from the Alaska State crime lab. We spoke earlier."

"Yes." Tanner recognized the woman's voice from their short conversation on the plane. "Hi."

"I know it's after hours," she spoke fast, "but I just had a new result come through my email that couldn't wait."

In the other room, Trooper Downing's voice rose. *"The Teacher Killer?"*

Tanner put his finger to his ear and stepped farther into the hall. The technician must've gotten a result on the blood samples taken from *inside* the cabin.

Lisa breathed into the line. "When Sergeant Waska submitted the DNA profile last week for us to compare to the DNA evidence from the 1999 Fairbanks murder that I called you about earlier, he also submitted some new evidence for testing from the 1997 Tok murder of Amy Clarke."

Tanner stared at the floor, holding his breath. *Had Louie Prescott, after he'd killed that woman in Fairbanks, also killed the two women in Tok in the nineties?*

"That evidence from Amy Clarke came back a match to the DNA sample Waska submitted: Alaska State Trooper Patrick Nelson."

Tanner brought his hand to the back of his head.

"Detective? Are you still there?"

Tanner started down the hall. "Yes, I am. Thank you. Can you email me that result?"

"Of course."

Tanner dropped his phone to his side after ending the call.

When Tanner returned to the main room, Morton and the two troopers were still talking in low voices, expressions serious.

"DNA evidence from the murder of Amy Clarke in 1997 just came back a match to Trooper Nelson," Tanner announced.

All eyes snapped to Tanner.

"The crime lab technician said that Waska submitted the profile last week, along with some forensic evidence on Amy Clarke's clothing that had never been tested for DNA."

Trooper Downing's eyes widened. *"Nelson?"*

The wildlife trooper gaped at Tanner. *"Shit."*

Tanner nodded. "Yes. I'm having the technician email me the DNA results. We need to get a warrant for Nelson's arrest. *Now.* How far away did you say he is?"

Downing flashed a look at the wildlife trooper, who stood from his folding chair. "About an hour." She put her hands on her hips, her gaze traveling from Trooper Webb to Tanner. "Wait. If Waska submitted that DNA sample, and the old evidence, how can we know he didn't tamper with it? If Waska's guilty, he could be framing Nelson."

Tanner's phone chimed with the email from the crime lab technician. "That's possible, but we can't wait to arrest Nelson." Tanner thought of the white SUV Nelson owned in the nineties. "If Nelson *is* guilty, then every second he's free is a chance for him to kill again."

"I can't believe it." Downing's gaze traveled to the whiteboard. "Nelson always seemed so…*nice*." She folded her arms across her vest. "Although so did Sergeant Waska." She looked between the two detectives. "So, this means Waska is innocent."

"I'm inclined to think so at this point," Tanner said. But they wouldn't know for sure until they had both men in custody.

"How long has it been since you heard from Nelson?" Morton asked.

"About an hour ago. I tried him over the radio, but he didn't respond. So, I texted him through our satellite phones." She turned to Tanner. "Nelson replied that he was still in Northway Junction. Waska's girlfriend told him earlier today that Waska was headed there."

"Wait," Tanner said. "Nelson went to see Cameron Prescott? At her home?"

Trooper Downing met Tanner's gaze. "She goes by Jenkins now. But yeah, that's what he told me before he left."

"When was this?"

She pressed her lips together. "Late this afternoon."

Right around the time Tanner texted her and she didn't respond. Knowing her, it surprised him that she would tell Trooper Nelson where Waska was rather than going in search of him herself. Thinking of Nelson alone with Cameron made Tanner's skin crawl, even though he knew Cameron could handle herself.

"I can text Nelson again," Downing said, "but I don't want to tip him off that we're coming for him. We need to leave now—before the roads get any worse." She started toward the door then turned to Tanner and Morton. "You both coming?"

"I'll stay here," Tanner said. "I want to check on Cameron. I don't like that she's not answering her phone after Nelson paid her a visit earlier."

When they stepped outside, the snowfall had lessened. Tanner got behind the wheel of Morton's Expedition, then followed the state trooper SUV out of the parking lot, turning the opposite direction on the Alaska Highway toward Cameron's house, hoping the gut feeling he had was wrong.

CHAPTER FIFTY

Tanner pulled Morton's Expedition beside the Howling Wolf Motel's lit-up vacancy sign. It hadn't

taken him long at Cameron's home to be certain she wasn't there. Her long driveway was empty, and the house was dark.

Her front door was unlocked. After calling her name, he'd let himself in. He checked every room, glad to see there were no signs of a struggle—or a body—especially after hearing about Nelson's visit that afternoon. Still, her disappearance disturbed him. Greatly. Since learning that Nelson killed Amy Clarke, Tanner was filled with a growing certainty that John Prescott was dead. But that didn't mean Cameron was safe.

Before leaving, he'd gone next door to the neighboring home, which was also dark with an empty drive. There'd been no answer. He debated going back to Cameron's and waiting for her to return, then decided against it.

He'd driven through the parking lots of each business that lined the Alaska Highway before stopping at the motel. There'd been no sign of Cameron or her truck. As far as he knew, Cameron still had a plane, but she wouldn't have gotten far in this weather.

As Tanner stepped out of Morton's SUV into the lightly falling snow, he thought about Cameron telling Nelson that Dane was at Northway Junction. Had she gone there too? Or had Nelson hurt Cameron? Had she figured out what Nelson had done? Tanner pictured Nelson attacking Cameron inside her home, handcuffing her, and dragging her out to his vehicle.

Had Nelson done something to both Waska and Cameron?

Now, he wished he would've gone with Morton to arrest Nelson. He hadn't heard yet whether they'd found the trooper. With the weather, he guessed they probably hadn't reached him yet. And if there was no cell signal out there, he wouldn't hear until they got closer to town.

He should be looking for Cameron rather than checking into the motel, but the lack of visibility killed his chances of being able to spot her from his car.

Tanner climbed the snowy steps of the motel's front office building. From what he could tell, the rooms were all detached, small cabins. There was a dim light coming from inside the office. A waft of heat hit him when he opened the door.

A gray-haired woman looked up from behind the desk at the back of room. Tanner caught a looming shape in his periphery and spun toward a pair of eyes boring into him. He stepped back at the sight of the mounted wolf's large, white fangs, only inches from his face. *Is that thing real?*

"You sure you're in the right town?"

Tanner turned to the woman's voice. She cocked her head to the side, making no effort to hide the way she sized him up from head to toe.

"I'm sure." Tanner approached the desk, thinking the woman looked tired. "I just need a room for the night."

The woman took off her glasses and rubbed her eyes. Tanner guessed she was around sixty. She wore a short-sleeved t-shirt despite the snow outside. A wolf howling beneath a full moon was imprinted on the front of her shirt beneath the words *The Howling Wolf Motel.*

"Well, you're lucky I'm still here. I'm Valerie, and I'm the only one working the motel this week." Her voice faltered, and she cleared her throat.

It was then Tanner realized this was where Sienna Lovell was working when she was killed. The news article he'd read said the young woman was in Tok for the summer, working at her aunt's motel. The woman behind the desk wasn't tired—she was grieving.

"I had to catch up on some bookkeeping, and I lost track of time," Valerie continued. "Normally, I would've closed up for the night by now. Especially with the storm and all. How is it out there?"

"Not snowing as hard as it was earlier." Tanner pulled out his wallet, but she made no move to check him in.

Instead, she crossed her arms. "What brings a city man like you into town so late during a snowstorm?"

In Seattle, he wasn't used to being asked questions from strangers. He debated before telling her the truth.

"I'm a Seattle Homicide Detective. Here on business."

The motel owner leaned forward. "Seattle?" Her wide eyes searched his. "You know who killed my Sienna? Because I know it wasn't Waska. Don't believe that for a second. You don't believe he did, either. Do you? That's why you're here," she added.

"No, I don't believe that he did."

"Then who?"

"We have a couple of leads, but I'm afraid I can't be more specific than that. Do you know a woman named Cameron Prescott? I mean, Cameron Jenkins. She's a dentist in town."

She stared at him, and he knew his question was pointless.

Just because Tok was small didn't mean they knew each other. Cameron was a woman who kept to herself.

"I know her well."

Tanner's pulse quickened. "She's not at home. You have any idea where she might be?"

"You could try her boyfriend's place. That's Sergeant Waska. He lives next door to her."

"I went there. He wasn't home."

Valerie appeared to think, her eyes traveling to the mounted beast behind him. Tanner followed her gaze and suppressed a shudder. The wolf looked too big to be real.

He tore his eyes from the vicious animal. "Could they be somewhere together?"

"The sergeant has a cabin on Hunt Lake. He might've gone up there to escape everything after making bail. It's what his father does."

Tanner straightened. "Where's Hunt Lake?"

Valerie pointed behind her. "North of here."

"How far?"

"About an hour, but you can't drive there tonight with all the fresh snow we've gotten"—her gaze traveled down his suit—"even if you were a local. Those back roads wouldn't be plowed. With the wind we've had, there's likely some fallen trees too."

Tanner exhaled. A remote cabin lake. Had Cameron gone there in search of Waska?

Although, if Nelson killed Amy Clarke, the odds of him having recently killed the two women in Tok in the same manner were high, making the odds of Prescott being alive slim.

"You think Cameron is in danger?" she asked.

Tanner met Valerie's gaze. He thought for a moment before giving her the truth. "I do."

The motel owner's eyes narrowed. "Why do you think she's

in danger if you believe Waska is innocent?" She leaned toward him, pressing her stomach against the desk and bringing her face closer to Tanner's. "You think there's someone else up there?"

When Tanner didn't respond, the motel manager's face darkened. She grabbed a coat off her chair and reached behind the desk. "Come with me. I've got a snowmachine that can get us there. I'll take you right now."

"A snowmachine?" Tanner took in the sight of her slinging a rifle over her shoulder before she rounded the desk.

"A snowmobile is probably what they call them in Seattle." Valerie waved her hand through the air, glancing at Tanner's small duffel bag. "You got a hat and gloves in there?"

"Um. Yeah."

"Good. You're gonna need 'em."

Tanner followed her to the door, staring at the rifle strapped to her shoulder and keeping as much distance between himself and the mounted wolf as he could. Despite his repulsion, he found himself homing in on the dead animal's fangs.

"That's quite the décor," he said as Valerie held the door open for him.

"Décor?" She laughed. "Never heard her called that before. But she's a beauty, ain't she? Shot her myself."

Tanner stared at the motel owner in disbelief before stepping outside.

If she registered the shock on Tanner's face, she didn't show it. "Come on, city boy. Let's go."

CHAPTER FIFTY-ONE

When Cameron opened her eyes, her face lay against something cold. Her vision blurred as she pushed herself off the wood floor, trying to make out her fuzzy surroundings. It was dark beyond the windows, but a kerosene lamp lit the cabin from the corner of the room.

Something crackled behind her. She twisted around. Flames flickered inside the wood stove.

She sat up and spotted Dane sitting on a wood chair on the far side of the room, hands still bound behind him, head hanging to the side. The lamplight illuminated the beads of sweat on his brow.

"Cameron." His voice was soft. Weak.

His face was ghostly pale. The right side of his blue uniform shirt was completely soaked with blood. His eyes fluttered, and he blinked them open, straining to stay conscious.

"Dane. I'm so sorry."

"Glad to see you're awake," Nelson said from behind her. "Wine?"

She spun to see Nelson sink onto the couch beside the

wood stove with a glass of red wine in his gloved hand. She was reminded of the first time she came here with Dane, except it had been Dane sitting on the couch, not Nelson. It was the day they'd met. She'd offered to fly Dane here to check on his father, hoping to glean information from Dane about Bethany Long's murder. She'd had no idea at the time they'd end up together, how close she and Dane would become.

Her throat tightened, visualizing George lying dead on his cabin floor next door. *Had Dane watched his father die? Or had Nelson killed George before Dane got here?*

Nelson swirled the wine in his glass. Cameron studied his profile in the dim light. He was shorter than Dane, but only by an inch or two. She could see now how she'd mistaken him for John when he attacked her outside her house.

"Why did you leave me alive that night? You could've easily killed me if you'd wanted to."

Nelson crossed one leg over the other, meeting her gaze. "I needed to give you an added motive for what you're about to do." He lifted the glass to his nose. "Because the only way at this point for me to get away with what I've done is to catch you, drinking wine, on the verge of killing Dane after murdering his father. After you found out Dane killed those women—and his dad helped him cover it up."

"Dane didn't kill anyone. You're not going to get away with this."

A sly grin spread across Nelson's face, reminding her of John, when she'd seen the evil behind his eyes for the first time that day at the remote cabin. A wave of revulsion slithered down her spine.

"I'm afraid that's not what the evidence shows." Nelson swiped an open palm toward Dane's slumped form. "He's already been arrested, and now he's *failing to cooperate!*"

Cameron recoiled as Nelson's voice morphed into a shout. Dane moaned as Nelson thrust the wine glass toward her face.

"Drink."

Cameron shook her head.

Nelson snarled, exposing his teeth. *"Drink!"*

Cameron pressed her lips together. She wasn't about to make this easy for him.

Nelson bent over until his face was inches from Cameron's. "Don't make me shoot Dane again."

Cameron glanced at Dane. His jaw was clenched in pain. A bead of sweat dripped down the side of his face, which had grown even paler. She grabbed the glass from Nelson's outstretched hand and took a sip.

"Good girl." Nelson grinned, taking the glass when she extended it back to him. "Luckily for me, you have quite the track record for vengeful killings, don't you?" Nelson shook his head, returning to the couch. "That was some Kill Bill shit you told me about. And I overheard you tell Dane that Seattle detective found the cabin that your ex-husband Miles owned, where apparently your not-so-dead-serial-killer husband was holing up—until you killed him." Nelson pointed a finger in the air. "Plus, there's that very suspicious death of that first husband. Anyway, when Detective Mulholland learns that I found you up here and witnessed you killing Dane, he'll understand I had no choice but to kill you before you shot me too." Nelson chuckled, his gaze drifting out the window toward the lake. "It's almost too perfect."

Nelson reached into his pocket and pulled out his phone. Looking at Cameron, he wiggled it in the air. "I also recorded your confession about what you did to John while I was at your house." He slid the phone back into his pocket. "Just in case anyone needs more proof of what you're capable of."

Dane let out a pained grunt. His head still hung slack to the side.

"Let Dane go. You've already framed him for murder. You don't need to kill him to get away with this."

Nelson's expression darkened. "You know that's not true. Dane suspected me ever since I killed Madison. And he's been coming up here, picking his father's brain on those old murders too. I knew I had to take care of them before they found evidence that could put me away. It's over, Doc. For both of you." Nelson set down his wine.

She started to stand, but the room spun.

She spotted her Ruger lying beside Nelson on the couch. A moan emitted from Dane as his head bobbed. She needed to keep Nelson talking while she figured out a way to gain the upper hand.

"Why did you risk everything to kill again after getting away with murder for nearly thirty years?" Cameron thought of John. If he *were* still alive, she doubted he could ever stop killing. It was a disease to a man like him. In his blood.

Nelson turned pensive, seeming to enjoy her question. "I hadn't planned on killing again in Tok. But Bethany Long's murder last fall triggered something inside me. When her case went unsolved, it felt like an opportunity." Nelson's gaze moved to the window facing the lake even though there was only darkness beyond. "I might've stopped after that, until I heard you try to convince Dane that Madison's death was the work of your husband. And I admit that once I got a taste for it again, the urge only became stronger." Nelson cocked his head, meeting her gaze. "I admired it when I discovered what you'd done. A woman who'd killed and gotten away with it. I felt…a connection if you will. A kinship. Most people aren't like us, Cameron."

Behind her, Dane wheezed. She glanced over her shoulder to

see him lift his head, eyes closed and barely conscious. She turned back to Nelson, rage spreading through her veins like wildfire. "I'm nothing like you."

"We're more alike than you admit, Cam." He smirked. "You told me so yourself."

She pictured John, how she'd shot him in the leg, made him walk into the bear trap, then tied him to a tree. How he cried in pain when she drove the knife into his abdomen when she should've left his fate to the wolves. Then Miles' head soaring backward after she shot him in the temple.

No. Those times were different. She hadn't done those things for enjoyment, but out of necessity.

Beside her, Dane had gone silent. Cameron twisted to see his head hanging to the side, his eyes closed. *Just hang on a little longer, Dane.* She turned back to Nelson. Her eyes traveled to her Ruger now in Nelson's hand.

He shrugged. "But you're wrong about what you said. I didn't go nearly thirty years without killing. There were two more."

Cameron stared at him, thinking this was likely the first time he'd ever been truly honest with anyone about who he was. "Who?"

Nelson's gaze traveled out the window toward the dark lake. He didn't respond.

"So, what?" she asked. "You're going to kill us both, then?" She scanned the room for something she could use as a weapon, hoping to keep Nelson talking until she did.

Nelson set the wine glass on the antique coffee table. Cameron's eyes settled on the corkscrew beside the opened bottle.

Nelson laughed, throwing back his head against the couch before turning serious. "I'm not going to kill him, Cameron. You are."

CHAPTER FIFTY-TWO

TANNER GRIPPED THE handles on the sides of his seat as Valerie sped along a back road, the snowmobile vibrating beneath him as its headlight beams cut through a haze of white. Tanner leaned around the rifle on Valerie's shoulder to see their speedometer as they neared a bend in the road. His body tensed, seeing they were traveling at over sixty miles per hour.

Valerie's speed hadn't scared him as much when they were on a straight stretch of road off the highway, but they'd turned onto a narrower, winding road lined with trees, and the motel owner hadn't slowed down. He fought the urge to ask her to ease up, trusting that her speed was an indication of confidence. She knew what she was doing, but it still terrified him every time they came around a bend.

After they made a turn, Valerie let up on the throttle. Tanner leaned to the side as she slowed to a stop in front of a large, uprooted tree that had fallen over the road, completely blocking their path. Valerie lifted her helmet's visor and turned toward Tanner. "That's Cameron's truck. We'll go around."

She veered into the neighboring woods, thankfully at a slower speed, and maneuvered through the trees until they were back on the road. After another minute of speeding through curves at a breakneck pace, she slowed again, pointing through the trees on their left.

"That's Hunt Lake. And Waska's cabin," she yelled over the engine.

Through the woods, Tanner could make out faint lights. Valerie cut into the forest. Tanner grabbed his handles as he was thrown against his heated seatback. Valerie leaned into her turns around the trees as they moved toward the lake.

At this rate, it was going to take them much longer to get around the lake. Unless there was a bridge that he couldn't see in the darkness.

"Couldn't we stay on the road?" Tanner asked.

Valerie didn't respond, probably unable to hear him over the engine. She continued down the embankment, and the trees cleared. Tanner got the uneasy feeling they were headed straight for the water. She was probably planning to cruise around the shoreline where there were no trees.

But at the bottom of the hill, she kept heading straight.

"Where are we headed?" Tanner called out, louder this time, wondering if the lake was frozen. Recalling how warm it had been in Tok last week, he knew it couldn't be. At least not thick enough to hold a snowmobile.

The engine revved as Valerie squeezed the throttle. Tanner's heart nearly stopped as water sprayed into the air on either side of them.

CHAPTER FIFTY-THREE

"Shoot him." Nelson held her Ruger with his gloved hand, then stood and unholstered his duty weapon with the other. He lifted his service pistol, aiming the barrel at her head. "Or I will." He stepped toward her, extending the Ruger toward her. "But the evidence will look better if you're the one who pulls the trigger. So, I'll give you an incentive. If you shoot Dane, you can end his suffering. If you don't, I'll make it ten times worse for him."

Cameron's gaze traveled to Dane. He was unconscious, life fading from his body. She gritted her teeth. "No."

Nelson sighed. "Oh, please. Don't act like you're above this. It's nothing you haven't done before. And you'll be saving him a lot of pain and suffering."

Cameron turned to Nelson. "You're sick."

Nelson pursed his lips. "Well, that's a bit judgmental." He motioned to Dane. "I didn't make him step in a bear trap now did I?"

Cameron stared at Dane's chest, watching his breathing slow, as Nelson let out a snort at his own joke.

"There was one thing you told me at your house that I

couldn't relate to. About not knowing whether you were capable of killing until you were faced with it. I've always known. I've wanted to kill for as long as I can remember. Suppressing it is what's hard. It's who I am." Nelson wiggled the Ruger in front of her face. "Come on, Doc. I don't have all night."

"You're not going to get away with this. Detective Mulholland knows it wasn't Dane that attacked me. He also knows that Dane suspected someone in town. Plus, those texts you sent from Dane's phone will prove I was lured here." Cameron tore her eyes from Dane, meeting Nelson's gaze. "If you kill us, Mulholland will know you're lying. And he won't stop until he proves it—trust me."

"*You* sent those texts from Dane's phone, remember? After you killed George and sedated Dane, you came back to town with Dane's phone to make it look like Dane lured you up here, pretending to be John." Nelson grinned. "Those texts were sent from your house. I remember you texting when I was there. In fact, now that I think about, I saw Dane's phone on your kitchen counter." He tapped his pistol against his chest. "*I'm* a state trooper. You're the disgraced wife of a serial killer. No one's going to doubt me."

Nelson crossed the room to stand over Dane, then slapped the side of his face. Cameron's face burned with rage. Dane moaned without opening his eyes.

My truck. "Wait!" She threw her hands in the air. "I left my truck parked behind a fallen tree that blocked the road. It will prove you got here before I did."

Nelson smirked. "Nice try. That tree was already down when I came back here. I tucked my SUV into the woods just off the road and came the rest of the way on foot, just like you did. Fortunately, there's a snowmachine parked on the side of the cabin for me to take back." He patted his pocket. "And the keys were easy to find." Nelson pressed his pistol to her temple and nudged the Ruger closer. "Last chance if you don't want him to suffer."

Cameron stood still, looking down at her gun. She was tempted to take it and shoot Nelson, end him right now. But with his gun aimed at her head, he'd also get a shot off.

She stared at Dane, praying for him to hold on a little longer as Nelson pressed his pistol into her skull.

She lifted her hand to take the Ruger, knowing what she had to do. She'd have to take her chances that Nelson wouldn't kill her first.

An engine droned from across the lake. Nelson's head snapped toward the sound as he withdrew the Ruger from her reach.

She turned toward the window. On the other side of the water, a light moved between the trees. It couldn't be headlights, Cameron thought. Not with the fallen tree blocking the road. The drone grew louder, and she recognized the hum of a snowmobile's engine.

The light zigzagged, nearing the lakeshore straight across from them. Had Trooper Downing come looking for them? Nelson stepped outside onto the deck, keeping a gun in each hand. Cameron watched Nelson raise her Ruger toward the moving light, leaving Cameron alone with Dane.

"Hang on just a little longer," she whispered to Dane before turning for the coffee table.

A shot rang out from the deck. She closed her hand around the corkscrew and made for the opened deck door.

CHAPTER FIFTY-FOUR

"What are you doing?" Tanner screamed as water splashed his helmet.

Was she crazy? He'd been a fool to let her take him up here. He held his breath, preparing to go under.

To his surprise, they didn't. They sped atop the lake like a jet ski. Tanner exhaled in relief just as a blast rang out from across the lake. *Whip. Whip.* There were two splashes beside him as bullets impacted with the water. Valerie killed the lights as they continued to speed toward Waska's cabin.

Tanner spotted a figure standing beneath the cabin's porch lights, but he couldn't make out the features. Valerie lifted her visor and yelled something Tanner couldn't make out aside from the word *throttle*. She grabbed his hand and tugged it toward the right handlebar.

"Hold the throttle!" she shouted.

Tanner wrapped his hand around the handlebar, squeezing the throttle with his thumb as Valerie stood, shouldering her rifle and aiming it at the figure on the cabin's deck. Tanner strained to keep the throttle engaged, knowing if he let up, they'd sink.

As they neared the other side of the lake, Valerie's body jerked from the blast of her rifle. Then another shot rang out, this time from a distance, and she jolted back into him. Valerie grunted, leaning so far he was afraid she'd slide off the seat. Tanner reached for her coat with his left hand, trying to keep her upright.

But Valerie's left foot was already off the snowmobile as she toppled over the side. Tanner lifted his thumb from the throttle, preparing to wrap both hands around her leg. The snowmobile immediately slowed, and cold lake water rushed over his shoes. Valerie hit the water with a splash.

CHAPTER FIFTY-FIVE

Cameron crept onto the deck. Nelson kept his back to her, aiming her gun toward the sound of the snowmobile's engine echoing off the water. He fired, and Cameron quickened her pace.

She lifted the corkscrew, preparing to drive it into his neck like she'd planned with the paring knife. When she reached him, a blast sounded from the lake. Cameron thrust the bottle opener toward Nelson as he twisted sideways from the impact of a bullet to his arm. The tip of the corkscrew tore into the meaty flesh of his shoulder instead of his neck.

Her Ruger landed in the snow between their feet. Cameron kicked it off the edge of the deck.

Nelson seethed a grunt and gripped her wrist, freeing the corkscrew from his flesh before he slammed her hand against the deck railing. Cameron heard a splash when the corkscrew hit the lake as Nelson's pistol spun toward her face. She grabbed his arm holding the gun with both hands, thrusting his arm against his chest as he fired the gun. A bullet buried itself into the wall of the cabin.

"Ahhh!" She swung Nelson's arm into the side of the deck

railing and dug her thumb into the bullet wound in his upper arm.

Nelson cried out and the gun slipped from his grip, flying onto the snow-covered deck. He lunged for it, and she jumped onto his back, hearing the snowmobile reach the shore beneath the cabin. She wrapped her forearm around Nelson's neck and squeezed, pulling her arm against his throat with her other hand.

Nelson stumbled back, slamming her into the side of the cabin. Her breath left her lungs as he thrust her against the wall a second time. Her grip on his neck loosened. Nelson doubled over, throwing her onto the deck. She rolled over with a grunt and scrambled to her feet.

Cameron raced down the slippery steps, nearly losing her balance on the last one. She glanced at the cabin, picturing Dane on the other side of the wall—barely alive.

Help was here, although she had no idea what condition they were in after being fired upon by Nelson. She needed to draw Nelson away from Dane. And Nelson's plan wouldn't work without her.

She rounded the corner of the cabin as Nelson fired a shot in her direction. Chunks of wood splintered off the side of the cabin, hitting her cheek.

CHAPTER FIFTY-SIX

TANNER SQUEEZED THE throttle. The light from the cabin window was close. If he kept going to shore, he could come back for Valerie without sinking the snowmobile.

He sped onto the shore and killed the engine. Another blast sounded from the upper cabin deck. Tanner spotted two figures engaged in a struggle moving in and out of the shadows. He recognized the way Cameron moved, and the other had to be Trooper Nelson. *She's still alive.*

There was shuffling on the deck. Cameron let out a scream. Seconds later a shot rang out.

The sound of someone struggling in the water drifted over the lake. He jumped off the snowmobile and waded into the frigid water, torn between helping Cameron and saving the woman who'd taken him here. Tanner swam toward the sound of Valerie's gargled cry.

He was a strong swimmer, but it took all his strength to swim against the drag of his suit. He took rapid, shallow breaths as he fought to reach the motel owner. She gasped when he reached her, then sank beneath the surface. Tanner reached below, wrapping his hand beneath her armpit to pull her up.

Valerie coughed as he pressed her back against his chest, keeping one arm around her as he swam backward with the other, hyperventilating from the cold. Tanner dragged her onto the shore before collapsing on the ground next to her, catching his breath.

"Leave me," she choked out the words.

Tanner sat up. Valerie shoved her palm against his chest. "You go."

Tanner got to his feet and ran toward the cabin, eyes adjusting to the dark. He darted to the far side of the deck, where a set of steps were faintly illuminated from the light coming through the window. He withdrew his gun, dripping with lake water as he climbed the snowy porch steps.

The deck was quiet. The faint light from the cabin's window cast a dim glow outside, and he saw no movement. Gun outstretched, he stepped inside, steeling himself to face off with Nelson.

But the cabin was still, empty aside from Sergeant Waska's limp form tied to a chair in the middle of the small space. Tanner swore. Waska looked to be dead.

Tanner spotted a door on the far side of the room. He crept toward it, gun aimed straight ahead. He swept the empty bedroom with his gun before turning back for Waska.

"Waska! Can you hear me?"

No response. The sergeant's head hung slack, his uniform covered in blood. Tanner bent over and felt his neck for a pulse, which was weak and thready.

A figure appeared in the open doorway to the deck. Tanner swung his pistol toward the movement.

"Easy." Valerie's teeth chattered as she put up a hand, hair soaked from the lake. She stepped inside, blood seeping from the bullet wound in her shoulder. Her gaze darted to the sergeant. "Dear God. Is he dead?"

"Not yet," Tanner said, lowering his gun.

Outside, an engine revved. Both of their heads jerked toward the noise. It sounded like Valerie's snowmobile but came from the other side of the cabin.

"That's a snowmachine," Valerie said, her eyes wide. She stepped toward Tanner. "Take mine. I'll stay with the sergeant." When Tanner reached the door, she added, "Remember, throttle's on the right and brakes are on the left."

"Got it."

"And Detective?" she called.

Tanner turned.

"When you reach them, promise me you'll kill that bastard."

CHAPTER FIFTY-SEVEN

Cameron ran toward George's cabin, relieved when she reached his carport before Nelson fired another shot. She went inside and climbed onto the parked snowmobile. Her heart pounded against her chest as her fingers fumbled to find the keys in the dark. When her trembling hand found the key protruding from the ignition, she let out the breath she'd been holding in. She twisted it, and the engine rumbled to life.

She reversed out of the carport, waiting until she was facing the road to turn on the headlights. A shot rang out from the side of Dane's cabin as Cameron sped across the snow-covered gravel. She veered into the woods, tucking behind a row of trees and squeezing the throttle to power up the side of the hill.

As she'd hoped, she heard Dane's snowmobile engine rev on the other side of the road behind her. She shot a glance over her shoulder to see the snowmobile's headlights. She ducked beneath a low hanging branch as she accelerated up the hillside.

Cameron clenched her handlebars tighter, her fingertips going numb from the cold, as she dodged between the scattered trees. The lights from Nelson's snowmobile illuminated the ground beside her. She didn't need to turn around to know that Nelson was gaining.

She swore under her breath, swerving to the left and narrowly missing a tree. She'd been stupid to think she could outrun Nelson. The last time she'd been on a snowmobile was last winter, when she'd gone out in the wilderness to find John; Nelson had likely been using one his whole life. She pressed her thumb into the throttle. The cold stung her face, making her eyes water. She blinked to clear her vision as she sped up the hill.

Feeling Nelson's headlights on her, she cut to the right as a deafening blast sounded from behind her. She braced herself for the impact of a bullet but felt nothing. She exhaled. Nelson's bullet had missed her. But she couldn't outrun him much longer.

A beam of light flickering through the trees caught her eye. She cocked her head to the side to see another snowmobile heading toward her and Nelson at increasing speed. Its headlights, emerging from the trees farther down the hill, kept her from seeing who was behind the wheel. Cameron glanced behind her, seeing Nelson swing his gun toward the other snowmobile. He fired a shot.

Cameron faced forward. She laid into the throttle with her thumb, numb from the cold despite the rage boiling inside her at the memory of George lying dead on his cabin floor. And how Dane looked when they left his cabin. Would he even be alive if she managed to return?

She spotted the ridgeline too late. Her eyes widened as she reached the edge of the cliff. Squeezing the brake, she twisted her handlebars to the right as Nelson collided with the back of her snowmobile.

Her snowmobile toppled over, sending Cameron over the side of the ridge. As she fell, Nelson's snowmobile flew through the air before landing on its side, spraying snow over her when she landed beside it on her back. Her legs flew over her head, forcing her into a backward somersault. Pain radiated through her neck as she slid down the hillside.

The snow burned cold against her skin as her sweater slid up her back. A broken branch protruding from the snow scraped her arm. Air left her lungs when she landed face first at the bottom of the hill with a *thud.*

She sat up, disoriented and fighting the sensation that she was still tumbling down the hill. She swiped the snow away from her eyes and ran her hands over her head and limbs, surprised to find that everything felt intact and unbroken. A few feet from her, Nelson's snowmobile lay on its side. On the other side of it, Nelson let out a grunt.

She couldn't see him, but her gaze settled on the handle of his pistol sticking out of the snow, illuminated by the snowmobile's headlights. She crawled toward it when the movement caught her eye.

Nelson staggered in front of the beam, eyes fixed on his weapon. Cameron reached for the snowmobile's handlebar, flicked the headlights off, and dove into the snow.

CHAPTER FIFTY-EIGHT

Tanner eased his thumb off the throttle of Valerie's snowmobile and veered behind a tree. An ear-piercing sound of metal screeching filled the forest. Tanner steered around the trunk, no longer able to see the other snowmobiles. He edged forward, spotting a ridgeline ahead.

He braked beside the cliff and climbed off his seat. The unmoving beams from a snowmobile's headlights lay at the bottom of the steep hillside, casting a glow through the thick layer of fog. Beside him on the edge of the ridge, an idling snowmobile lay on its side in the snow. Tanner withdrew his weapon, straining to find Cameron or Nelson amidst the white haze below. A figure moved in front of the headlight beam. Recognizing Nelson, Tanner trained his gun on the trooper.

He was about to shout at Nelson to put his hands in the air when the headlights turned off. Tanner lowered his weapon as Nelson disappeared in the darkness.

"Trooper Nelson, drop your weapon and put your hands on your head! You're under arrest!"

No response. If Nelson had survived the crash, Tanner's

headlights put a spotlight on him and made him an easy target. He killed the lights and listened.

Tanner lifted his gun in the direction of Nelson. "Trooper Nelson, I need you to respond and come up the hill with your hands on your head!"

"Nelson, do you hear me?"

A blast rang out from the base of the hillside, the gunfire's bright muzzle flash cutting through the darkness. Tanner gripped his pistol as a consecutive shot sounded with another flash of light.

Tanner stood still, staring into the darkened valley. Had Nelson fired the gun, or Cameron? It was too steep for him to climb down. He strained to pick up any noise coming from below that would tell him who fired the shots. Besides Tanner's own breathing, there was nothing but dead silence.

Tanner's heart thumped against his chest when he heard the trudge of snow being crunched beneath someone climbing the hill.

Tanner aimed his weapon toward the sound. "Trooper Nelson? Drop your weapon!"

A grunt.

Tanner waited for the person trekking up the ridge to announce themselves. If it were Cameron, she would've done so already. Tanner retreated behind the snowmobile, gun outstretched.

In the moonlight, he recognized Cameron's slight frame. He flicked on the snowmobile beams. She squinted from the light.

"Cameron."

"Tanner?" Her jaw fell open.

Tanner lowered his gun. She slipped and fell to her knees. He moved around the snowmobile and extended his arm. She grabbed his hand, allowing him to pull her to the top of the ridge.

She got to her feet and handed him Nelson's gun as she brushed the snow from her jeans.

"Are you shot?"

She shook her head. "Just a little banged up. I was wrong about John. It was Trooper Nelson this whole time." She glanced over the ridge. "I shot him. Twice. He nearly got the gun away from me. I think he might still be alive, but I'm not sure." She turned toward the snowmobile. "Since when do you know how to drive one of these?"

"Valerie brought me."

"I heard a splash in the lake when you arrived. Is she okay?"

Tanner holstered his gun and climbed on the snowmobile, sliding forward to make room for Cameron on the back. "She was shot, but she seemed like she's going to be okay. Tough as nails, that one. I left her at the cabin with Dane."

"Was he…still alive?"

"He was when I left to follow after you."

Cameron swung her leg over the seat behind him. Tanner put the snowmobile in reverse.

"Hurry. Dane has a satellite phone that we can use to call for help when we get back."

Cameron glanced over her shoulder, wondering if Nelson would still be alive by the time help reached him. She gripped the sidebars and prayed that Dane could hang on a little longer as Tanner maneuvered between the trees and started down the hill.

CHAPTER FIFTY-NINE

THREE DAYS LATER

Cameron stood beside Trooper Downing in the tight-quartered viewing area at the Fairbanks Police Department. They looked through the one-way mirrored glass to the interview room where Dane sat across from Trooper Nelson. Dane's crutches leaned against the metal table beside his seat. Looking at her boyfriend, she hated the thought of how close she'd been to losing him.

By the time she and Tanner had returned to Dane's cabin, Valerie had found Dane's satellite phone and sent a message to Trooper Downing. An hour later, a medevac helicopter had arrived from Fairbanks and taken Dane and Valerie to a Fairbanks hospital. A rescue team had been dispatched to find Nelson, who was amazingly still alive when they found him—despite Cameron shooting him in the shoulder and chest.

Using fuel from Dane's cabin, Cameron and Tanner then took Valerie's snowmobile back to Tok. While Dane, Valerie, and Nelson were treated at the Fairbanks hospital, Tanner and Cameron were interviewed at this same station by Morton and another detective about what happened at Hunt Lake. Valerie had been discharged from the hospital yesterday, while Dane and Nelson weren't released until today.

Cameron stared through the glass at the two men facing off. That morning, Tanner and Detective Morton flew back to Miles's remote family cabin to conduct a thorough search for John's remains. Cameron's stomach churned at the thought of what they would find. If they found John's body, would they charge her with murder? And if they didn't, would she spend the rest of her life looking over her shoulder, expecting John to come after her at any given moment?

She suppressed the shudder that coursed through her and focused her attention on the two troopers on the other side of the glass.

Cameron surveyed Nelson in his orange jumpsuit, still coming to grips with the fact he was a killer. Nelson's handcuffed wrists were secured to the top of the table. Before leaving the hospital, Dane got permission from Morton to speak with Nelson before the trooper's court hearing tomorrow morning for the murder charge of all four female Tok victims and George Waska, along with the attempted murders of Dane, Cameron, Valerie, and Tanner.

Beyond the glass, both men assessed each other without a word.

Beside her, Trooper Downing folded her arms. "Nelson almost seemed relieved when we found him and said we were arresting him for murder. Like he'd been waiting for that moment for a long time."

According to Morton, Nelson had given a full confession to the murders of Amy Clarke, Erica Lavine, Madison Youngblood, and Sienna Lovell shortly after Nelson woke from surgery. He also confessed to killing a young woman in Glennallen, a town over one hundred miles southwest of Tok with a population of five hundred, in 1998. Nelson offered to tell authorities the location of her body in the outlying forestland in the hope of negotiating a plea deal for his cooperation.

Nelson admitted to another killing in 2018, but stated he would only confess if he could speak to Dane about it first.

Cameron watched through the glass as Nelson looked at his hands before breaking the silence. "I gave her those pills."

"Who?" Dane asked.

"You know who." Nelson lifted his gaze. "Your wife."

Dane straightened in his seat.

"I overheard your fight that day at the station, when she told you she was going to leave you for that prick doctor. She was going to ruin your life. Drag you through an ugly divorce." Nelson shook his head. "Trust me, I've been there. If I hadn't slipped her those pills, you would've seen the two of them around town together forever. Been the center of town gossip. It would've been awful." Nelson's gaze returned to his hands. "I had those pain pills in my car, left over from that knee surgery I had. Lucille was crying when she came out of your office, as I'm sure you remember. I crushed up a handful of them, along with several benzodiazepines I'd been prescribed for anxiety and put them in a coffee I gave her." Nelson paused, looking up. "That way the Narcan wouldn't do anything to revive her if she passed out at work."

Nelson lifted his hands, but they jerked to a stop from the cuff link securing them to the table. "And don't judge me for taking meds. It weighs on you. The fear of being caught at any moment, especially with DNA advances."

Cameron's brows knitted together at Nelson worrying about what Dane would think of him taking anxiety medication when he was confessing to killing his wife.

"You killed my wife." Dane stared at him in horrified awe.

Nelson leaned forward. "I did you a favor."

Dane scooted back his chair and reached for his crutches.

"The urge to kill isn't something you choose. I've tried to fight it all my life, but there was that period in the nineties when I just…couldn't."

Above her, Cameron heard the rhythmic *thwip* of a helicopter's rotor blades landing on the building's roof. Her pulse quickened. It could be Tanner and the Fairbanks detective back from their search for John's remains.

"We're done here." Dane got to his feet, pushing off the table to stand on his leg that hadn't been shot.

Cameron could see the betrayal written all over his face. Like she'd felt when she learned who John really was. He'd lost not only his father, but his longtime friend.

"Wait." Nelson's eyes pleaded with Dane as he tucked a crutch under each armpit. "You were the one who submitted my DNA profile, right?"

Dane's left eye twitched as he stared down at Nelson silently.

"What made you suspect me?"

Cameron could tell he was debating whether to answer. "After Madison Youngblood's murder, I found an old photograph of you, your dad, and my father standing in front of a white SUV. My dad said it was taken in ninety-two, shortly before your dad's heart attack—when you inherited your father's car. I didn't remember you driving it since I'd only seen you in your trooper vehicle. When I looked up the registration records, I learned that you kept the vehicle for less than a year, selling it right around the time Karl came forward saying he saw me leaving the lake.

"After my car was searched by police and nothing was found, my dad said authorities believed Karl had made the whole thing up. You were never even questioned regarding it, even though you had a nearly identical vehicle at the time. So, I took your coffee mug from the station and submitted it for DNA testing."

The side of Nelson's mouth upturned to a half smile. "Never thought it would be a photo that did me in. I guess it's the little things, the details, that can get you caught, you know?"

Cameron's phone vibrated in her pocket as Dane started for the door of the interview room without responding to his long-time colleague and friend. Downing glanced at Cameron as she checked the caller ID. It was Tanner.

"Excuse me," she said, stepping past him into the hall. "I need to take this."

CHAPTER SIXTY

She drew in a deep breath and pressed the phone to her ear. "Hi, Tanner."

"We just returned to Fairbanks PD from our search of the surrounding area of your late husband's cabin. I'd like to speak with you about what we found."

Cameron's body stilled. *They found him. He's going to charge me with murder.*

"Where are you?" Tanner asked.

"I'm at the Fairbanks police station."

Dane stepped out of the interview room at the same time Tanner emerged from the stairwell at the end of the hall with his phone to his ear and the Fairbanks detective at his side. Dane turned to the sound of the two detectives coming down the hall. Tanner's eyes locked with Cameron's as he lowered his phone.

She swallowed as they strode toward her.

Tanner nodded at Dane when they approached. "Glad to see you're on the mend, Sergeant."

"Thanks." Dane leaned his weight on his crutches as the two men shook hands. "I owe you one for coming to my rescue."

"I'm sorry about your father," Tanner said.

Dane nodded, and Tanner turned to Cameron.

"Cameron, can we speak with you for a few moments?"

Cameron searched the detective's slate blue eyes. As usual, his expression was unreadable.

"Okay."

The Fairbanks detective opened a door next to the interview room containing Nelson. "We can talk in here." He glanced at Dane. "Alone, if that's all right."

Dane held her gaze when she turned toward him.

He's worried, Cameron thought. *This is bad.*

"That's fine," she said, trying to look relaxed.

Dane nodded. "I'll be in the waiting area at the end of the hall."

Cameron slowed when she reached the doorway, seeing it was another interview room, identical to the one holding Nelson, apart from the one-way mirrored glass. She entered the small space, taking a seat across the metal table from Tanner and Morton.

Tanner interlaced his fingers atop the table, reminding her of the times when he'd questioned her at the Seattle Police Headquarters.

"First of all," Tanner said. "Is there anything you want to tell us?" His jaw flexed as he chewed a piece of gum.

Cameron leaned back in her folding chair. "No."

The two detectives exchanged a look.

Tanner cleared his throat. "We found a snowmobile less than a mile from your late husband's cabin. We couldn't lift any prints from it since it was out in the elements for some time, but we found partial skeletal remains a few hundred yards from the snowmobile."

Her breath stuck in her throat.

"They appeared to be male," he added.

"We've submitted them to our forensic lab for identification."

Tanner's eyes remained on her as the Fairbanks detective continued.

"But it will take some time, weeks if not months, before we have an identification."

Tanner leaned forward. "You want to tell us what happened up there when your prints got on the door?"

Cameron looked between the two men. "Am I under arrest?"

"No," Tanner said.

Cameron straightened. "Then I have nothing more to say."

Cameron was lost in her thoughts as she and Dane walked to her truck parked in front of the Fairbanks police station. Dane hadn't yet asked her what they'd told her, knowing what they were likely to find. She would tell him as soon as they were in the privacy of her truck.

While she'd been relieved to learn that John hadn't survived, her steps were heavy with dread imagining the moment when Tanner would return to arrest her for John's murder. She had no doubt that he would as soon as he verified the skeletal remains belonged to John.

When they got to her truck, she spotted Tanner as he stepped out of the building and donned his sunglasses.

"I'll be right back," she told Dane after unlocking her truck.

She jogged across the parking lot, reaching Tanner's rental car at the same time he did.

"Tanner!"

He turned. "Cameron. Is there more you want to tell me?"

There was no point in beating around the bush. She had to

know the answer to the burning question in her mind. "Are you going to come back and arrest me if those bones turn out to be John's?"

Tanner slid off his Ray Ban's, meeting her gaze with his slate blue eyes. "Arrest you for what?"

Be careful what you say. He could try to trap you into a confession. "For my prints being on the door to that cabin."

Tanner brought his hands to his hips. "Last I checked that's not a crime."

"Oh, come on, Tanner. We both know you're never going to let this go. And I don't want to live in fear of being arrested for murder at any given moment. I came up here to be free." She crossed her arms. Maybe she should tell him everything. Tanner could help sway a prosecutor to be lenient. "I need to know what you're planning to do. I can't—" she exhaled, looking at the ground. "I can't keep living my life looking over my shoulder." It was part of why she killed John.

"Based on the condition of the remains, it's going to be very difficult to determine whether a murder took place, if in fact one did. Secondly, it will be almost impossible to determine whether you were at the cabin while the deceased was still alive."

Cameron looked up. "And what do *you* think?"

Tanner chewed his gum, casting a glance at her truck on the other side of the parking lot. "I think that if those remains turn out to be your husband, then John got what was coming to him." He redonned his sunglasses. "One way or another, it seems that justice has already been served."

He opened his car door. "Goodbye, Cameron."

"Goodbye, Tanner."

Cameron watched the detective pull out of the parking lot before she started for her truck where Dane waited in the passenger seat. Maybe she hadn't known that detective as well as she'd thought.

Tanner's car disappeared around a corner when she reached her truck.

"Everything okay?" Dane asked when she got behind the wheel.

"They found John's remains. Part of his skeleton. At least they think so. They still have to confirm that it's him." She started the ignition. "But Tanner said so far, there's no proof that John was murdered. And that it would also be difficult to prove I was at the cabin before John died." She turned to Dane before throwing the truck in reverse. "Tanner told me just now that he thinks justice has already been served."

Dane sank against his seatback as relief flooded his face. "That's great news. I agree with him on that."

She smiled at her boyfriend seated beside her, thinking how lucky she was to have him in her corner. And how grateful she was that their time together wasn't over. Hopefully, it wouldn't be for a very long time.

She pulled out of the parking lot, still shocked that Tanner wasn't planning on arresting her. They rode in silence for the next few minutes.

"Valerie told me at the hospital that she's thinking of selling her house in the spring," Dane said, changing the subject when Cameron merged onto the highway that would take them back to Tok. "She's planning to move into the caretaker cabin at the motel."

"Oh, yeah?"

She was surprised Valerie would move into the place where her niece was murdered, but maybe Valerie would find comfort in living in the cabin where her niece spent the last three months of her life. Cameron recalled her visits to John's hunting cabin in Washington to feel close to him after she thought he'd died, the first time. Then how hard it was living in her Seattle home after she learned the truth about him—John was everywhere inside that house.

"I thought maybe Valerie's house could be a place where you and I could have a fresh start—together," Dane said. "Not that I don't love being your neighbor."

Cameron glanced at Dane. This wasn't where she expected the conversation to be headed.

"We don't have to decide now. But I thought it might be something to think about." He put his hand on her leg. "Her house has three bedrooms. Room for a family eventually…if we wanted." When Cameron didn't respond, he added, "Unless you think it's way too soon."

We've only been together for six months.

Dane pulled his hand away. "Sorry, I didn't mean to spring that on you. And I know the last two weeks have been…crazy… to say the least. Losing my dad and thinking I might die too made me want to make the most of the time I have. With you."

"It *is* soon." Cameron shot Dane a smile. "But I can't think of anything better than a fresh start. With you."

EPILOGUE

THREE WEEKS LATER

Tanner rubbed his eyes at his desk at Seattle Homicide. He'd tossed and turned all night, unable to shut off his mind from his unsolved cases—and whether the skeletal remains he'd discovered in that remote Alaskan wilderness belonged to Prescott. At nearly four in the morning, he gave up on sleep and decided to come in earlier than usual.

He'd enjoyed a few hours of working in silence before his colleagues began to shuffle in, their presence and conversation of what they did over the weekend bringing with them their usual distraction.

Tanner straightened, taking Morton's call on the first ring. "Hey, Morton. You got news for me?"

"I do."

Tanner held his breath.

"The crime lab just called me to confirm that the remains we found were those of John Prescott."

Tanner sank against the back of his chair. It was what he

expected but still a relief to know without a doubt that Prescott was dead. And could never harm anyone again.

The medical examiner had been unable to determine Prescott's cause of death from the remains they'd found. Which wasn't surprising. His body had been so picked apart by wild animals and scavengers that only skeletal fragments remained.

"The media is going to have a heyday when they find out."

"Does Cameron know?" Tanner asked.

"Yeah, I called her right before I called you."

"Did she sound surprised?"

"No. I'm thinking about bringing her back in for questioning."

"You can try, but she won't talk."

"You think she killed him?"

Yes. "I don't think we'll ever know. I think we're best to let this one go. John Prescott is dead. For the rest of the world, that's a good outcome."

"You're probably right."

A short laugh emitted from the adjacent cubicle when Tanner ended the call. The desk behind his was empty. He'd overheard his sergeant say that Detective Richards and Suarez had been called out to a double homicide in the middle of the night.

He pulled on his noise-cancelling headphones without looking up from his desk. He reached for a folder on top of the stack he'd gathered that morning, the unsolved casefile of young women who'd been murdered in Seattle between the years Louie Prescott lived in Tacoma.

Movement at the edge of his desk caught his eye, and he looked up to see Richards standing beside his desk. She plopped the skull bobblehead onto his opened case file.

Tanner slid his headphones off his ears.

"Hope you caught up on your beauty sleep this weekend," she said. "You're next up."

Tanner slid the jiggling bobblehead toward the back of his desk as Richards retreated to her own. He folded a stick of gum into his mouth and readjusted his headphones, refocusing on the casefile from 1985.

He'd never know for sure how many victims were killed by John Prescott's father, but he was certain there were more than two. Probably several, and likely more than one in Seattle.

He wouldn't stop digging until he found them all.

NOTE FROM THE AUTHOR

CODIS is an acronym for Combined DNA Index System, which is a computer software program that operates local, state, and national databases of DNA profiles from convicted offenders, unsolved crime scene evidence, and missing persons.

For the purposes of this story, Tanner used CODIS to perform a familial DNA analysis on John Prescott's DNA, which linked John's father, Louie Prescott, to unsolved crimes. However, in reality, there are currently only twelve states (Arizona, California, Colorado, Florida, Minnesota, New York, Ohio, Texas, Utah, Virginia, Wisconsin, and Wyoming) that are allowed to utilize familial DNA analysis within CODIS to link unsolved crimes to the DNA profiles of convicted offenders.

Some of the most famous cases that were solved using familial DNA analysis are the "Grim Sleeper," arrested in 2010 in Los Angeles and convicted of killing nine women and one teenage girl; and the 2016 Utah arrest of a man later convicted of murdering 69-year-old Evelynn Derricott in 2011 after his DNA was found on the hammer used to kill her. In 2017, familial DNA analysis was used by the Los Angeles County Sheriff's Department to solve the 1976 strangulation murder of Karen Klaas, the ex-wife of Righteous Brothers' singer Bill Medley.

Note: Familial DNA analysis using offender databases (i.e., CODIS) differs from the strategy of identifying suspect DNA profiles using genealogy databases.

ACKNOWLEDGMENTS

Huge thanks to my editor, Leslie Lutz, for your tireless work in helping me to make this the best draft possible.

To my agent, Jill Marsal, thank you for your support and faith in me, and for your invaluable insight and advice.

Traci Finlay, thank you for your guidance with the plot developments during the early stages of drafting this novel.

Thank you to Nancy Brown for your attention to detail in proofing the final manuscript.

Detective Rolf Norton, thank you once again for your willingness and patience in answering my long list of procedural questions for this story, and for weighing in on the ending when this book was in the early stages. As always, any errors are completely my own.

Alaska State Trooper Cody Webb, thanks for answering my questions about Tok, coyotes, and Alaska State Troopers.

Huge thanks to the team at Spotify for producing a fabulous audiobook. Leslie Howard, your engaging and talented narration is a perfect fit for this story.

To my parents, thank you for your endless support, reading my draft, and watching my children in the mornings when I ended up having seven more chapters to write on our family vacation.

Elise and Anders, thank you for being my biggest cheerleaders and for eating frozen pizza and chicken nuggets so I could make my deadline.

To my favorite brother, Cary, thank you for answering my medic-related questions for this story.

Clay Richmond, thank you for sharing your wealth of knowledge with me about wolves when I was working on The Final Hunt. Your insight into their behaviors stuck with me while I was writing this book.

To Jack Lawson and Keira Henson, thank you for all the work you do behind the scenes.

To all my readers, bookstagrammers, and bloggers, I am incredibly grateful for your support. I couldn't do this without you. Thank you, thank you.

Keep reading for an exclusive preview of *The First Hunt,* a prequel to *The Final Hunt,* coming June 2025! Available for pre-order now.

Also, don't miss Audrey's newest thriller, *Missing In Flight,* coming January 2025! Available for pre-order now.

PREVIEW

THE FIRST HUNT

PROLOGUE

Seattle, 1984

The boy eyed his father from the backseat of the Ford Escort as it turned off the Pacific Highway and pulled up to the curb of a dingy side street. He turned down the volume on his AC/DC cassette that played through the Walkman his dad had given him last month for his eighth birthday. When a young woman with dark undereye circles and heavy makeup approached the passenger side of the car, he didn't have to ask what they were doing here. Her fishnet tights and cut-off shorts way too cold for the middle of winter in Seattle.

His dad rolled down the window. The woman leaned inside. She eyed the boy curiously in the back before speaking to the driver.

"Are you lookin' to have some fun this afternoon?"

His father leaned across the seat and opened the passenger door. "Get in."

She climbed inside without another word, and the Ford Escort pulled back onto the Pacific Highway.

She rubbed her hands together and held them in front of the heater. Her knuckles were red and cracked.

"I'm not used to being picked up with someone's kid in the back," she said. "And I've seen a lot of weird shi–" She looked back at the boy. "Stuff."

The boy's father didn't respond.

She smiled at the boy through her bright red lipstick. "Hi," she said. "I'm Sally."

"Don't talk to him," his dad said from the driver's seat.

Sally obeyed and turned back around. The boy looked out the window at the cars in the adjacent lane as they sped along the highway. Families. Commuters. None of which, he guessed, had a hooker in the front seat.

The boy knew his dad had picked up women before. Before his mother died, he'd heard his parents arguing about it, although at the time, he'd been too young to understand what it meant.

Last year, his dad had picked up another hooker by the airport. They'd driven to a rundown motel, and his dad told the boy to wait in the car while he and the woman went into one of the rooms. The boy had fallen asleep, and when he'd woken, his dad had driven the woman back to the street where he'd picked her up.

Afterward, his dad had never spoken of it, and the boy had never asked.

They turned off the Pacific Highway onto a winding road lined with towering evergreens. They hadn't passed a single car when his dad finally pulled into an empty gravel parking area surrounded by green woods.

The boy pulled off his headphones, hearing the gravel crunch beneath the tires before the car came to an abrupt stop.

"Get out," his dad said to Sally.

Sally glanced at the boy before opening her door. "What about your kid?"

"He's fine," his dad said. He gave the boy a stern look. "Stay in the car. Me and her are gonna take a walk."

He slammed the door and motioned for Sally to follow him. She gave the boy a sheepish look before following his dad into the woods until he could no longer see them.

The boy waited in the car for as long as he could until his curiosity got the better of him. He knew this wasn't normal. With his Walkman in hand, he climbed over the front seat and opened the side door. The boy left the door ajar, afraid the *wump* of the car door closing would alert his father of his disobedience.

He stopped when he reached the edge of the forest, straining to hear what his father and the woman were doing. He took a few steps into the woods, wincing when a branch snapped under his foot. He paused before moving forward, following in the direction he'd seen them go.

A woman's scream pierced the silent forest. The boy stopped in his tracks. It was a different kind of scream than he'd ever heard before, high-pitched and keening, almost like an animal.

Sally appeared in the woods ahead of him. She was naked, her eyes wide with sheer terror. Branches cracked under her feet as she ran. The boy took a step back and stumbled onto the damp flora.

Sally's petrified eyes met his when his dad appeared behind her. He was too focused on Sally to notice his son in the distance. He gripped her arm with such force that she flew backward onto the ground. The boy gaped at the dirty, bloodied soles of her feet.

He watched his father grab her by the hair with gritted teeth. Sally shrieked and whimpered as he dragged her deeper into the forest, branches breaking under her naked body, until they were out of the boy's sight.

The boy sat still, paralyzed with fear as he listened to Sally's screams and pleading cries grow farther away. He heard his father grunt. Then there was nothing other than the rapid beating of his own heart. The silence was worse than Sally's screams for mercy, even though he hoped it meant she was okay. But his gut told him there was only one reason Sally was no longer begging for her life.

The ground seemed to move beneath him. His father's face, when he'd come out of the woods and pulled Sally off her feet, was that of a stranger. Pure rage. Evil. He'd known his father to be a stern man, but nothing like that.

The boy covered his face with his hands. He should've helped her. But he'd been so afraid. And after seeing the look in his dad's eyes, he knew there was no way he could've overpowered him. But it didn't lessen his shame.

The sound of twigs snapping under footsteps caused the boy to leap to his feet. He turned and ran for the car, tripping where the forest turned to gravel but catching himself before he fell. He didn't dare turn back as he scrambled toward the faded blue car. He got in and closed the passenger door harder than he intended.

The boy fell into the back seat and tried to catch his breath as his dad emerged from the woods. Alone. The insane look was gone from his father's face as he crossed the gravel parking area toward the car.

His dad reached the car and opened the driver's door. He held something square and blue in his hand, and the boy's heart sank when he recognized it. His father held it out for him.

With a shaking hand, the boy took his Walkman.

"I told you to stay in the car, John," his dad said, his voice strangely calm.

John swallowed. "Sorry." The words came out in a croak.

His dad took a deep breath and put both hands on the steering wheel. John was desperate to ask about Sally. What happened to her. But, after what he'd seen, he didn't dare. And, deep down, he already knew.

His father turned and put his hand on John's leg. John looked beyond the wet spot around the crotch of his pants to his father's hand. He was sure his father could feel his knee trembling.

"How about pancakes for dinner?" His father's expression had softened, his demeanor restored to the man he'd known all his life. "It is Christmas, after all."

John nodded, afraid if he spoke, he would break out in sobs. His father patted his leg and turned forward in his seat. With trembling hands, John connected his Walkman to the headphones that still hung around his neck and pulled them over his ears.

As he stared out the window and turned up the volume, tears blurred his vision. Almost certainly, Sally was dead. His father threw the gearshift into drive and sped out of the empty gravel parking area onto the winding, paved road—leaving Sally alone in the woods.

ABOUT THE AUTHOR

Audrey J. Cole is a *USA TODAY* bestselling author of ten novels. She resides in the Pacific Northwest with her two children. Before writing full time, she worked as a neonatal intensive care nurse for eleven years.

Want to hear about Audrey's next release and get free bonus content to her books? Visit *www.audreyjcole.com*